The Lost Sole's Club

DEBBIE RAE

For anyone who has left their soul in Thailand…

Or their flip flops at a Full Moon party.

With Special Thanks to:

All of the friends I made in Asia, who shared in the adventures and experiences that inspired this book.

Lucia, Sarah and Ben, my time spent with you led me to discover my true self; and to my husband who made it possible for me to follow my dreams.

The monsoon rains hammered into her back, insistent and driving. The river flowed about her ankles, the swirl pulling toward the cliff edge. She held her breath, swallowed the pain, and forgot her loss. Then she ran.

The looming jungle palms flew past, panic rising as the edge drew closer, the heavens hung grey and furious above. She jumped, leaving everything behind on the cliff. For a heartbeat she was free, floating on the breeze before she hit the blackened waters and the world stopped.

Chapter 1

Shuffling down the aisle, she picked at the edges of her passport, trying not to think about her sister. Would Claire be frantic or relieved to find her gone?

She checked her boarding pass and looked at the seats. A pale man in his sixties sat by the window, vacuum squeezed into the chair. His vest was decidedly too skimpy for both the season and his ample form. With a large hairy hand he swept crisp crumbs from his chest and protruding stomach. He smiled at her, mouth full, spilling more debris downward.

One last glance at his beading neck rolls, oozing sweat into the headrest and she decided not to argue for her reserved seat. Instead she stood in everyone's way trying to decide where to sit. She didn't like to deviate from what she had been told to do, she never had. Her ticket said 34A not 34B or C. A dilemma.

A man in a Yankees baseball hat stopped next to her and put his things in the overhead locker. He glanced at his ticket and took the middle seat, 34B.

He had unkempt brown hair which crept from beneath the hat, reaching for his shoulders, greying at the temples. He was riddled with eclectic tattoos, Thai writing and symbols that made no sense. She was trying to decipher what was etched over his neck and hands when he caught her staring.

She flushed crimson and tumbled into the isle chair, a tangle of long loose hair and arms full with hand luggage. 34C it was then.

'You want a hand with that?' the man offered, with a faded New York accent, nodding to her bag.

'No thanks.' She mumbled, shoving the bag into the foot well, leaving precious little space for her feet.

She smoothed a magazine on her knee and tried to look interested in it before realising it was upside down. She swung it around quickly, slapping her knuckles against the tray on the back of the seat in front. It slipped from its clasp, crashing onto her knees, 'Shit!' she muttered, thrusting it back up.

Eyes were upon her, when seconds later, it smashed down again. 'For fuck's sake.' She moaned.

Maybe it was a sign she should get off?

Her heart began to beat to the frolic of a thousand thrashing butterflies. She swallowed the familiar knot which writhed in her throat. Blood rushed to her head, her breath quickened. She dragged a damp hand across her cold waxen forehead, sweat crawling up through her contracted pores. She grappled for control.

She had not fainted in public for over a month, but she had not ventured anywhere unfamiliar in over six. *Go back to your room, go back to your old life,* her internal voice pleaded. *No chance* she wanted to scream, but buckled forward instead battling for breath.

The American rested his hand gently on her back, 'Hey are you ok?'

She wasn't used to being touched and didn't like it. She twitched, trying to shake him off while fumbling in her bag, retrieving a couple of Valium tablets. She longed for her stronger anti-anxiety pills, but she'd been off those for a month and her prescription had run out. They had always worked to still her mind when she had been in a perpetual state of mania, but consistent stability and calm had helped her to come off them.

Her mental health relied on her living a life that was boring and predictable. This was not a predictable situation.

Something cool nudged against her arm, the American again, 'Here, take this.'

She accepted the bottled water, 'Thanks,' she stammered, surreptitiously slipping the pills into her mouth before gulping the water down.

He was close, his breath on her cheek. It was hardly the spot to demand more personal space so she stayed quiet.

He spoke quietly, 'Just take a moment. There's no rush, we don't have anywhere to be for at least ten hours. Sometimes the most important thing in a whole day is the rest we take between two deep breaths.'

He sounded so like her psychiatrist that it made her laugh between jagged breaths. She stared, he certainly didn't look like a doctor.

He sat back in his chair, unfazed by her outburst, 'I can't take credit for that one, that's Etty Hillesum. She knows a thing or two about calming a restless mind. I've read a lot of her books. Used to be a bit of a stress head myself.'

Willow didn't know what to say. His eyes transported her to the oceans of dreams, a calm surface masking a dangerous rip tide? She looked away.

He blundered on in his, very un-British, manner, 'You're not a good flyer then? I used to be the same, but it's an occupational hazard, I travel a lot. I've had to work out how to relax.'

As a woman who spoke six languages she had surprisingly little to say when it came to conversing with the opposite sex. Her head swam with questions, none of them managed to reach her lips.

He pulled a piece of gum from his mouth, reached across her, his shoulder pushing against her chin and squashed it onto the fallen tray. He fixed it back in place, 'There good as new!' the peak of his hat hit her on the nose as he fell back into his seat, slipping his hand into hers and shaking it, 'Sorry about that. Not much space. I'm Aaron by the way.'

Unable to keep up with the casual chat, the likes of which she had actively avoided for months, she stayed silent, feeling like a moron. Eventually he tired and turned his focus to his entertainment system.

'Sorry. I'm Willow,' she blurted, her name sounding like it didn't fit; perhaps she should have used the other one?

Aaron smiled in response and went back to selecting a film.

That's that then. Willow twisted her engagement ring which hung on a chain around her neck. Despite it no longer symbolizing the promise of a marriage, wearing it made her feel as if she still belonged to someone, as if she was still loved and safe.

What would James think of her running off, chatting to strange men on planes?

She put her headphones in and let the Valium take over, guiding her to sleep.

Sometime later Aaron shook her arm, 'Hey Willow wake up! I thought you might like something to eat?' he accepted two trays from the stewardess without waiting for a response and passed her one.

The man in *her* chair had already torn off the foil sleeve and launched into his food with unrefined gusto.

Willow was foggy, but hunger had crept up with vigour. While on medication she had found that the pleasure of consumption had been lost, a month later and even plane food invoked a primal urge. 'Yes thank you,' she accepted, pulling her tray down, exposing long tendrils of Aaron's chewing gum. She stared at it and laughed, relaxing slightly.

'God sorry,' he muttered, smiling as he reached across to remove it with a napkin.

'Don't worry.' She waved away his apology, opening the food boxes. It was a sad nod to a Thai noodle dish, but she devoured it with a smile on her lips, pausing only when the tray was empty.

Aaron looked on.

'I love Thai food, always have.' She reddened, wiping her face with a wet wipe.

Aaron grinned, continuing his own meal, 'Don't mind me. You'll love the food in Bangkok. Have you been to Thailand before?'

'No, I haven't seen any of Asia, I'm ashamed to say.' The tension that she had been carrying continued to lift. It was nice to talk about normal things.

'Are you heading to the beaches for a holiday; maybe some partying?' Aaron asked with amiable charm.

The mere mention of beaches and Willow beamed, 'Maybe later. To start with I'm going straight to a hotel in Bangkok where I will make a plan.'

There hadn't been time to consider how she was going to go about searching for one man in a country of nearly seventy million.

Aaron's eyes were intent, 'No time schedule? No job or boyfriend you need to rush back for?'

She thought of James and admitted, 'No there's nothing, there's no one.'

Aaron hummed in contemplation, 'Lucky you, no restraints, It's the best way to travel. You never know who you'll meet and where they may lead you, best to keep your options open, otherwise you could miss something. Let the road guide you,' he gestured, waving.

Lucky you, Willow turned the words over. Could it be that way?

'What do you do back home? Sorry; what *did* you do?' Aaron corrected.

Willow wasn't used to people being so upfront, it was unexpectedly refreshing. 'I was a hyper polyglot linguist lecturer,' she said feeling somewhat fraudulent, she had not worked in six months and her boss would not be offering a reference anytime soon.

Aaron's eyebrows shot up, 'Cool; so you're a linguist?'

Willow was amused by his interest, men were usually indifferent to her career, 'Yes and no. A linguist is a scholar who analyses languages, they can break them down and work out the mechanics of what makes it work the way it works. I never liked that, I prefer to accept it as it is and go with the idiosyncrasies. I like the way that my tongue wraps around Latin-laced romantic French, how my hands seem to fly into life when making Italian observations.' She stopped her mouth running away. He probably wasn't interested in *all* the details.

Like a wound toy unleashed Aaron began animatedly chatting in Thai. Laughing and kissing his fingers. Willow looked on, clueless.

He slowed as it dawned on him, 'You don't speak Thai do you?'

'No I don't, but in my defence there are seventy-four dialects and don't get me started on the romanised inconsistency of Thai spelling.' She stopped before she slipped into a lecture.

'Actually 94% of people speak Tai-Kadai Thai so if you learn that you'll get by just fine.' He quantified.

Willow was impressed, 'How do you know that and how do you speak it so well?'

He raised his eyebrows 'Ha, if you could interpret what I was saying you may disagree, I make lots of mistakes, but I get by. I live in Thailand, have done for nearly twenty years. My wife was Thai,' a tight smile. 'So how many languages can you tell me to shut up in?' he changed the subject.

'Ten, but only seven with any semblance of elegance, all European I'm afraid,' she stated not wanting to sound too showy.

'I know a great guy in Bangkok who could teach you a bit,' Aaron rummaged in his bag and held a card out, 'If you get stuck on your travels, call me, I may be able to help you.'

She wriggled it into her pocket with no intentions of calling, she didn't want any help, no matter how tempting it or *he* was.

'My work takes me away to London every month. I don't like it much, but my publishers are based there so I don't have a choice.' He conceded.

Her interest rose, 'So you're a writer?' That made sense, he was so inquisitive.

'Sort of. I review hotels, restaurants and tourist attractions, but I'm better known for travel blogs, audio tour guides; you know the type of thing?'

She didn't. How did a man carve out a career from bumming around Asia? It seemed a bit sad to be living in a beach hut and partying with students in your late-thirties, no matter how beautiful the scenery was supposed to be.

A beautiful air stewardess appeared, smiling and patting down her immaculate hair, 'Aaron! I tried to get to you earlier, but it's been such a busy flight. How have you been?'

'Oh, hi Nang, great to see you! I was hoping that you'd be on this flight. I've been good thanks. How's your brother doing at Uni?'

The stewardess leant unnecessarily closer, 'He's in his final year and has a lovely girlfriend now. Have you met anyone special?' she exposed the slightest tip of tongue through her teeth while waiting for his answer.

Willow looked away, uncomfortable with the shameless flirting, but listened for his answer with too much interest.

Aaron scoffed, 'Nang you know no woman would put up with my lifestyle. I'll be a bachelor until I die.'

Nang professionally excused herself when a colleague signalled for assistance.

7

He turned to Willow, 'I met Nang on a night out in Bangkok, she's a wonderful girl. I should have introduced you properly. I'll get her back.' He moved to turn on his *assistance* light.

'No. No thanks!' Willow exclaimed too quickly, 'I'm sure she is great, but I think I'm just going to lay low for a few days and find my own way.'

He sat back, relaxed, 'If you change your mind, she could show you a really good time.'

'I'm sure she could.' Willow said with more judgement than she intended. 'I'm going to watch a film now. Let you get on with your work.' She nodded at the laptop he had produced, searching out her headphones.

She busied herself watching a bad movie and reading mundane magazines until, finally the plane touched down and she stepped off in Bangkok.

She had begun.

Chapter 2

Willow heaved her backpack off the conveyor belt and squeezed the straps over her delicate shoulders. Her muscles protested with each step, the buckles pressing uncomfortably around her waist and chest as she tilted forward, staggering toward the exit.

Thinking about the contents, she cringed.

Claire would be furious to find her hangers stripped bare, but Willow couldn't have risked running into James had she gone back to her own flat and she could hardly have left England with nothing to wear. There had been no time to go shopping, just a couple of hours.

Noise resonated from every direction; Loud speakers, touts and tourists, all vying for air space. Willow pushed through the exit and was hit with a wave of heat so intense it took her breath away. Wearing jeans had been a mistake.

The queue for a taxi snaked down the pavement, disorganised and chaotic. If only she could throw her bag on the floor, collapse upon it and cry until she was magically transported to the hotel. Doing things alone was too hard!

'Hey Willow; where are you staying?' Aaron called.

Be careful what you wish for she noted.

She turned, hobbling a few steps in his direction, 'It's written on a pad, in the front pocket of my bag,' she indicated with a flick of her head, unable to reach around, feeling like a kitten chasing its tail.

'Come on, let's have a look.' He unzipped her backpack, pulled out the note pad and turned his nose up theatrically, 'No you can't stay in this place. The air con is either non-existent or arctic. Three of my friends got food poisoning from the breakfast buffet last month.'

She knew she shouldn't have trusted Google, 'But the online reviews were good.'

Aaron shrugged, 'It's changed hands recently. Don't worry I'll take you somewhere else, same area, but much better and it won't give you Bangkok belly.' He grimaced. 'You haven't paid upfront have you?'

'No,' Willow lied, flinching as a large van screeched to a halt at the curb by her feet.

The long-haired Thai man behind the wheel honked his horn aggressively, flashing a vibrant white toothy smile. Was he friend or foe?

He jumped from the vehicle, denim shorts and a *Guns and Roses* T-Shirt, swamping his slight frame.

'Mr Aaron, Sawardi krab!' he shouted, jumping onto Aaron, hanging on like a limpet, slapping him enthusiastically on the back.

'Che I've missed you man, but it's only been a few weeks!' Aaron exclaimed with visceral joy.

Willow watched, bemused, as their conversation flipped and skipped along in nimble Thai. Aaron far more gifted with the language then he had let on.

Was she intruding on their reunion? She fidgeted with her bag straps, knees feeling as if they might buckle; should she sneak away?

Suddenly Che was pawing at her bag and pulling it off. She was grateful to be free of the weight, but it crossed her mind that she might be getting mugged in a strangely friendly way? She'd been warned at check-in to be mindful of her possessions.

'Phew lady, you no travel light no?' Che griped, throwing the bag onto the back seat of his van, shaking the suspension.

Had she had agreed to go with them? She looked around, unsure what to do.

Aaron gave a reassuring smile, 'I don't want to force you to come with us. I get a bit too enthusiastic. I'm like a proud home owner, I only want you to see the best of Thailand, not inside all the messy drawers. Come on let me be your tour guide, at least for your first thirty minutes; it's what I do after all.'

'Rescue maidens in distress?' she muttered, feeling pathetic.

He laughed, 'I'm no knight, I'm a tour guide remember?'

The Valium, the sleepless nights, the strangeness of it all was making her slow, but she did recall their earlier conversation, 'Of course you are. Sorry.' She glanced at the gargantuan taxi queue, 'I don't need saving, but I could do with a lift.' She granted. She'd envisaged being a strong independent woman upon arrival, however she was woefully out of practice.

'Good choice lady! Those drivers bastards!' Che broadcast at an uncomfortable volume.

Aaron slammed her door closed behind her and took his place in the front, 'There's no safer driver in Thailand, hardly ever kills a tourist, it's been bad for business in the past.'

Che beamed at the *almost* compliment, clambering into the driver's seat and switching on the most aggressive air conditioning Willow had ever encountered.

'You meeting friends in Khao San?' Che stared keenly in the rear- view mirror, oblivious to the rising traffic, forcing the van in and out of impossibly small spaces.

'No. It's just me, but lots of people travel alone.' She justified unnecessarily. She looked out of the window at the sprawling motorway, modern bill boards and skyscrapers, creeping in to view. Where were the Tuk Tuks, temples and dusty tracks?

Aaron nodded, 'You'll be hard pressed to spend a moment truly alone here. Everyone is looking to share their experience. You'll find that people talk far more freely then they do in England. You may have noticed that already?' he spoke with an unapologetic self-aware smile.

'You'll go out expecting a quiet dinner and end up on a tour to Loa with three Australian surfers before you know what's happening. There was this one time I had to get a boat from Phi Phi to the mainland, a taxi, a speedboat to another island and then a longtail boat to another, just to outrun all the people looking to make friends. I wound up in a hotel that only had four German guests, on a tiny island in the middle of nowhere. Bliss.'

Who had time for friends and random road trips? Didn't anyone have jobs or lives to get back to? Maybe she wasn't the only one with nothing?

Despite enjoying Aaron's company she had no intention of meeting anymore people. She wanted to go quietly about her business, see a bit of the country, sort her head out and get back to her rebuilding her life in London as soon as possible. He might have the time to play at being eighteen again, she did not.

Aaron turned to look at her, 'What I mean is that travellers tend to band together. The transportation can get pretty overbooked and once you've spent fifteen hours in a mini-van with Emma from Reading, hearing all about how much she misses her boyfriend, you'll be best friends, sharing a room for the night.'

Willow was only half-listening, watching the city grow out of the skyline, the rocking van lulling her toward sleep. She hadn't slept in a bed for more than thirty hours. 'Sorry who's Emma?'

'Someone I met a few years ago. Anyway that's not the point. I just mean that you will meet a lot of interesting people and most likely make some great friends,'

She yawned, unable to suppress it. 'I guess I could? Are you staying in Khao San?' she asked, politely trying to stay awake.

'God no, I couldn't stand it, It's a flying visit for me. I have a few friends to catch up with, then I'm back to work. I've got some audio guides that need updating for Koh Tao. A new hotel has changed the forest quite a bit and new paths have been put in all over the headland. Then I will head home.'

Did he mean America? Willow was about to ask, when Che swore loudly, hammered on the horn and slammed on the breaks. She stared aghast as a family of four, one carrying a dog, cut in front of them on a moped. Aaron didn't blink an eye, clearly he'd seen it all before.

'We don't have far to go now.' He reassured her, pointing into the distance. 'See how the urban landscape is changing? We are coming out of the financial district and heading toward backpacker territory. Bangkok is pretty much in the middle of Thailand; did you know that? Lots of people in the Khao San area will be planning their travels around the full moon dates and when they want to be on Koh Pang Yang. It's sad really, central Thailand has some amazing attractions and scenery that most visitors never take the time to explore,'

Willow sat back, enjoying his guidance more than she had expected. It was easy to imagine that he'd be good at his job. 'I would love to see central Thailand, but I'm on a deadline, I'm not sure where I will be going yet.'

Her mind reeled with the recent events that had led her to be there, unfortunately she wouldn't be enjoying much sight-seeing.

When her family's farm sold, Willow had been grateful to go back alone. She needed to work out what she was going to do with her life and it seemed like a good place to think.

She slept in her old bed, surrounded by trinkets from her youth, teddy bears and posters of ponies. The days passed and the memories unfurled, the house grew sparse and the skip filled. The quiet fresh air and remembrance lifted her spirits after months spent without leaving the city.

London had been home for over ten years, but every road and coffee shop held a memory of James. Being at the farm was a respite and made it clear that she needed to get away; but where to?

On what was to be her last day, she was clearing her mother Caroline's beloved potting shed. It was heart-breaking to see her treasured plants had wilted after months of neglect, their desecration another part of Caroline lost forever.

Willow found a storage cupboard at the back. Inside was Claire's childhood bike, the adored electric blue streamers still flowing from the handle bars, faded and dusty. Willow's old bridle, which still smelled of her first pony, Skyla, sat above her baby mobile. It was like a shrine to their past, keep-sakes only a mother would treasure.

Willow cleared the larger items and set about uncluttering the shelves. Tucked away on the highest one, behind binders packed with school reports, was a damp cardboard box. It was battered and buried, but wrapped in a beautiful silk scarf. It must have meant something to someone once? The scarf was familiar, Aunt Rosa's; her mother had kept it on her bedside table for years and then one day, just after Christmas, it was gone.

Rosa, her mother's twin sister, had been absent from Willows family since before she was born; tragically lost to cancer as a teenager. Her mother's usual soft and smiling face would crumple with pain at the mere mention of her name, so Willow knew nothing of her at all.

She stroked the scarf, interest swelling, scooped up the box and ran in to the house.

She slumped down on to the rug, fire licking against the logs that her father had cut the previous autumn, in the hearth. His presence was in the woody scent, urging her to leave the box closed, *whatever was in there was none of her business.*

She couldn't resist. Inside lay a copy of her mother's will, which Willow discarded; Claire had dealt with their inheritance. Of more interest were the letters and photographs, which were crammed in; each one addressed to her mother in an unfamiliar hand, carrying a postal stamp from Thailand.

Willow removed one from the envelope, the pages yellowed with age. She checked the date and then swept to the last page, where the sender had signed off. There must have been a mistake?

She opened another and then another, they were all signed, *Rosa* and dated up until November 2004; over thirty years after she had *died*?

Willow searched the box. Beneath the last letter was a Death certificate, along with an official government letter. She scanned the first line:

It is with regret that we inform you of the death of Rosa Chuglin and Wan Chuglin, who were reported missing...

Who was Wan? Rosa's maiden name was Whittaker, she can't have been married, Willow's mother surely would have mentioned that? The letter continued, but Willow was disorientated, hungry for clarity.

She turned to the next page, taking a moment to work out what she was looking at, the prominent script was Thai with smaller English translation. She picked out the key details:

NAME: Rosa Chuglin. December 26th, 2004. OCCUPATION: Teacher. CAUSE OF DEATH: Drowning.

Willow immediately recognised the date: the Boxing Day Tsunami that had decimated much of Asia, when she was still a child. If Rosa hadn't died as teenager, then what had she been doing for all those years in Thailand? Had her father known the truth?

The questions kept coming; perhaps the answers were in the letters? Willow tore open another one. It was nearly 10 o'clock by the time she'd read the last, more questions formed than answered.

The letters told of Rosa's years as a young woman, teaching in Thailand, later of marriage and then of her precious son, Jay. Laced through the accounts of her life were the words of a tormented and ostracized woman, who, in the earlier years longed to return home and never stopped craving forgiveness for some terrible wrong.

Infuriatingly she never mentioned what it was that she was apologising for. Willow could not imagine what had kept Rosa away from her twin, from all of them for all those years?

Amongst the decaying declarations of regret were Rosa's poetic observations of the country around her which, as time went by, seemed to heal her broken spirit.

The photos spanned her life, spent in paradise, wild characters smiling out from backdrops of idyllic beaches and Asian ruins, colourful and vibrant. Tales waiting to be told. Then there was Jay, her cousin: a beautiful, golden faced child who clung to Rosa no matter how old he grew.

Why had Willow and Claire been denied knowledge of this enigmatic explorer and their extended family?

Willow absentmindedly picked up the Will. A copy was with the lawyers. There was no need to keep the duplicate. She was about to abandon it to the embers of the fire when something caught her eye and she froze.

Willow fled the farm and jumped into her car with a burning fury in her stomach. She gripped the steering wheel, knuckles white with rage, the box of photos and letters on the back seat.

She burst through Claire's front door, slamming it closed, not caring that her nieces and nephew were asleep. She wanted to scream away her rage.

The Will was clear: they were to find Jay within a year of their mother's death and deliver him a reserved portion of the inheritance. If he could not be found, his money was to be shared equally between the sisters.

Claire shuffled into the hallway in her dressing gown, bleary eyed. Willow held up the Will. The look on Claire's face was one of resigned acceptance, not of surprise and Willow hated her for it. Her mother's last wish had been kept from her.

Had Claire stolen the money for herself? She had certainly tried to steal a cousin from Willow when she needed family more than ever.

There were only twenty-four days left to find Jay. Claire had robbed her of over eleven months. Time which Willow needed to try to locate the boy who would have become a man, without an address or contact number.

Willow was jolted back to the present. Che was hammering on his horn again. She must have dozed off.

She considered her predicament and decided that it was worth asking for help if it meant succeeding where Claire wanted her to fail.

'I need to find someone as quickly as possible. He is, sort of, missing. I have something that I need to get to him.' Willow spoke up.

'I knew there had to be a man!' Aaron celebrated.

'Why do men always believe that a woman's life revolves around one of them?' he was infuriating. 'The man is my cousin. I recently lost my parents and they left something for him in their will. He was orphaned a long time ago and I am hoping that maybe we could mean something to one another.' That was the truth, she realised for the first time, it wasn't just about getting the money to him, she wanted a family again.

Aaron turned, interested, 'Sorry about you parents. That's rough. I'll help you find your cousin if I can. What have you got? An email? Address?'

She shook her head.

'Surname?'

'I'm not sure what his surname is. I've searched online for people with my aunt's surname, but I haven't found a match.' She hadn't had time to try anything else.

'Don't think of what you don't have. What do you have? You must have something to go on, or you wouldn't be here?'

Willow's hand tightened on her bag, protective of the letters inside.

'My aunt wrote home every few months for years, from the places that brought her the most happiness. She had used a PO box in the beginning, but then nothing. Some of the photos have landmarks in them, others have named buildings or sign posts. There are a couple of places she seemed to go to a lot. I thought I might start with those. Maybe I can find some people that knew her or could lead me to him?'

she looked at Aaron, grateful that he hadn't written off her chances immediately.

'Let me and Che look at the photos. We've seen a lot of this country, together we might be able to point you in the right direction at least?' Aaron stretched out his hand expectantly, 'A dripping tap will finally fill a glass, *so it begins*,' he said theatrically, 'What have you got to lose?'

Willow let herself imagine that first bulbous droplet falling and unzipped her backpack, pulling out the box, 'They're twenty odd years old, please be careful with them,' she warned, handing him the photos and retrieving her note pad and pen.

Aaron flicked through, taking time on each one, 'Wow some of these are really beautiful and these ones,' he held up a few, 'These ones were taken in Ayutthaya; the same hotel pops up again and again; right Che?'

Aaron handed the bundle to Che, who turned away from the rushing traffic with an ease that made Willow grip on to her seat belt.

'Yep. Floating markets. Don't know hotel though.' Che pointed at one of the other photos, 'This is school. She's older in one of these. She go there many times?' Che glanced casually back to the road, leaping to another lane; causing a cacophony of horns to sound.

A flicker of hope flared in Willow's stomach; 'I think it is where my Aunt lived and worked with Jay? If I can find the school it would be a huge help. Could it be near the floating markets?'

Che grunted 'I think no. School sign in Dambro.'

Aaron nodded, 'Dambro is a rare southern dialect, Ayutthaya is central so they don't use it there. You should talk to my friend Eric, he speaks it well. He owns a tour company which runs outreach programmes for disadvantaged children across Thailand. He has travelled to that region a fair bit as well as knowing many schools.'

Eric, Willow wrote down. 'Can I have his details?'

Aaron searched through his contacts on his phone and pulled a face, 'I don't have his new number. His shop is based in Koh Tao; it's called *Longecrang travel,* I'm sure you can find him online. Let me look you up on Facebook and I will send his details. What you full name?'

She couldn't say it aloud, there would be questions to answer. 'It's on a private setting. I will find you from your business card later. What does *Longecrang mean?*' she asked, keen to deflect his questions.

'It means, *Try Again*. Eric says that his extreme sports and travel company was his second chance in life. We all get one of those right?' Aaron ventured, hopeful.

Che bowed his head to a small carved Buddha that was stuck to his dash, 'More than one. Thank Holy Buddha.'

Aaron patted him on the shoulder, 'If your driving is anything to go by.'

Willow liked the sound of the word, *Longecrang*, repeating it over and over, perfecting the rise of the E and the roll of the last G. She wanted that more than anything; a second chance.

'Willow do you want me to look at the letters? There may be more information in them?' Aaron asked.

'No! The letters are personal between my mother and her twin and they don't mention specifics. They're more emotional then informative.' Willow didn't feel comfortable sharing such personal details of the lady's lives with a near stranger.

Aaron nodded, 'Sorry, I love an adventure. Hopefully Eric can help you more.'

Willow siled, grateful, 'You've given me something to go on which is more than I had a few hours ago.'

She returned to looking out the window. The skyscrapers had made way for stubby eclectic buildings, squeezed together in tight rows. Nothing was as she had expected. What other surprises were waiting for her in Bangkok?

Chapter 3

Willow's heart sank as they approached the Khao San Road.

The first thing she saw was the Golden Arches of McDonalds. Shoals of men wearing football shirts like a uniform and women in hot pants bustled along. The throngs of tourists writhed from market stall to stall, eager for fake sunglasses and wallets. Rogue motorbikes and persistent Tuk Tuks flew in every direction.

The colours, sounds and smells were distinctly Asian, but scrubbed with a western soap. The vivid yellow and red Thai iconography on the walls and shop fronts bled into *Coca Cola* signs and advertisements for boat trips.

Young women, who despite it being mid-afternoon, paraded outside several bars. They wore tiny skirts and crop tops, exposing trim and perfect bodies as they chatted with passers-by. Willow's mouth fell open. 'When my Aunt was here this was a rice market. She'd described it as *spirited!*'

'Don't let the ladyboys worry you. They're after men with money, they won't do you any harm.' Aaron dismissed.

'They're men?' Willow self-consciously smoothing her unbrushed hair.

'Sort of. Look it's not all bad, give it a chance. Like the ladyboys it's not what it seems on the surface.' He assured her.

Che stamped on the breaks, narrowly missing a drunk, shirtless man, who had fallen from the pavement, sunburnt and glassy eyed. Che muttered something under his breath and went back to speeding down the road swaying and swinging around Tuk Tuks, abandoning all forms of indication.

Willow struggled back into her seat, stomach swirling and bile burning. Covering her mouth she burped and hiccupped.

Aaron seemed used to the slalom driving. 'Don't look sad. It's not so awful; Most trips start and end here. It's full of hope and loss, optimism and sadness; anything is possible on these streets. It's a melting pot of people telling their tales or those who are about to embark on adventures that may shape who they later become. The streets are paved with stories.' He was clearly enjoying his soap box.

'You should have been in PR.' Willow laughed, he could sell her almost anything. It was a shame she wasn't in the market for a man.

She pointed to an older man who was picking up one of the lady-boys, 'What's his story do you think?'

Aaron tutted, 'Come on be open minded! You'll meet some interesting people and sample some great food. Left just here Che,' he yelled forward.

The van sped around the bend without slowing. The colour drained from Willow's face. She was about to be sick, 'Can we pull over?'

No-one answered.

Aaron was looking at the road ahead, 'The hotel is just down here. It's much quieter on this road, but still walking distance from the main strip.'

Willow's stomach gurgled, winding down the window she glanced up, relieved to see how much quieter it had grown. At least she wouldn't shower pedestrians with vomit. She took a deep breath, feeling less claustrophobic, the high hotels of the ominous dark metropolis were behind them. They could have been in a different city.

Che, heavy on the breaks again, stopped the van. Willow jolted forward, thrusting her hand into his head rest, bracing her arm in time to keep herself in her seat. She had given Che a good shove in the back of his head, but she was learning.

'Now you used to driving in Thailand,' Che grinned, rubbing his neck.

Aaron leapt from the van, 'Excuse me one minute.'

He began chatting with a woman who could have been over a hundred years old. She was precariously perched on a rickety stool, dwarfed by her ramshackle stand which bowed under the weight of high-piled King coconuts. She hopped up with surprising dexterity.

Willow was reminded of Yoda.

The lady grabbed one of the orb shaped fruits, produced a huge machete, wielded it above her head and brought it down upon the coconut in her other palm. Three loud cracks of the blade against husk and the top flew off, juice spraying through the air. She popped a straw into the juicy fruit and limped to the van, thrusting it towards Willow.

'No thank you. My stomach. I'm not feeling well.' Willow declined, unsure why she was putting on a strange, probably insulting Thai accent.

Che observed her, 'You green, coconuts very good for green tourist.' He indicated for her to drink up.

Bowing to the peer-pressure, Willow accepted it and sucked the warm sweet liquid. Her eyes widened, mouth tingled and stomach thanked her. She'd had coconut water from the supermarket but a fresh one was a totally different experience, her first real taste of Thailand.

Aaron returned to the van slurping a coconut of his own, 'Start your day with one of these and your stomach should keep in check. Bex works that same patch every day. I've never been to this road without seeing her in over fifteen years.'

How many other women had he taken to the same place?

Che started the engine up again.

Willow peered at the road, the few awnings which hung out into the street were torn and sun bleached. The western-style advertising and modernisation had stayed firmly behind them. At first the road seemed neglected; but when she looked more closely she could see something quite beautiful beneath the tired veneer.

They pulled up outside a small terraced building with an enormous, intricately carved entrance. Aaron got out and opened the van's back door and hoisted Willow's bag from the seat, 'Christ, I better carry this inside for you.' He declared, before she could object.

Willow stepped out of the van, relieved to be back on the safety of her two feet.

'Do you like it?' he asked, leading her inside.

'I love it!' she gasped, feeling like Alice stepping through the looking glass.

The walls were adorned with teak statues of Elephants and religious icons. The floor was covered in a sprawling array of pot plants, giving off a gentle perfume; a reprieve from the city smog. Large fans whirled on the ceiling, circulating the soft scent. A gateway to what she had imagined would be waiting for her when she stepped off the plane.

Aaron rang a large ancient bell which hung above the front desk and a Thai lady, with deep laughter lines and white grey hair appeared from nowhere.

'Aaron and beautiful guest come to stay with Apple.' The lady greeted them with a warm smile, wearing lashings of long fabric, moving with grace.

'Just one beautiful guest, this time thanks Apple,' Aaron corrected, avoiding Willow's disparaging look.

Clearly there had been many women.

Willow wanted to explain that they were just friends, she wasn't anything like these *other* women, but Apple was already cupping Aaron's face in her hands.

'Ah, such a shame. So beautiful, so lonely.' Apple kissed him and patted his cheek, 'Come, come; let me show you to your room. Aaron don't be so slow with bag.'

Willow's basic room was homely with hand-painted floral wall murals, hanging plants and quilted throw pillows filling the space.

Her room at Claire's house belonged to Barney, her three-year-old nephew. Moving into that space rocket-themed hole had been the lowest point in a year which had been crammed with them.

It wasn't just the decor she was tired of, it was the screaming kids, lack of personal space and weekend dinner parties. She would perch at the end of the table, quietly praying that Claire's friends wouldn't offer her unwanted advice about her single or unemployed status, but it was preferential to the hospital.

'You happy?' Apple queried.

'Very happy, thank you,' Willow said, truthfully. She could *feel* Rosa there, in a way that she couldn't in the madness offered on the surrounding roads. She was on the right path, she knew it.

Apple winked, 'So polite. Aaron you keep her please.'

Aaron put his hands over his face and shook his head, 'Apple Bai.' He chuckled, shepherding her out and shutting the door behind her.

Willow could hear her giggling as she walked away and could imagine what she was thinking. It was clear that Aaron was a lady's man, but he had helped her and she was grateful. 'What did you say to her?' she enquired.

'I told her to go away,' he was still smiling, 'Don't worry it's not rude here, you'll be told to go away a lot, no one means anything by it.' He let her bag drop to the floor and stood in silence for a moment, 'So…'

'So…' she echoed; was he waiting for a tip?

'Thank you for all of your help today.' She wasn't sure there was anything left to say.

Why was he looking at her? She squirmed, uncomfortable under scrutiny.

Thankfully he seemed to remember that it was rude to stare and averted his eyes. 'No problem, it was a pleasure. Now this is where I leave you. I hope you find Jay and whatever else you are looking for. Apple can help with booking trips or recommending restaurants, anything you need, but don't believe everything she tells you about me, it's only half true.' His easy smile, spread to his ice blue eyes, he tilted his hat and bowed out the door.

As quickly as he entered her life he had left.

Chapter 4

The sun was standing proud in the clear morning sky. A gentle breeze whispered through the surrounding palms. They were blissfully isolated. Aside from chatter of the resident monkeys as they danced through the foliage, the beach was quiet.

Rosa stretched; her husband's T-shirt rising up, exposing her tanned naked flesh. She yearned for more sleep, but the morning was too beautiful, the ocean air too enticing.

She groaned, her eyes adjusting to the brightness, the view bringing a smile to her face, as it always had, regardless of the hangover.

She grabbed her iPod, hopped off the rickety terrace onto the baked sand and flung herself upon it, ever the sun worshipper.

She should be preparing to head back to the school, there was a mountain of marking waiting and it was hard to be away from the boys, especially Jay, but he had begged to stay with his friends.

She closed her eyes, trying to forget about packing. Her music soothed her back to sleep.

Later Rosa wriggled her fingers, smiling as Wan interlinked his with hers, kissing her neck. She pulled her headphones from her ears and brushed the sand from her hair and shoulders.

'Good morning my love,' she murmured, looking up into his amber eyes, loving him every bit as much as she had the day they'd met. She was envious of his skin which held its youth against the sun in a way that hers had not. She had recently turned forty, a day which should have been celebrated with Caroline, instead it had been another day that she was forced to miss her.

Wan stroked her long hair away from her face, 'You're up early this morning. How's your head?'

She thought back on their evening spent on the other side of the island, drinking and dancing with their closest friends, as they had done every Christmas for the past twelve years. Her hair still carried the scent from the bonfire, Mac's guitar music and questionable singing still looping in her consciousness. 'Pounding. I think I'm getting too old for this.'

He sat up, looking out to sea, 'You have said that every year since you were twenty-five,' he reminded her, distracted by something.

'One of these years it will be the truth,' she said, following his gaze. 'The tide is really far out; I've never seen it like this, have you?' Rocks that were normally under a few feet of water were visible, the sea bed sodden and exposed.

Wan got to his feet, 'No I haven't.' He meandered, closer to the water, squatted and turned back holding a writhing fish. He flung it back into the sea, looking to the horizon.

She lay back down, intrigued but not concerned and yawned. Just a few more minutes rest. Moments later she sat up, bewildered, water was lapping up her legs clawing its way to her waist at unsettling speed. The air was too still, even the monkeys had fallen silent, Wan, breathless from running, grabbed her hand and pulled her up.

'Run,' he screamed. A wall of darkness, behind him, where there should have been only sky, the ocean growling up into the air, rushing toward them.

The sand was like wet concrete, Rosa pushed on to the hut, the water was at her thighs when she reached it. Over the roar she could make out distant cries and screams, from the neighbouring bays and hotels?

She didn't see the wave that engorged them, she saw the panic reflected in Wan's eyes as he stared, aghast, over her shoulder; then she was drowning.

Chapter 5

Willow woke with a start, sitting up, sweat cloaking her like a veil.

She was in hospital. The nurses must have called lights out while she was sleeping? Her door would be locked for another six hours. No permitted toilet breaks, no trips to the kitchen. She couldn't be trusted with access to razors or knives.

She sat up and rubbed her eyes. The room did not smell right. Where was the medical scent of bleach? Her senses began to clear as she woke fully.

The sun had set and little light penetrated the slatted window blinds, but once her eyes adjusted she could make out the soft furnishings of Apple's room.

She lay back on the bed, relieved, she was free.

Clashing street music was playing nearby. Threads of *Kings of Leon* could be picked out from amongst sitars and street drums. She got up, stumbled across the room, pulled the blinds back and swung open the window. The heat, noise and life of the night swept in.

The sill was large enough to sit on, so she pulled her legs up, and stared at her phone, which had been turned off since leaving London. Was it anything more than a shackle to an unhappy life? Resigned, she switched it on.

An assault of beeping, ringing and vibrating message alerts sounded, each chime escalating her panic and an undeniable thrill. Maybe James had made contact? Claire's name came through over and over, she pressed delete against each message, without reading one, then the screen was blank.

James had been part of her life's plan, her happy ending was within grasp when she, or both, had blown it. If he came back life could go back to normal; that's what she wanted wasn't it?

She closed her eyes and could feel him there, her arm linked through his, palm pressed up to his shoulder. Safe. She had been totally unprepared for how awful it would feel to walk into a party alone, she never knew what to do with her hands, so she had stopped going, stopped going out entirely actually.

She tried to imagine what it would be like to go out onto the streets below, alone. She could be a carefree traveller for the evening, making idle chat drinking in a bar, but what would she talk about; why would anyone want to spend time with her? Everyone was with partners and friends.

Her stomach let out a loud hungry grumble, she weighed her options: venture out in search of food or try to get back to sleep and wait for daylight? She slipped on her trainers and stepped towards the door, rested her hand on the handle and paused.

She could get lost, or attacked, no-one would take care of her. Her hand shook, she pulled it away, as if burnt, her heart drumming with an intensity that caused her to sink to her knees, cowering from the door, heaving one laboured long breath after the next. Who wanted to risk fainting and injuring themselves again?

Laying on the cold floor, she closed her eyes and counted slowly to ten, then twenty and on to one hundred, just as the doctor had suggested. Her breathing slowed as it usually did. She pulled the sheet from the bed and stayed, where she was, until sleep offered her rest from fear.

When the sun began to brighten the room she cautiously opened her eyes. What had she done? Why was she thousands of miles from home, lying on the floor, aching all over and starving hungry with no idea what to do next? Maybe she was still crazy?

She observed out the window that the streets were dormant, save for a few tired looking travellers, guidebooks at the ready. It was 06:15, Bangkok was clearly not a city that woke early. The bottle of water Apple had supplied was nearly finished and the guide book's warning had been clear: *Avoid drinking the tap water at all costs it WILL cause diarrhoea and vomiting.*

Willow didn't fancy dying in her room, in a pool of her own sick, or worse. She was thirty years old, there were girls straight out of college traveling all over Thailand and they weren't cowering away. She grabbed her keys and wallet, quickly opened the door and chucked herself through, slamming it behind her before she could change her mind.

She warily stepped out on to the deserted street, the emptiness of the city giving her space to breathe. Shutters were firmly in place, hatches were down, but there had to be food somewhere; didn't there?

To save herself from getting lost Willow walked in a straight line until the road came to an end and she realised she'd have to find a more commercial block. She took a left and walked toward the Khao San road. A street cleaner glanced at her and nodded in greeting.

Inexplicably there were a high number of discarded children's beach buckets in an assortment of colours, littering the floor, minus the spades. Bangkok got stranger and stranger.

A small group of weary tourists were huddled outside a travel shop, off on some excursion she guessed. She contemplated asking them for a tip for finding a meal, but crossed the road, giving in to social anxiety. Then she saw the illuminated lights of a Seven Eleven convenience store.

Elated, she wandered the isles, satisfied that she was an intrepid explorer who had found sustenance against all odds. Her basket was full with familiar crisps and drinks, a comforting reminder of home. When she saw a pair of scissors she threw them in, she would need to cut her jeans into shorts.

She wanted to stay in the safety of the shop, but once she had circled the goods for the fourth time it was time to go.

The cashier smiled at her, 'Welcome to Thailand!'

'Thank you.' Was it that obvious she'd just arrived?

As if reading her mind the cashier elaborated, 'You really white and…' she nodded at her snack selection.

Willow had to laugh. She was *really white,* the winter in London had not been kind and her skin had fallen sallow with many days spent inside.

She wandered back to the hotel, squinting in the sun, she needed to buy sun glasses amongst many other things. Despite her fears, she could hear the city calling, begging her to scratch beneath the surface, but when she saw the hotel the relief was intoxicating.

Back on the window ledge, surrounded by snacks and fizzy drinks Willow watched as Bangkok rose its sleepy head. The shutters lifted, couples walked hand in hand, young groups joked loudly and sauntered about, buskers and fruit sellers set up for the day. Women her age set off for days filled with adventure while she played puzzle games on her phone, walked around like a caged animal, read and reread Rosa's letters, showered; ate a dry croissant from a vacuum-packed bag, five bags of crisps and a melted Mars bar.

Finally the sun fell, floss pink light blanketing the city and she settled herself in for another night.

'Willow; Willow are you there?' It was a female voice, from the hallway, heavy with a Scandinavian lilt. Swedish perhaps?

Willow grabbed the bedside lamp, still tethered to the wall, 'Hello. Who is it?' Who the hell was this person and how did they know her name?

'I'm a friend of Aaron's.'

Swiss. She was definitely Swiss, Willow decided, still teetering in bed. Should she open the door or call Apple for protection?

'He said that you might be interested in a trip I'm going on?' the girl was unfazed by talking to a door and sounded friendly enough.

A trip; intrigue began to replace her fear. Desperate to escape the hotel and craving a proper meal, Willow made her way to the door and hesitantly opened it.

The girl had long icy blonde hair, tamed into braids that twisted down either side of her head, licking up at her hips. Her eyes were a piercing shade of blue, surrounded by fair pearly white lashes. Her skin was tanned and freckles fell across her nose, the type brought out by prolonged sun exposure. She wore a crochet top exposing a taut youthful mid-rift accented with a bejewelled belly button and fairy tattoo up her side. Her legs were covered in a long silk painted skirt. Her orange painted toes peeked from worn out flip flops.

Smiling broadly, the girl waved a hand, riddled with silver rings, wrists rattling with reams of tinkling bracelets. 'Hi there lady from the plane, it's nice to meet you, I'm Lucia.'

Lucia was the most curiously beautiful girl Willow had ever seen. An ethereal pirate/elf. What impression could Lucia possibly have of her? Wearing an office shirt, undone and exposing a faded bra. Her face was free of makeup and her hair was in a knotty bundle. 'So Aaron told you to find me?' she asked, flattered that he had thought of her.

Lucia nodded enthusiastically, 'Sure did. I've just come from dinner with him. You and I are neighbours. I'm staying down the hall. He loves this place. Recommends it to everyone.'

Lucia filled the silence that followed, 'It's a shame he had to leave, he knows all the best places. I'm sure he would have liked to have shown you around himself; he's great don't you think?'

Willow couldn't ignore it, she was disappointed, he was gone. 'Yeah he is perfect. I mean this place it perfect, the hotel.' Heat rose in her cheeks.

Lucia took her hand and squeezed her fingers conspiratorially, 'I don't know what I would have done without him when I first got here, he says I helped him, but I don't remember it being that way at all. I didn't have a clue where to go or what to do, I was so lost. It's a bit embarrassing really.'

'I think I'm one of those embarrassing people right now,' Willow confessed, 'I wanted to do everything alone, now I'm not so sure.'

The reality of setting off into the unknown alone was not as appealing as it had been when she had been fleeing London.

'Stuff that! Everyone needs a bit of help. If you knew everything about this place you wouldn't have the joy of stumbling on the gems. Look, I'm planning on going to Ayutthaya in two days, I'm the only one going and I hate those big group excursions. We could split the costs of a taxi or something? I mentioned it to Aaron and he seemed to think you might be keen? It's the ancient capital of Thailand, a beautiful city, well it's an island really at the confluence of three rivers. Pretty special,' Lucia kept nodding enthusiastically.

Sold! Willow ushered Lucia inside and grabbed her box of letters, pulling out the photo that Aaron had recognised as being in Ayutthaya. 'Yes, I want to come!' Willow blurted, holding up the photo, 'I need to find this hotel, the one in the background.'

Lucia examined the photo, 'I can help you find it, or at least find you someone who can. We can do some cycling at the same time, it's the best way to get around the place and Aaron told me that you get a bit car sick.'

What a fabulous impression she had left on him. She silently thanked a God she'd given up on, grateful for a companion, for the first leg at least, 'So when do we go?'

Lucia scrutinised her, 'Bangkok hasn't left a good impression on you has it?'

Willow looked away, 'Mostly I've been chilling here. It must be the jet lag.' She lied.

'That won't do. We leave in two days, by then I will have shown you plenty of reasons to love this city. Starting from now, you are not allowed to spend another waking hour in this room. No offense, but you look like you could do with a drink. Are you hungry? Let's go out and make some plans.' Lucia delivered her invitation as a demand.

Willow could have hugged her, it was the push she needed. 'A drink would be great!'

'Awesome! Grab your purse and follow me!' Lucia was already turning to leave.

Galvanised, Willow was half way out the door before she realised she was in her sister's shirt, 'Hang on a minute, I've got no trousers on, I've got to get changed,' She uttered, unable to imagine she had anything suitable to wear.

Lucia waved her hand, 'Half the people here won't have got changed this week. It's far too hot for trousers. You're fine as you are.'

Willow doubted that but didn't want to disagree. She pictured the awful looking street that they had passed on the way to the hotel, her motivations ebbing, 'Are we going to Khao San Road?' she would be grateful to be out, regardless of where but needed to mentally prepare herself if they were entering the eye of the storm.

Lucia bit her lip, 'We can if you like, but I know some far better places on Soi Rambuttri, still lively but far more relaxed, nowhere near as many prostitutes or men in football shirts.'

'Less prostitutes; sounds good to me.' Willow tied a belt around the waist of her shirt, trying to ignore that it flitted precariously short. She grabbed her wallet then phone, paused and chucked it back on the bed, slamming the door behind them. The last thing she needed was to be checking it for messages from James all night.

Willow was in the twilight zone, *Soi Rambuttri* was unlike anywhere she had ever been.

She was only able to go away during the school holidays, so overseas trips were expensive and her wages couldn't cover anywhere outside of Europe. Not when she inevitably ended up paying for James as well.

James was an actor and would spend every penny he had and quite a few of hers, on his annual three-month trips to LA for *pilot* season, January through to April, when she could not leave her students and going to see him meant crashing on his friend's sofa.

Each year he went to find his fortune, returning home broke and depressed with stories of celebrity parties and near breaks. Despite all the auditions and ever-changing agents, James had never made the grade. Now finally her money was her own.

Willow turned in every direction, nearly spinning, eager to take it all in. The people and places were wrapped in a cloak of otherness; like the petrol station which had been taken over with fold out tables and chairs. A man was selling the colourful children's buckets that had littered the road that morning. They were full with various bottles of alcohol and energy drinks.

When someone bought a bucket the vendor emptied in the contents of the bottles and packed it with ice and straws. She had never considered a bucket a drinking vessel, but it was very popular, judging by the amount of them she saw in the hands of tourists.

She wandered over, picked one up and examined it, one of the bottles was a mysterious 500ml of dark alcohol, *Sangsom* read the label, there was also a can of coke and a bottle of something that promised to be ten times stronger than Red Bull. Christ.

'Five hundred baht,' the vendor called to her, while serving a group of giggling girls.

Lucia took the bucket from her hands and put it back on the stall. 'Easy tiger there'll be time for one of those later. Drink one now and you will be a wreck within an hour. They are absolutely lethal, I never go near them, well hardly ever. They're for the tourists.'

'Aren't you a tourist?' Willow realised that she had no idea who Lucia was.

Lucia shook her head vigorously 'I live here, I have a coffee shop on Koh Tao.'

Willow was impressed. 'Wow that's amazing.' She was about to ask about it, when she saw a woman filling up her motorbike with fuel from one of the pumps, she had assumed they were dormant. Tourists were crammed around a table, feet from the pump, smoking. It was time to leave.

Lucia shouted, 'Verpiss dich,' at a man who bumped into her.

'You speak German?' Willow asked, hoping that Lucia's language skills went further than, *fuck off*.

Lucia shrugged, 'Yep a bit.' She hustled Willow toward a bustling bar, 'Come on I'll ease you into the drinks, save the buckets for when you want to get really messed up!'

The bar was full with people smoking scented shisha pipes and drinking beer from large plastic towers. The walls were pasted with magazine cuttings from old copies of NME, Melody Maker and Rolling Stone. A DJ perched in a corner playing Guns and Roses, like in an American biker bar. Then she noticed the beautifully embroidered cushions and low tables, carved wooden ceiling and the multilingual chatter.

She filled her nose with the warming sweet chilli aroma wafting from the kitchen, cutting through the smoke like a knife. She had waited nearly all her life to be in Thailand and she would be damned if she'd let fear bind her to a hotel room again.

Lucia returned from the bar, an expert in juggling, holding two bottles of beer, a whiskey bottle, a jug of soda and two glasses, 'There are two things you need on your first night in Bangkok. A Sangsom Whiskey and a Chang beer.' She deposited the bounty on the table, 'Drink up!'

Intrigued, Willow sniffed the Whiskey, her face crumpled, 'Wow that is something else. It smells like drain cleaner! Thank god I didn't buy a bucket of the stuff!'

Lucia poured them a glass each, ignoring Willow's protests, 'Trust me after you've had one you lose your ability to taste. The buckets actually taste marginally better, if you like the taste of madly sweet cola and amphetamine laced *Red bull*?'

Willow pictured her alternative evening, tucked up in bed and braved another sip, then another, and another. Her lips tingled, growing numb as she relaxed. They chatted in a peculiar mix of Swiss, German and English. Lucia was fluent, despite her modesty.

To be flexing her linguistic muscles again was energising. She'd spent too long in the company of her nieces and nephew discussing *Play Doh* and *Peppa Pig*.

Willow was enthralled by Lucia's life, she had come away for a gap year at eighteen and six years later was still there. She had been unhappy with life so she had changed it, just like that. Could it be so simple?

Willow's head began to fog so she left the half empty whiskey bottle and moved to sipping a cold beer, settling further into the cushion, laughing as Lucia poured another whiskey, 'I'll stick to the beer thanks, I'm getting drunk.'

Lucia drained her own glass, 'You can do that, but it's not much safer. The alcohol percentage on the front is more like a guesstimate then a fact.'

Willow discreetly spat the beer back into the bottle, 'Do they have any wine?'

Lucia hooted, 'Don't ever drink the wine! I had some once on Koh Phi Phi. It was the end of low season. We hadn't had a wine delivery for months and were all excited when one of the bars got some in. It tasted a bit weird, but like I said, it had been a while.'

Willow wrinkled her nose, she had been hoping for a nice dry white Rioja, 'Did you get really sick?'

Lucia put her hand over her mouth theatrically, 'Sick as a dog, but that's not the worst of it. I'd shared three bottles with a diver I was momentarily dating. We were so smashed that I woke up with an engagement ring tattooed on my finger and fuzzy memories of a proposal. There had been some dancing on a table with half a rugby team who wanted to help us celebrate; at least I think it was a rugby team it could have been a gaggle of nuns, I could hardly see!'

Up until she had boarded the plane for Thailand Willow had never done anything reckless and wasn't sure if she should laugh or console her new friend.

Lucia held up her hand, exposing a small pretty pink heart etched on to her engagement finger, on the reverse was a small black bird, 'The bird is a cover up. It used to say Dave.' She belly laughed, 'Thankfully a friend of mine is a tattooist and managed to cover it quickly. Now I quite like it. The bird reminds me that I am free from Dave and all the others like him.' she took another swig of whiskey, raising her glass in the air, 'To Dave, thanks for the cool tattoo!' she yelled.

James hardly ever drank and had made Willow feel foolish if she was even a little tipsy. She hadn't wanted to upset him or show him up, apparently her behaviour was *embarrassing*, so she'd stayed away from alcohol. What would he have done if she'd ever gotten a tattoo, drunk or otherwise?

She picked up the Sangsom-filled glass, tipped her head back and swallowed the vile liquor in one. *Fuck James.* She poured another.

Lucia held her glass aloft, 'To new friends,' she sang.

Three more whiskey's, two beers, a bowl of scrumptious noodles later and nature had called. Willow staggered back from the toilet to find Lucia had been joined by four men. As she got closer she detected strong South African accents.

Lucia was three sheets to the wind, glassy eyed and smiling wildly, 'Willow, look who I've found, my friends!' she was jubilant, 'We had the most amazing few days together in Koh Pang Nang last month. These guys know how to party!'

Everyone was whooping and congratulating themselves on an amazing time as Willow stood on the outside of the circle. Maybe it was time for her to go back to the hotel. She shuffled awkwardly, Lucia and the men oblivious to her discomfort and her in general.

'We sure did,' drawled a particularly handsome sun kissed young man, 'This one dances like no one's watching!' he winked at Lucia, 'Do you remember when you fell off the bar?'

Another eruption of laughter at the shared memories followed, Willow feeling truly out of the loop.

A smaller muscular man with deep dark skin chimed in, 'I didn't get to bed until 9:00 A.M and I had a boat to catch at 10:30! I'm still not sure how I made it or why I was wearing a sombrero when I arrived on Koh Tao.' He flashed Willow a huge smile.

The men continued to laugh, while Willow stood, unsure if she should let herself be swept along by their fun and youthful spirits, or if she was eaves-dropping. Should she pretend she hadn't been listening? Her hands grew sticky.

'I'm Neo,' said the smaller man, stretching across the table with his hand outstretched.

Willow wiped her sweaty palm on her leg and took his hand, grateful.

'This is Chris,' he shook her hand, nodding at his gorgeous friend who was slumped across her cushion, 'That's Grae and that's Jesus,' he pointed to the others.

Her heart rate returned to normal. Emboldened by whiskey she smiled. 'Hi I'm Willow. Is Jesus really your name?' she reassured herself that making conversation did not have to be an ordeal.

The one that they called Jesus bowed his head.

Neo let out a hearty chortle, 'We went to his hut one day, just as I was about to knock the door, I heard a girl screaming *"Oh Jesus, Oh Jesus"* and so the name was born.'

It was like being in a boy's locker room, but she liked it, feeling part of the team.

Chris addressed her, 'Don't stand on parade. Sit Down!' he patted a tiny spot on the cushion next to him.

Willow tried to sit as delicately as possible, but collapsed the last few inches, rolling against his hard-muscular body. Wow, she'd forgotten that men could be made like that, young, fit, a head full of thick unkempt hair. He put his arm around her and shuffled about so they could both squeeze on.

She was surprised at how comfortable she was sitting on that grubby floor with a stranger, more at ease than she ever had been on a bar stall, alone, in London, waiting for James as he *networked*.

'Let's finish these, buy buckets and go dancing!' Lucia announced, throwing her arms in the air exuberantly.

The men protested, they had a plane to catch in the morning, but they were playful in their rebuttals and were downing their drinks readying to go before they had finished their sentences. Willow's immediate thought was to object, but why? She was having fun and had nowhere to be for the next thirty-six hours.

'Willow is an awesome dancer,' Lucia winked at her, pulling her to her feet.

Willow almost choked on her drink and pulled a face at Lucia, urging her to retract the statement. She couldn't recall the last time she had set foot on a dance floor, she didn't like to embarrass herself or James. On a night out she was the girl sat in the corner, the one who no one could remember being there.

Lucia whispered in her ear, 'Don't be scared. In Thailand you can be whoever you want to be!'

Willow squeezed her hand, she wanted to move on, she wanted to feel happy again, 'Let's go, show me the best Bangkok has to offer!' She shouted, confidently leading the way, vowing that on that night she would be remembered as the girl who loved to dance.

Chapter 6

Willow groaned loudly, head pounding and blinked hard, half asleep. She knew she was in her hotel room but wasn't sure how she had got there.

A moment later she realised she wasn't alone. She watched for a moment as Chris moved, a whirlwind throwing sheets and clothes around in a frenzy.

'Oh Crap!' he yelled, his guttural South African voice booming in the tranquil space.

He was naked, deep tan lines leaving his white bottom illuminated in the morning's half-light.

'Sorry I was trying not to wake you, I'm just so bloody late, I have to run or I'll miss my plane!' he smiled with a sparkle in his blood-shot eyes, pushing his sun-bleached hair back, whipping his pants on, half hopping across the room and kissing her on the cheek.

She remembered something about the boys having to get a plane to Laos in the morning. She sat up and shuddered. Was it morning already?

The men were going tubing. It was a *once in a life time mind fuck,* or so Neo had shouted. She couldn't see how sitting on a giant rubber ring, floating down a river and being pulled into bars and opium shacks that lined the banks was that earth shattering, but clearly they did.

Parts of the later evening were coming back with embarrassing clarity. kissing Chris in a nightclub as they danced, skipping down the road holding hands and singing, taking him back to her room and pulling his clothes off. Oh no, that was not the behaviour of a university lecturer, then again she wasn't one anymore.

Chris looked at her approvingly, 'You were worth being late for,' he gently stroked her face before erupting into activity again, grabbing his t-shirt and shoving his wallet into his pocket while slipping on flip flops.

In the furore Willow's sheet had been pulled off. She was face down on the bed, naked. If she moved to grab the sheet she'd have to offer Chris a full-frontal show of untended nether regions. Without inebriation she was not as bold as she clearly had been a few hours previously. Instead she chose to leave her pasty buttocks and unshaven legs on display to the ceiling and the gorgeous man. She was not *summer body* ready.

With his arms risen to the skies he laughed, 'Last night was awesome!'

'Awesome.' she whispered feeling silly. She hadn't used words like that in years. She studied him; how old was he? Early twenties? Was she a cougar?

'Those ladyboys loved your moves, hell I loved your moves, so much fun!' he testified moving to the door.

Willow was hit by more flashbacks. A back street Go-go bar, questionable pole dancing and a rather ambitious hanging upside down by one leg trick. Oh no, she cringed. Miraculously she had escaped any serious injuries, she wasn't aware of any lingering pain. She flushed pink, the flamboyant girl of the night ebbing away with the clarity of the morning light.

Chris stepped toward her and grabbed her phone, from the bedside table, checking the time. He winced.

'Sorry, I've really got to go. You're still coming right?' he stared with puppy dog eyes full of hope.

'Where? For what?' she wanted him to slow down, he was making her dizzy.

'Tubing. Opium all the way down the Vang Vien river. Just you and me, and the rest of the guys and a whole travel party of course, but I could make time for us just to be together.'

'We'll see. I'll Facebook you,' she agreed, bemused, certain that she was too old to be experimenting with drugs and drifting down a river even if the offer to escape with a man like that was very tempting indeed.

Chris gave her a thumbs up, 'Cool. I'll put up some photos from last night when I get to some Wi-Fi. My surname is Gregson, you'll find me on Lucia's friends list.' He threw her phone back on to the bed, then quickly kissed her on the cheek.

She didn't even know his last name. She needed to get new social media sites set up as soon as possible. New place, new friends new....

Chris stopped and turned back, 'Your phone has been beeping all morning, someone really wants to get hold of you. Time to wake up and phone home gorgeous.' He blew her a kiss and slipped out the door.

In the sudden-still she thought of James, she couldn't help it. She longed to leap for her phone, feeling awash with guilt, she hadn't been with anyone since him. What if he had phoned while she was out behaving like a slut? She picked up her phone, but before she turned on the screen she put it back on the side table. Whether it was Claire or James no good could come of hearing from either of them.

Willow had never deemed herself to be sexy or particularly sensual. She was not the girl to turn heads; that had always been Claire's job, elegant and tall with plump lips and orange brown eyes. Claire had married a handsome soap opera producer at twenty-three and quickly was surrounded by a brood of children. Claire got everything she had ever wanted, a family.

Willow had been surprised when James had asked her on a date. She was not oblivious to the more glamourous girls who regularly called or turned up to the parties he frequented. His Instagram was laden with likes and heart emoji's, things he brushed off and made her feel crazy for every worrying about.

Was it her intellectual arrogance that had led her to believe that James loved her for her humour, political insight and knowledge of current affairs? He had proclaimed to find it incredibly sexy when she spoke to him in a different language, of course he had no idea what she was saying, but she had been flattered.

She hadn't wanted to see James's keen interest in her sister's husband Paul for what it was. A sad attempt to progress his career.

He had pretended to run marathons so he could bond with Paul over his upcoming triathlon. It had worked until he got swept along with his own deception and found himself signing up to take part. It was hard to picture James out of his leather jacket and in Lycra, but she was proud and supportive of his efforts, until, smoking on their balcony the following month he admitted to never considering taking part, he was just after *a part*.

Paul had seen through James, he met chancers like him all too frequently. That had been the moment her relationship with Claire had shifted. When Claire had ceased to embrace Willow's happiness and instead pitied her. *Poor Willow can't find a decent husband, this man doesn't love her, he is just using her.* Willow so badly wanted to prove Claire and herself wrong that she'd turned herself blind.

She couldn't deny it, James had never looked at her in the way that Chris had, in the way that a man should, with desire. Chris hadn't cared what was in her bank account or what she could do for his career, he had just seen her, a woman he wanted to fuck.

Regardless of any feminist inclinations, she had to admit, that made her feel good.

She closed her eyes considering the silliness of the morning. She knew that she wasn't a slut, she had the right to do whatever she liked with her body. She rolled about, enjoying her recklessness nakedness, shaking away her exhaustion in the cascading rainbow sunlight that crept across the bed.

She could not get back to sleep. She was in Thailand! Her mind was racing with the possibilities for the day.

She rose to her feet, an excited current flowing through her body as she skipped to the bathroom, stopping in front of the mirror, something she usually avoided. The change took her breath away.

She had lost a lot of weight, physically growing weaker as her mental health deteriorated. Over the months her face had grown gaunt and drained, happiness gone from her soul; but that morning she saw another *her* was coming to the surface, bringing back the light.

She stepped into the shower, gasping as it spluttered to life with cold water, which failed to ever grow warm. Her nipples hardened and goose bumps rose. She lathered her hair and watched as the bubbles fell over her collar bone, scented suds slithering over her dormant engagement ring necklace. She considered taking off. Not yet.

She towelled herself dry and look down upon the contents of her backpack, strewn across the bed. She hated all of it, she didn't want to dress up as Claire; but what was her style? Who was Willow?

She might not be capable of choosing clothes for herself, but there was something she could do. She signed into the Wi-Fi and hurriedly set up a new Facebook account. *Willow Brady* read the name. A new beginning was at her finger tips.

A loud banging on the door disturbed her thoughts.

'Coming,' she yelled, throwing on a huge men's t-shirt and opening the door, to find Lucia grinning on the other side.

She was effortlessly bohemian, wearing enormous canary yellow sunglasses, hair piled high and no bra on under her colourful long dress which skimmed over her body perfectly. Her toenails were a freshly painted electric blue, glistening next to her tanned skin like sapphires. There was a woman who knew her style, who knew who she was!

'What's up? You look worried,' Lucia peeked out from over her sunglasses, outstretching a cup, overflowing with icy pink mush to Willow. 'It's a watermelon shake, fresh from the street, it will help rehydrate you. If you are going to handle Bangkok today, you'll need this.'

'Thanks.' It smelled incredible. Willow took a long slurp, the explosion of taste refreshing her from the core. She stopped and considered the wild, carefree beauty stood in her room and had to ask; 'Why are you doing all this for me?' She couldn't remember the last time anyone had made her a cup of tea or taken her for a night out without agenda.

Lucia's confident veneer abandoned her. 'Because I was you. I was lost when I arrived, it took me a while to find my feet and I was miserable. Aaron helped me in the beginning and I don't know, I guess I wanted to help you on your way?'

Willow was touched, there was no sinister motive, just one friend helping another.

She motioned Lucia to look toward the bed, 'I didn't exactly have time to pack properly. I've not got a thing I can wear, nothing for a bar, a day in town, or for the beach and certainly nothing for riding a bike in!'

Willow pushed Claire's clothes around on the bed, letting them cascade onto the floor, sitting on the bare patch on the mattress. She picked out some jeans: thick, heavy duty, at least four sizes too big and held them toward Lucia laughing at how wrong they were.

'Well they would keep you covered-up, they are definitely not sexual in any way; you could wear them to a

49

temple?' Lucia couldn't stifle her laughter, 'Are they even yours? They look huge!' she snatched them from Willows hands.

Willow scoffed, 'I think they may be my brother-in-law's.'

'…And these? what are these about?' Lucia held up two pin-stripe, work blouses.

'They are Tommy Hilfiger!' Willow defended Claire's taste without knowing why.

Lucia turned her nose up, causing Willow to laugh

'They're my sisters. She's a bit of a soccer mum. Nothing on this bed is mine.'

'I should hope not,' Lucia cackled, flinging a pair of greying faded knickers at Willow.

Willow flinched away, 'I'm ashamed to say that those are mine, but no one's been looking at my undies in a long time.'

'I don't wear any, it's too hot.' Lucia stated.

Of course she didn't. Willow was beginning to fear that she was like an old frumpy cast-off herself, but sauntering about with her fanny out seemed a bit new age, not to mention breezy. 'You know this trip was not exactly well planned?'

'You did mention that a number of times last night! Don't worry I'll help you sort this out. There must be something you can wear in that lot?' Lucia grabbed a few tops from the top of the pile.

They leafed through the clothes, a discarded pile growing on the floor. Black fitted trousers, a couple of men's T-shirts, a sports swimming costume, some fine knit jumpers; not a hint of summer dress or shorts.

Willow huffed, 'You can tell so much about who you are by your style. I'm not sure of who I am anymore?' she kicked the pile of clothes, a pang of sadness as she saw James soft black Calvin Klien T-shirt, the one she had slept in since the split. 'I see my sister here, my brother-in-law, my ex, but nothing of me.'

Lucia flung a kitten heeled boot on the pile, 'So package it up and post it home. It's crazy cheap here, just buy things that you love and not what your sister loves! You my friend are not a soccer mom! We've got a whole day before we need to leave. It's Saturday and the best shopping in the world happens in Bangkok on a Saturday!' Lucia exclaimed as if addressing a crowd.

'We need to leave right now or we will be too late!' She grabbed at the hem of Willow's t-shirt, tying it in a tight knot above her navel and handed over a pair of jeans, which she'd cut off into shorts with nail scissors. 'You can borrow a pair of my flip flops, you can't do this kind of shopping in heels!'

Willow rubbed her eyes, the hangover lingering. she had lost all concept of time, 'What time is it?'

'Nineish. I wouldn't have come over so early, but I knew you'd be up. I saw Chris. Well done with that by the way he's bloody gorgeous! He came to my room to collect Neo about half an hour ago. I'll tell you about that later. Now come on we need to move!' She grabbed Willow's hand and pulled her out into the hallway, nearly toppling Apple over; who had been polishing the wooden statues of Buddha.

'You crazy girls,' Apple chortled, 'You need taxi?'

Lucia waved, 'No thanks Apple. We are going to take a Tuk Tuk.'

This was news to Willow.

She slowed, trying to find a reason to avoid travelling by a precariously balanced cage on three seemingly mismatched wheels and being lugged about the perilous roads by a spindly motorbike.

She was about to speak up as they burst out of the front door, Lucia immediately hailing a passing Tuk Tuk.

'Chatuchak, kap kun ka,' Lucia shouted over the coughing engine to the driver as she got in. 'Come on; what are you waiting for?'

Willow took a deep breath and climbed onto the tiny seat, clinging on as the driver shot out into the road, careering noisily away. Her bare midriff felt incredibly exposed as they rattled along the uneven streets. There were rules about wearing crop tops in your thirties weren't there?

'You don't mind taking me do you? Will you help me choose the right things?' Willow shouted over the engine. 'Ahhh!' she screamed as they bumped over a particularly deep pothole.

They came to an abrasive halt at traffic lights, giggling as they took off again without warning. Willow clung to her passport and wallet, not ready to lose those along with her stomach.

'Of course I don't mind, it's one of my favourite places on earth! I was going anyway. I've got to get more coffee for my shop. I won't have time to go with you. Get what you like; how can that be wrong? If you smile in sequins and glitter, go for it! Give those ladyboys a run for their money! If you want to get those gorgeous legs out, buy obnoxiously small hot pants, if you are more of a boob girl get tiny vests. Never dress to impress, dress to be the kind of person that others want to impress!'

Lucia patted Willow on the shoulder, 'Don't look so doubtful, Chris was impressed when you weren't wearing anything!'

Willow couldn't argue with that.

They turned onto another busy stretch of road, reams of Tuk Tuks and bright pink taxis, packed with tourists, coming from all angles, all headed in the same direction.

Willow counted six people bulging out of one Tuk Tuk and reassessed her own situation, grateful for her relative spacious luxury. The air was heavy with exhaust fumes and engine noise. She wiped the sweat from her face with the back of her hand, realising too late that they were filthy from the hand rails.

'I want to wear beautiful colours, floating fabrics, nothing that resembles tailoring or anything that Claire's mumsy mates would wear. I don't want to look like the woman that I left behind!'

'What's wrong with that woman?' Lucia asked as she snitched Willows passport from her fingers, quickly examining the photo, 'I think she looks nice,' Lucia smiled.

Willow grabbed her passport back, her face burning, 'No one, including me, thought she was very special.'

Lucia took the passport back gently, scrutinising it more closely, 'That woman was called Sarah?' she said with a raised eyebrow, reading aloud 'Sarah Brady?'

Willow wanted the ground to swallow her. Why was she making up names and pretending to be someone she wasn't? 'God it sounds crazy, but *Willow* is a name that comes from my childhood. I was trying it on, like a dress that makes you feel fabulous, but not quite like yourself. I only told Aaron my name and I never expected to see him again or for him to tell weird girls,' she smiled at Lucia, 'Call me Sarah if you prefer?'

'What do *you* prefer?' Lucia pushed.

'Willow.' She concluded, definitively.

'So Willow it is. You know Aaron's name is really Mike, his middle name is Aaron and he started using that for equity card reasons in the US, it stuck. My friend Coral, who works as a faith healer is really called Sue and owns an apartment she rents out in Swanage to supplement her earnings. The beauty of being here is that no-one knows or cares who you were. I'll call you Roger if you like?'

Lucia stared at her for a long time, before grabbing her by the shoulders, 'You have eyes that look as if they are laced with honey, your hair is like spun bronze. You're incredibly smart and you dance like a bloody maniac,' she struck a *Saturday Night Fever* pose, nearly falling from the seat as they flew around a small round-about. 'You're a lot more than you think you are.' Lucia yelled at the top of her lungs, 'We will germinate that bulb inside of you and you will burst like a flower!'

Chapter 7

Willow stepped out of the Tuk Tuk on shaky legs, with dry dust-filled eyes and wind-rushed hair, feeling as if she had been freed from a hamster ball which had been fired around a pinball machine.

The streets were alive with shoppers arriving and leaving. Motorbikes, Tuk Tuks, taxis and buses all bustling for their spot near the pavement.

Lucia paid the driver, walked to Willow's side and stretched with a mighty groan, 'Well that will wake you up!'

Willow surprised herself, beaming, 'That was amazing.' Stifling a sick burp, her fingers came to rest on her engagement ring. She snapped her hand away, stung by the memories it conjured.

Lucia reached for the chain, taking the ring gently in her fingers, 'Where's this from? It's really beautiful.'

Willow closed her eyes.

To tell someone that you *were* once engaged was to say that you no longer were. Someone had loved you enough to want to spend their life with you, but after careful consideration and getting to know you better they had decided that you were not good enough after all. They could do better. 'It's my old engagement ring. I know I should get rid of it but…' she had no explanation.

Lucia dropped the ring gently, 'When you're ready it will be a damn-sight easier to get rid of than a tattoo!'

Willow relaxed, feeling fortunate to have found a friend who knew just the right thing to say. She pushed thoughts of James away, appreciating the alien landscape that awaited.

The market was an immense thatch of canvas awnings, stretching as far as she could see, a sprawling medley of colour, scent and sound. People flocked from all directions. There was no obvious way in, she watched amused as customers appeared to launch themselves at it through a succession of small gaps between the stalls.

It was a bazaar of the bizarre, alluring in its oddity. Part of her wanted to run to a familiar clean and bright shopping mall with changing rooms perhaps? But when she inspected more closely she was enticed. She wanted to dive in and wrap herself in the fine fabrics, douse herself in the exotic scents, fill her stomach with the sumptuous flavours, roll around in all the spender and eclectic fun that was on offer.

Lucia turned around, saw something in the distance and gathered up her bag, decisive.

'Right I have to go and get this coffee or I won't have anything to sell when I get back to Koh Tao. The stallholders are ruthless so don't you go taking the first price on offer either.' She patted her shoulder, reassuring, 'Trust me it's so much fun to get lost by yourself. Take your time and enjoy, but keep your money in your bra, you don't want to get pickpocketed and don't sit on the squat toilets. Absolutely always hover. I could tell you many a story of why but just trust me.'

Willow shook her head at the thought. She hadn't seen a 'squat toilet' up until that point and had hoped that they had died out sometime in the last century.

'Here take my phone,' Lucia got out her handset and headphones, opened an app and handed them to Willow, 'Listen to this, it's amazing. He's good at what he does, irritatingly brilliant actually. Never tell him that I said that.' She started to move away.

'Wait!' Willow called out, 'Who's brilliant? How will I find you when it's time to leave?' confused and panicked to be left standing unaided. *Get a grip*, she told herself.

Lucia waved over her shoulder, a bird in the wind. 'Meet back here in two hours or thereabouts, by the taxi side on the left,' she pointed to a mound of patchy grass where a few people sat waiting for friends to join them.

'Which is it; two hours, or two-ish? Is that more like three?' Willow yelled after Lucia's retreating figure.

She was routed to the spot, stupefied by indecision.

Regular panic attacks had crippled her over the past year, she had learnt to manage them but they still crept up at the worst of times. She took three deep breaths and closed her eyes, put the head phones in and pressed play, she immediately recognised Aaron's voice and smiled:

Approaching Chatachak is terrifying, especially if like me you are daunted by the most mundane and mainstream of shopping experiences. Thankfully I'm accompanied today by Phoenix, my son, who looks at the world in a way which makes it a less scary place. When he saw the sea of tent stalls he said, "It's the biggest grotto in the world!" before running in to explore, with a broad smile and eyes wide open with wonder. I could hardly be outdone by a six-year-old.

Don't let the dust and pushy vendors scare you. Get inside, get lost in the layers of the weird and keep your eyes open for Santa; you might just find him hiding behind the bongs and statues of Buddha.....' Aaron's audio blog rolled on.

Aaron had a child. Where was Phoenix while his father was away on business? with his mother perhaps? Did he share Aaron's soft curly hair and ocean blue eyes? It made sense that Aaron would be a father, with his easy manner and interest in others' wellbeing.

He was paternal and nurturing, rather than flirtatious, she realised with a warm heart. He had wanted to help her after all, he wasn't looking for anything in return.

Aaron's boy wasn't scared; what reason did she have to be? If she couldn't face a bit of shopping alone; what chance would she stand of finding Jay?

She fell in with the sea of people, bumping into her and rushing about. Her pulse quickened, but she kept her breathing controlled. She spotted a gap between two tents to make her entrance into the market. Fear eclipsed by eager expectation, she stepped through it.

Aaron's voice was a cushion against the strangeness of her surroundings. She was enclosed, wading through the sea of questionable *antiques* and knock off t-shirts, above her hung goods for sale from parasols and awnings.

She didn't feel claustrophobic as she thought she would, she felt embraced, drifting from seller to seller, intoxicated by the variety, buying every-single-thing she desired without one thought to what other people would think.

Skirts and vest tops, shorts and sunglasses, wraps for hair and beaded jewellery, beach bags and bikinis all went into bags as Willow parted with her Thai Baht. When the cash left her hand and found the sellers palm she was buying back a part of herself. Her favourite purchases were her new pants and bras, in vivid hues with soft delicate lace detailing, a far cry from the grey ones in her hotel room.

She could have shopped all day, but her fingers were numb from carrying bags and her feet puffy in the heat, when mixed aromas pulled her from her buying odyssey.

Thai basil and galangal transported her back to the family farm. Her mother had cooked the family Asian dishes regularly, finally she knew why. Caroline had done it to feel close to Rosa. Willow spotted the busy food stalls, 'Thanks Mum,' she whispered, feeling her guidance at work.

The selection was overwhelming, rows upon rows of cold beverages in a choice of bottles, cups, bags and more of the dreaded buckets. Willow's stomach lurched. Instead she went to the BBQ's, which sizzled with honey scented meats and whole fish. Vendors shook and thrashed noodles together with vegetables and sauces in enormous woks. Gleaming white rice was being served under a mountain of fresh mango and sweet cream.

She opted for a King coconut to drink, Pad Thai noodles with a fried egg on top, an undiscernible ugly whole white fish and a BBQ beef skewer which may or may not have really been beef. Even the flies hanging around the stalls did little to dull her appetite, she longed for something to soak up the previous night's alcohol.

She piled the food containers high and wedged the coconut between them and her chin. She floundered toward a seat, desperate not to drop her lunch or shopping. Both were too precious.

Someone tapped her shoulder. She couldn't turn around or open her mouth without running the risk of spillage so she grunted, hoping they'd find someone else to bother.

'Hi; do you speak English?' a Dutch, voice came from behind.

She shuffled around, surprised to find herself looking into the faces of two smiling, tall, boyishly handsome men who had to be brothers. They wore battered and frayed vests with rock climbing logos on, long wild blond hair and deep ruddy tans.

Suddenly she didn't mind being bothered one little bit. 'Yes I do, I mean I am, English I mean,' she mumbled as best she could with a coconut under her chin.

One of the two men took the coconut from her, whilst the other motioned toward a bench where three seats sat vacant. 'Do you want help with your things? Would you like to sit with us?'

'Yes please!' Her day was getting better and better. Lunch with two handsome young men. She put down her feast next to their own huge selection of boxes.

'I'm Jake and this is Kane,' Jake raised his hand in welcome and pointed at his brother. 'I hope you don't mind us jumping you like this. We have a baby sister and we'd want people to look after her if she was alone in a crazy place like this. Are you coming or going from Bangkok?'

'I've just arrived, two days ago,' she found it hard to believe that so much had happened in only forty-eight hours.

'We're heading home tomorrow,' Kane told her, as they pulled matching faces of exaggerated sorrow. 'You will have the best time! I wish I could do it all again. Ah and the food...' he rolled his eyes in ecstasy, biting into a piece of pork, reddened with spices.

Willow nodded in agreement, raising her coconut to her parched mouth and glugging back the juice.

'What made you come to Thailand?' Kane asked, between mouthfuls, 'Let me guess; you're a diver?'

Even the thought of diving evoked a primal fear, the breathing equipment, sharks, jellyfish. She loved the sea, but she was no adrenalin junky. 'God no! I have family here and I needed to get away. Messy break up at home.'

Chatting to strangers was surprisingly liberating. They would be out of her life in moments and would never care enough to judge.

'I *completely* understand.' Jake agreed with an expression that showed he really did.

Kane grinned at Willow, 'We came for the rock climbing.' Without warning they high fived, whooping like kids.

Willow was enjoying their enthusiasm, then stopped, trying not to stare, shocked to see that Kane's left wrist was a rounded stub of flesh covered bone.

Kane nodded towards his handless arm, 'You wouldn't think it would be the best sport for me, but I like a challenge.'

She was so impressed she didn't know what to say. He was so strong, his shoulders broad and biceps bulging.

Jake scoffed, 'He's not lying, last girl he tried it on with was a lingerie model!'

'Hey that number she gave me was legit, I must have taken it down wrong,' Kane shoved his brother playfully.

'He's really good, at climbing I mean, not pulling girls, he's rubbish at that. He's a Paralympian. You'll see him on a podium one day,' Jake stated proudly.

'It is the best feeling in the world. Nothing makes you feel more alive than crawling up a rock face towards heaven, while knowing you could drop to your death at any moment.'

'It's a total rush. When you are up there you are alone with your thoughts the air even smells sweeter. You'll never appreciate the ground beneath your feet as much as when you've come down from a cliff in one piece. It sounds crazy, but it's like therapy.'

Kane threw his napkin at him, 'Ignore him. His childhood sweetheart dumped him before we came out here. He's mending a broken heart.'

'I'm all healed now,' Jake put his hand to his heart, 'I only call her two or three times a day.'

Kane smacked his head down onto the table.

She had been so absorbed in her own pain and loss that she'd forgotten that there were other people in the world suffering loss. The difference was that they were getting out there and making the most of it.

They continued their chat for a few more minutes before their drinks were dry and stomachs full. The brothers pointed her in the direction of the market's entrance and she waved them goodbye.

She put her headphones back in and snaked through the labyrinth of people, feeling part of the chaos instead of a bystander. Aaron's voice continued to from his blog. When he spoke of Phoenix, she could envisage him skipping through the market's aisles, eyes brimming with youthful wonder.

When a lady walking with a beautiful tiny puppy perched on her shoulder walked passed Willow wanted to point it out to someone. It was not James she yearned for, as she had in London, it was a companion. The lady came to a stop, the puppy staring at Willow straight in the eye, 'Hi there big guy,' she cooed looking into his adorable face and scruffed his fur with her fingers.

The lady turned, looking flustered, 'Hello, can you help me please?' her accent was Italian, her English faltering.

Willow would have bet she was from Naples. 'Che cosa c'e?' she asked, *what's the matter*, in the lady's native tongue.

The lady closed her eyes, sighed and smiled, relieved. She went on to explain that she was looking for somewhere to eat and was desperate for a drink but could not find her way and nobody understood her shaky English.

Willow pointed out the food shacks in the distance, taking time to recommend the scary looking BBQ fish.

The grateful lady moved on and Willow stood a little taller.

She didn't need James or anyone to enjoy a moment petting a puppy, to tell her that lunch was delicious or that her language skills gave her a gift. She could enjoy things without validation.

Thinking of friends, she checked the time, she was nearly forty-five minutes late. *Shit*. What if Lucia had left without her, angry, or gone looking for her? Willow attempted to jog, which was impossible with her shopping, so she wriggled through the crowd as fast as she could, spying the entrance, their meeting point, off in the distance.

Lucia was sat on a high wall, legs swinging and reading a well-thumbed book, Willow breathed a sigh of relief. 'Sorry, I got carried away,' she shouted as she approached, holding her bags up by means of explanation.

Lucia glanced up from her book, 'Already on Thai time and enjoying the markets, you'll fit in here just fine!' She jumped from her perch, 'Let me take some of those.' She freed Willow from her purchases. 'You said that you didn't know what you wanted to buy. Looks like you found your groove!'

'It was pretty easy when I wasn't dressing to impress someone else,' she stated, triumphant, excited to get back and try it all on.

'Well halifuckingluyah, finally!' Lucia exclaimed, whisking her towards a waiting neon pink cab.

'Aren't we getting a Tuk Tuk?'

'If you fancy watching your new clothes go flying off all over the high way then we can? On my first night in Bangkok I bought a bag of deep-fried crickets….' Lucia started.

Willow stopped and stared, 'Sorry a bag of deep-fried crickets; why?'

Lucia rolled her eyes, 'To eat of course dummy.'

Willow imagined the winged little insects that used to plague the farm, 'Hold up, people eat crickets here?'

Lucia huffed, losing the thread of her story, 'No, not normally, not really. The Thais fry them up for the tourists. Although very poor Thai people will eat the critters, it is not common. You know what it's like, everyone comes here looking to try something new. Et Voila, most people have never eaten insects. Thai's aren't stupid, they can spot when an easy buck is to be made.'

Willow would be happy to miss that particular *delicacy*.

Lucia headed for the taxis, 'I was one of those stupid tourists once, trying to impress a guy, bought a bag, ate a few to prove how *worldly* and *wild* I could be.' She stuck her tongue out pretending to gag, 'Teenage boys are even more stupid than girls; he jumped into a Tuk Tuk with me, heading for my hostel. I put the bag on the floor, must have been at least fifty crickets left but I wasn't going to eat any more, he wasn't that cute,' she nudged Willow, 'Well that driver was a maniac! Went flying around a corner, the wind picked up and blew the crickets from under me. I hadn't realised that the base of the seat was a metal frame and not solid. I heard a racket of blaring horns and screaming from behind us. The crickets had been flung straight into the face of a moped driver. He was wearing my bugs like a mask, swerving about the road, trying to wipe them away, causing chaos! We turned down another road after that. I guess he was ok?'

Lucia pondered for a moment, but didn't seem too concerned, 'We'll swing past the hotel and put our things away and then we are going to a party!'

Willow groaned, 'I'd love to, but I'm exhausted.' The time difference, the alcohol and her exertion in the market had all taken their toll.

'You have one day left in Bangkok, you cannot spend it sleeping. I will not allow it!'

Willow was swayed by Lucia's eager smile and couldn't decline, 'Fine I'll come for an hour, then I'm off.'

Twenty-five minutes later, a quick change into a bikini and dress and they were back in the twilight zone. Willow had not imagined a place like it existing in Bangkok's back-packer district. She had thought it was all bunkbed hostels with bed bugs and thirty pence noodles. But there she was, ten stories above the busy streets, at a deluxe rooftop bar.

They found two poolside loungers, masseurs circulated, glamourous waitresses served cocktails on silver trays and impossibly tanned and toned young bodies basked in the afternoon sun.

Willow sipped a lurid green cocktail that was so overdressed with umbrellas, straws and gold foil fans that it looked ready for a night out. She closed her eyes behind her new large-lensed sunglasses, which made her feel like Jackie O. 'What time is it?' she yawned.

Lucia shrugged, 'Why are you always asking me the time? Have you got some place to be?'

'I've had no place to be for a year. Do you think it's too early to start drinking again?'

'By whose standards? Who do you have to answer to? Do *you* think it's too early?'

Willow downed her drink and slammed the empty glass on the table, laughing as the sticky liquid ran down her chin.

There was buoyancy in the air. The pool was a throng, overflowing with people sharing tales of parties, travels, far flung beaches and temples, moped accidents and dodgy tattoos.

All nationalities merged into one community. The transient nature of Bangkok meant that no one seemed to have the time to decide if you'd be their *type* of person or what you could do for them, they just wanted fun, company and others to share their adventures with, past, present and future.

Something had been bothering Willow since meeting Lucia, 'Your English is incredible as is your German. I've also heard you dabble in French and Thai today. Where did you learn all of these? I've had degree students who are not so gifted.' Willow considered Lucia's use of colloquial notes, diction and phraseology. Only her beautiful Scandinavian lull gave her away.

A blush spread through Lucia's cheeks. She was not good at taking compliments. 'I've never been good at anything else, I'm severely dyslexic, I can hardly read or write a word. Language is like a song to me, I find it easy to remember the lyrics no matter where they are from. I'm sure you speak a lot more than me?' she deflected from her own talent.

Willow was amused to see her confident companion shy, it made no sense. Intellect was something she had always been proud of. Looks would fade, style could waver, wealth could be fleeting, but no one could take your intelligence. It could not be garnered by force or luck, you had to work for it, 'Six European and a little mandarin, but I honestly don't know how you do it without text books. You have a real gift.'

'When I was busy failing all of my exams my parents never considered me gifted.' Lucia said, a discernible crack in her voice.

Willow hated the exam-based system, it failed some people miserably, but as it turned out, so did some parents. 'Your brain works differently, you can't measure your talent on a test paper so it can't be so easily quantified, but that doesn't make you any less brilliant.'

Lucia puffed herself up, 'I don't mind really. If I had been able to convince an employer to give me a go I may have never become my own boss. I had to give myself a chance when no one else would. I wouldn't have it any other way.'

'Neither would I.' Willow inhaled the incense and coconut cocktails and listened to the happy conversations that were bouncing on the air around her.

She had to admit that her painful year had led her to be sat on that roof with this wonderful person, ebbing towards the end of an amazing day.

Chapter 8

Willow and Lucia paid their hotel bills and bid farewell to Apple. It was six a.m. the sun was already up and the temperature was rising. Lucia jumped up and down, yawning loudly, shaking herself, 'Let's get to the train then,' she yelled with a transparent lack of enthusiasm.

Willow didn't want to be awkward, but she had other ideas. 'I had my heart set on the boat if possible?'

Lucia screwed her face up, 'It takes ages, I just want to get there and get back to bed as soon as possible! The boat is slow and full of Chinese tourists with cameras.' She was uncharacteristically grumpy with exhaustion.

Willow could sympathise with her desire to get the fast and efficient train and normally she would be happy to go along with the desires of others, but some things were too important. 'My aunt made the trip by the river. I want to see for myself: the temples and houses lining the banks and not just read about them from her letters. I want to see everything that she saw, I need to know what was so special that it kept her from returning to us at home and fighting to be part of our lives. Rosa's secrets are all over this country and I don't want to miss them sat on a train.'

Lucia resigned, 'Sheesh you are a hard woman to say no to. We need to get a move on, we're cutting it fine.'

When Willow saw their boat, it was exactly as Rosa had described. A solid teak vessel that could have sailed in on the tails of another century. Ornate carved rails ran around the edge and a heavy timber roof loomed above half, offering shade to most of the boat.

'You ok?' Lucia asked, breathless, running with their bags toward it.

Willow puffed along behind her, taking in the wonderfully weird creation. 'I was just thinking that you don't get boats like this on the Thames.'

'Yeah the ones in London are less likely to sink!' Lucia shouted as she jumped aboard, alarming their fellow passengers.

Willow followed, apologising as they pushed their way through to the deck. Once they found a vacant spot they collapsed upon the floor, relieved to be rid of the weight of their belongings.

Lucia had an amused look on her face, the cause of which she failed to articulate; instead she stared at Willow.

'What?' Willow had to ask, intrigued to know what her friend was thinking about her.

'Do you apologise when someone stands on your toe?' Lucia probed, still evidently tickled.

Willow was too embarrassed to admit it. 'Why are you asking that?'

'It's nice, you're just very British; intrinsically polite. Do you enjoy queuing too?' Lucia joked.

Willow wasn't sure how to respond, everyone she knew had been so careful when speaking to her that her conversations had been a bland forgettable dialog for months. It gave her a curious pleasure to be teased.

She thought of the stereotypes that were applicable to the swiss, 'Go yodel, Heidi.' She jibed, enjoying Lucia's surprised and hearty laugh that followed.

Lucia clapped her hands, 'This is going to be great! I've heard that the river is really beautiful this time of year.' Her weak smile telling of a girl who wanted to be in bed.

Willow was touched, Lucia was trying.

The engine grumbled loudly and the boat burred out into the water with a judder, kicking up a cool breeze around the deck. Lucia downed a large bottle of water, rubbed her temples, closed her eyes and lay back on the deck. The boat hiccupped along happily, Willow watching the lush banks, vivid with exotic vegetation,

'I can't believe we are so close to a city, this is like a different country,' she mulled.

Lucia was silent. Already asleep.

The other passengers were enjoying the view, tucking into an unconventional breakfast of rice and bisk soup with chicken. Willow thought of the dry sandwich she had forced down on the train from Vitoria station to Gatwick a few days previously. It was becoming clear just how far from home she was, and she was heading further away.

People on the banks were going about their business, unaffected by the urban bustle only a few miles behind them in the city.

River boats carried coal, sand and sugar; ferries and fishermen skirted around each other, dipping in and out of the many piers like bees from a hive. A man steering his long, thin wooden boat, with a small motor and hand operated rudder, stacked high with sugar, looking whimsically at a woman selling fruit on the shoreline; his lost love?

A woman berated a wayward child who started laughing and she embraced the impish boy; her son badgering her for another treat?

Willow knew as little of the people's lives as they did of hers and she liked it. She could hardly believe that the amazing world opening in front of her had been waiting while she had been holidaying in budget *all-inclusive* in Spain.

She spent happy hours sat on the deck in the wonderful sunshine watching the beauty of the river unfurl as Lucia slept in the shade.

She had surreptitiously downloaded one of Aaron's blogs about Ayutthaya and kicked back to listen. His strong voice guided her through the history of the surroundings as she fantasized that he was there. He was utterly enraptured by the wonders of the world he reported on, funny and intelligent in a way she had forgotten a man could be.

There had been a time when she had been swept along with James's words, he had been obsessed with where he was going and what his life could be, *one day*. She had wasted years ebbing toward a finish line, where his success would be waiting and their lives could begin, but it never came in to view. Then one day he was gone, there was no-one to follow or to tell her how to live her life. *Where was her finish line?*

The river snaked through thick jungle, every few minutes a fresh exploration into the unknown. Tall trees and shrubs overhung the water, hiding the curious creatures that lived among them. Birds chattered wildly and swooped for fish beneath the waters' surface. The air was fresh and light out on the river, the smog and petrol-seeping Tuk-Tuks' were a fading memory. Rosa's letters were coming to life.

In defiance of her desire to see absolutely everything Willow closed her eyes for a moment and awoke with a jolt as the boat came to a shaky stop at a pier an hour later.

Lucia stretching her arms wide, looked refreshed and ready to go. 'Oh my god!' she laughed, staring at Willow, 'You didn't put on sun lotion did you?'

Willow brought her hands to her face abruptly aware of the sting, 'When did you do yours? Does it look bad?'

Lucia removed her sunglasses to scrutinize her more closely, 'I do mine every morning after I've washed my face and my skin is used to the sun. *You* can't be out in these rays for a moment without burning. You are extremely pink. Come on let's have a proper look, take your glasses off.'

Willow took them off, heat radiating from her skin.

'Put them back on you look like you're wearing googles!' Lucia roared, before pulling herself together and handing her a baseball cap, 'We'll get you some Aloe Vera later to calm it, but you better keep covered up for the rest of the day.'

Willow knew the dangers of the sun, she wasn't an idiot, but she'd lost track of practicalities like sunscreen in the excitement. Thankfully she had worn a long kimono top over her shorts. Instead of being pink from head to toe, she just had a blazing lolly pop head. Luckily it was only Lucia looking at her, she thought, pulling the hat on.

Ayutthaya was bordered with jungle and river, the remanence of huge temples were everywhere, being reclaimed by the earth. Trees sprouted from the stones, strangling the bricks with their roots and branches. Whole buildings were framed, like pictures, with snaking vines and flowers. There was a stillness and peace to the place despite the crowds.

Ayutthaya had been so important to Rosa, it was the place where she had met her husband. It had been integral in guiding her life, away from loneliness and towards a new family. Willow rested her hand on Lucia's, grateful to have someone to share the moment with.

Not for the first time she thought that Rosa's letters were guiding her not just towards Jay but towards a better life of her own.

Lucia pointed into the distance, 'That's the island.'

The cluster of temples huddled together pointedly reaching to the heavens were stunning, 'I can't believe this was once one of the world's largest and most cosmopolitan cities, it just seems so…..left behind. like time stood still.' Willow wondered aloud.

Lucia appeared to breath it in, 'It's exquisite, strong, still standing despite war and attacks.'

Willow could see how Rosa could have fallen in love there, 'I'm glad that Bangkok took the shopping malls and motorways. Some things are better left behind.'

Lucia nudged her, 'To think that this place would once have been bustling with the finest minds of the Siamese kingdom,' she gestured towards a spectacular *Reclining Buddha* statue, it was at least forty metres long, lying in an open field, Light and dappled mosses peppered its sleeping form, serene. Against it perched a young western man, wearing a bright pink t-shirt, emblazoned with the slogan *"No I don't want a F##KING Tuk Tuk"*. He was smoking whilst playing on his phone, unaware of his surroundings or any offence that he was sure to cause.

Willow scoffed, saddened. His ignorance was astounding but sadly not isolated, the streets of Bangkok had been filled with more than their share of similar, 'Why do so many idiots like that come here?' She wished they kept themselves to Magaluf.

Lucia stared, 'Some people are idiots, and they are happy to go on that way. They don't come here to change, to learn about different cultures or to find themselves. They come for the booze, drugs, cheap women and sun. Don't be fooled, Thailand isn't all mysticism and self-enlightenment.' She walked away from the boat, scowling at the man, 'Let's get out of here, grab some bikes and get out exploring; or I can drop you at the hotel if you would rather crash?'

'What hotel? Do you have somewhere in mind?' Willow asked, relieved that Lucia had taken control of their sleeping arrangements, then concerned 'You didn't book a dorm, drunk last night did you?'

Lucia stuck her tongue out, 'It's all been sorted. I'm sure you'll like it. Do you want to go there now?' she was avoiding Willows eye.

Great, she had booked something drunk. Willow didn't want to waste any time or to spend the day in a dingy hostel, 'I need to warn you that I haven't ridden a bike in years, might be a bit rusty.'

'So are the bikes!' Lucia pointed out leading her to a bike stand.

Willow took in the tawny, flaking frames, flattening tires and threadbare seats that awaited unsuspecting tourist's bottoms. 'Can't we pay more and get better bikes?' she asked hoping for something more like the *'Boris Bikes'* of London. 'Oww.' She flinched as Lucia slapped her bottom.

'Your delicate derrière will have to harden up, you won't find any better bikes. This is the place that Aaron told me to use. it must be the best.' Lucia ribbed, examining the bikes, not looking too impressed herself.

Willow was reminded of something else that Aaron had mentioned on his blog, 'Apparently it doesn't matter how unfit you are, it's not that hard to cycle here, or so he says,' She repeated, trying to get herself into the mood. She glanced at a map, on the cycle shed wall. It seemed that they had a lot of ground to cover if they were going to visit all the monuments and places in Rosa's photos.

Lucia waved to the vendor, 'Who says that?'

'Aaron,' as soon as his name left her mouth Willow regretted it, she was bound to sound *fan girl* or worse.

Lucia's interest perked-up, she turned to look at her through narrowed eyes then grinned, 'If you want some more advice you can ask him in person later.'

Willow span around, irrationally panicked that he could be there, 'Is he here?'

Lucia was clearly enjoying Willow's discomfort, 'Keep your knickers on, he's not here yet, he's reviewing a hotel for some poncey New York travel rag.'

'At least I'm wearing some.' Willow deflected whilst cringing at her own transparency. She never had been able to hide her feelings.

Willow would have remembered if Aaron had said he was going to Ayutthaya, 'He told me that he was going straight to Koh Tao from Bangkok.'

Lucia shrugged, 'Change of plan I guess. I'm sure I told you all of this?'

Willow had the feeling that she was being set up and wasn't sure if she was annoyed or pleased about it, 'When exactly did you tell me about this?' her eyes narrowed, scrutinising her friends shifting expressions.

Lucia huffed, 'Yesterday in the toilets at the roof bar. I'd just downed a tequila and needed a pee, I was a bit wobbly so you came with me to the bathroom. You were shrieking about how excited you were about a girl's trip and I said, "*Yeah me too, but its Aarons trip that we are gate crashing*". Don't you remember?' She appeared confused, her eyebrows raised to the sky.

'I do not shriek!' Willow half shrieked, then adjusted her tone, 'And I didn't help you to the toilets, we didn't want to lose our sun loungers, I stayed put, you went with Chloe, that girl from Coventry!'

Lucia clicked her fingers, 'Oh yes that's right! I told Chloe about our trip. She was the one who was excited about *her* next girl's trip and we got chatting. I was hammered.' She shrugged, 'It will be a great hotel and free. I think he wants the company to be honest. Come on let's get our butts on these bikes.'

Lucia pulled out her money and waved to the vendor, who rolled two horrific looking bikes towards them.

Willow couldn't argue and didn't want to, there was no denying that she was happy to be seeing Aaron again. What would she wear to meet him, the blue dress or the floating trousers? Then she remembered, she'd have to wear a balaclava, her face was an inhuman shade of pink.

As if reading her mind Lucia produced a bottle of sun block, factor fifty and handed it to her, 'Cover yourself in that, you don't want the burn getting any worse. Grab your day bag, I'll send the rest of our stuff on to the hotel with one of the reps in that travel shop over there.' She pointed to a shop a short walk away and set off.

Willow slathered herself in the cream and sat herself on one of the lumpy bike seats. A wayward spring poked into her bottom, she got off, folded her spare shirt and positioned it as a cushion. Congratulating herself on her Bear Grills instincts until Lucia returned and tittered at her efforts.

'Come on princess are you ready for this? She called as she leapt onto her own bike, eager for a head start. 'I'll race you to the corner!'

Willow wasn't about to be beaten that easily, she flew off after Lucia, but the bike had a mind of its own, taking off on all sorts of unexpected preambles. To her delight Lucia was having problems of her own, her gears slipping as she bunny hopped along. After a laughter-fuelled shaky start, they slipped and skidded towards the corner.

'Move, move, move!' Willow screamed at a street dog, idly lifted its head and stepped out of her way, just in time. She was winning! She swerved to miss a coconut husk, the bike careering out of control and pulled on the brakes, narrowly avoiding an unsuspecting tour group.

'Look out!' screeched Lucia, just avoiding tail-ending her as she flew up behind. 'Maybe we should take a break from racing and concentrate on surviving the roads?' she laughed, taking a moment to catch her breath.

Willow was grateful for the excuse to slow down, she was feeling horribly unfit, 'So long as it's agreed that I won?' she asserted, amused to feel an old competitive spirit rising.

Lucia pouted in good spirits as they started up again, wobbling up and down many paths before they were moving along with any semblance of stability; weaving their way around meandering tourists and street sellers.

The temples were thankfully close together and by late afternoon they had taken on *The Reliquary Towers* and remains of huge Buddhist monasteries.

Willow considered herself an imposter at first, posing for photos in the places that her aunt had been, but after a few were taken the magic of the place began to take her on a journey. She was moving though Rosa's memories with her by her side. It was as if Rosa could materialize at any moment, as the young woman from her stories to guide her.

Lucia joined Willow on a bench, where Rosa had sat, a statue of Buddha in front of them, cloaked in striking orange robes, hiding the broken structure beneath. The bright and vibrant shade brought joy to the spiritual effigies as ethereal bald monks shuffled between them, never rushing, always calm. Some had a shoulder exposed and many had intricate tattoos, patterns that mirrored the temples around them.

'They look content, like they have life all worked out.' Willow marvelled. 'Maybe I should become a monk?'

Lucia studied the older monk, sat on a wall opposite, a wry smile on his lips, 'Hell no! You know they're celibate right? No relationship problems to get upset about, that's the only reason they look so happy with themselves.'

Willow wondered aloud, 'Could it be that simple, no love, no problems?' Her life certainly would have been simpler without the influence of love.

Lucia's face fell, theatrically horrified, 'You won't catch me turning celibate for a simple life. Do what I do. Have sex without love, the two aren't mutually exclusive! Ask your Saffer Chris!'

Willow blushed, 'Shut up, it feels weird talking about sex in a place like this.' She couldn't disagree that her night with Chris had been fun, but she couldn't see herself finding anything fulfilling in embarking on a trip filled with one-night stands.

Perhaps the monks had it right? Talking of sex inexplicably led her to think of Aaron. As she pictured him she remembered something unusual, 'Aaron has a tattoo like that monk doesn't he? On his neck, and I'm sure Rosa had something similar on the top of her back, I can just about make it out in some of her later photos. What do they mean?'

'It's Sak Yant. Very sexy. On Aaron, not on monks,' Lucia clarified.

Were her and Aaron a thing? Was she gate-crashing their date? Willow began to panic; had she been unwittingly blind to the obvious?

'The look on your face!' Lucia teased, 'He's a gorgeous man, but far too old for me!'

Willow wanted to defend him, he was only a few years older than her, but she was too relieved to manage any intelligent protest.

Lucia went on oblivious, 'For centuries the Thai monks would only tattoo Buddhist Thai people. Now you or I could get one done in any parlour, on any street, all over the country but they wouldn't be authentic. Aaron had his done in Chang Mai by a monk in a remote hill temple. The real ones, the ones done by the monks, are rumoured to be magical,' she waved her fingers in front of Willows face, with wide eyes, goofing around, 'The ink is a blend of cobra venom and charcoal, put into the skin using a bamboo cane with a needle on the end. They are designed by the monk to provide you with whatever you need the most.'

'Like bigger boobs?' Willow joked, looking down at her small chest.

Lucia tutted, 'No, they are for protection, to keep illness away, to bring you luck, things like that.'

Willow thought of her search for Jay, a needle in a haystack, 'I could do with some of that.' She had shown Rosa's photos to at least twenty people. No one recognised the hotel or Rosa.

Lucia became serious, 'Getting a true Sak Yant tattoo isn't easy, many of the monks still do not like to do them for foreigners, but I have heard of a guy not far from here. I've wanted to get a one myself for a long time. Would you like to come with me to find him, maybe get a tattoo of your own?' she said slowly, her eyes keen like a puppy impatient to play.

Willow had never considered having a tattoo, *forever* was a long time to be stuck with a picture on your body; but this sounded like so much more than a picture.

She had twenty-one days to find Jay, she should be searching the city for the hotel where he had stayed with Rosa and not traipsing about getting tattoos, but... 'Yes!' she spluttered, before she could change her mind, certain that Rosa would have approved.

Lucia clapped her hands, 'Let's go right now!' she announced, nearly tripping over her feet, racing to lock up the bikes.

They drove away in a Tuk Tuk, leaving the tourists to their photos. Willow squirmed in the heat, coughing on the dust, wondering what she had signed up for.

Their surroundings grew greener and the people fewer, then after about half an hour, Willow made out a village appearing in the distance. They screeched to a stop, a cow lumbering into their path, standing still, chewing on some grass. It cast them a glance, defiant, raised a bored furry brow and went back to its lunch. The driver mumbled and leapt from his seat, waving his arms and pushing against the cow. It didn't budge.

'Mai pen Rai,' yelled Lucia, to the driver.

He turned to her with obvious relief.

'What did you say?' Willow asked, impatient to learn more of the language.

'I told him, *no worries,*' Lucia said, climbing down, 'We can walk.'

Willow followed, unnerved: Would they be welcome?

Some scrappy goats bleated from down the road, accompanying a woman who ambled in brightly patterned robes. Before Willow could hold her back, Lucia had set off towards her, shouting a greeting. The lady turned and, even from a safe distance, Willow could see her features transform with a smile, her hand flying to Lucia's hair, where it rested a moment and she appeared to pray.

Lucia turned to Willow, beckoning her to join them.

'This is Bess. She is going to show us the way to the temple,' Lucia let Bess take her hand and lead her away. The goats skipped by their ankles and Bess smiled, rushing them toward the village which comprised around thirty rudimental houses.

Two young boys were kicking a football in the street but stopped abruptly when they saw Willow and Lucia. The older one, Willow guessed was no more than thirteen, stood up straight.

'Harry Kane,' he yelled patting himself on the chest, flicking the ball into the air, bouncing it up and down on his knee, grinning with pride.

Willow applauded, 'Well done, that's very good.'

The boys ran away laughing. Had she said something funny? Kids were a mystery. With them gone it was eerily quiet; where were all the people? Bess walked toward a building which was covered in carved icons and foliage. Bess pointed to the door, exchanging words with Lucia, hugging her tightly and going on her way, the little goats faithfully at her heels. Lucia explained, 'This is the temple, where Master Ajarn Toy works. He's inside. We just need to walk through the doors. You ready?'

No! Willow wanted to scream, but found herself mute, her feet moving forward.

Master Ajarn Toy was alone, his back to the door, bent over and lighting candles around a bright red, multi limbed stone deity. A Buddhist Garnesha Willow realised as they approached.

Toy was in orange robes and was covered in the Sak Yant markings, more ink than skin. If he was surprised to see them he didn't show it. 'You pray with me now, then tattoo,' he told them, placing three red mats on the ground and settling down upon one on his knees.

Willow's parents had enjoyed their weekly trips to church, but worshipping made her uncomfortable. When they had died she had blamed the God, that she had never put much faith in, for not saving them.

Lucia had joined Toy kneeling and she couldn't argue with a monk, so putting her reservations aside, she knelt. For a moment there was silence, Willow uneasy with her own company, Then Toy began leading the prayer for at least ten minutes, before he rested a hand on her shoulder. She blinked and adjusted to the light, unexpectedly calm.

'Hello, I am Toy,' he said, showing them toward a small room, away from the shrine. A woven straw matt covered the floor, bamboo canes lay on a wooden tray next to an ominous box of needles and a bottle full of black and red ink, pencils and papers. 'I design you Sak Yant now,' he stated.

Willow's eyes shot to Lucia, 'Can we see some pictures and choose one? I would like something small, maybe on my hip or somewhere not too visible?'

Toy burst into laughter, 'It OK I know what you need. I choose magic not you. You have tattoo on high point on body, respect for Buddha, no leg.' Toy shook his head, still laughing as he settled with his sketching materials on the floor.

Willow thought quickly, finding no argument to counter, British reserve preventing her from running out the door. She didn't want to appear rude, even if that did mean having a tattoo that she might not like. She sat on the floor, brimming over with anxiety, while Lucia bobbed up and down, excited. Toy continued to draw, f

rom time to time looking up at them analytically, then going back to his strokes and scribbles.

Willow surreptitiously crossed her fingers, she'd heard too many stories of people having Thai words for love or peace tattooed on them, only to discover later that they mean *curry* or something far worse.

Finally Toy passed Willow a leaf of paper. The design, a series of five lines, made up of Thai script, each topped with a wave design, reminding her of the peaked temples she had seen that afternoon.

Toy pointed at the first line, '*I ra cha ka ta ra sa*. This stop unfair punishment in life. This bit be more grey colour, it clean out bad spirit, protect the place you choose to live. This one,' he pointed to the next peak, '*Ti hang ja toh loh ti nang*. It protect against bad fortune.' Toy tapped the next peak, '*Soh ma na ga ri tah toh*. It protect from black magic and curse,' he rested his finger on the next peak and thought for a moment, '*Pi sam lah loh pu sa pu*. It will make good luck, bring you more success and fortune. Last one, most important, *ka pu bam too tahm wa ka*. It make you more charisma, good to attract a husband.'

Willow spluttered, 'How do you know that I don't have a husband?'

Toy took her left hand in his and pointed at what would have been her ring finger, 'No man who stay.'

Lucia couldn't hold in her laughter, 'Keep that tattoo away from me, I do not want one to stay.' Toy handed the other design to her, a pyramid of boxes, filled with symbols and topped with three ovals laid one on top of the other. There were eight in total. She examined the paper. 'This is a bit like Aarons. It's for good luck when travelling isn't it?'

Toy narrowed his eyes, 'Not only this. It bring good luck and protection from all directions of compass. A powerful tattoo to help you when you travel to your future.' Toy began to chant, taking a seat behind Willow, wielding his bamboo stick.

It was too late to turn back.

Willow gripped Lucia's hand. A sharp pain shooting through her right shoulder and then another and another. She tensed at the rhythmic tapping. It was like being stung by wasps, but it soon grew numb and the intensity lessened. She rested her head on her forearm, relaxing as much as possible. It took about half an hour for the pricking and prodding to stop, when it did Toy blew her skin and whispered at it, before announcing 'The spell finished!'

Exhilarated she wanted to hug Toy but refrained; her guidebook had made it clear not to touch a monk unless invited. It could have been the *magic*, the elation that the ordeal was over, or that finally she had done something for herself regardless of others judgement, but she was unable to speak.

She sat back as Lucia got in to position for her tattoo, chatting comfortably as the needle continuously poked her, clearly experienced with the art. Willow was spell bound by Toy's dexterous fingers, until he was finished and quietly led them to the door.

'How much do we owe him?' Willow whispered to Lucia, feeling foolish for not asking earlier.

'You have any cigarettes or food? I do not take money. Monk no take money. Please leave any money you like in donation box on way out. For the temple and village.' Toy said, unashamedly eavesdropping.

Lucia bowed to Toy and handed over a large carton of cigarettes, bundles of instant noodles and biscuits, much to his delight.

'Where did you get all that?' Did her friend always carry the contents of a high-school teachers confiscation drawer on the off chance she would need to pay a monk?

'Never travel without currency,' Lucia shrugged as if were the most normal thing in the world.

Willow gave generously to the donation box on her way out.

Toy smiled in thanks, 'Man on bike take you back now.'

As if by magic the thirteen-year-old football ace wandered around the corner pushing a motorbike.

Like all the modes of transport in Ayutthaya the bike was eighty per cent rust, twenty per cent cut and paste. Was it a joke? Surely a child was not going to drive a motorbike let alone one with her as a passenger?

Lucia explained where they needed to go to the driver and climbed on behind him, wrapping her arms around his skinny waist, readying herself for the off, unfazed by their precarious situation.

'Where's *my* ride?' Willow asked, relieved she'd have a different driver, hopefully one of legal age.

Lucia laughed 'You're hilarious! Come on hop on behind me.' She was serious.

It would soon be getting dark and Willow couldn't stay alone in a near deserted village, so she squeezed on, gripping onto Lucia.

She'd considered that the biggest risk when having a tattoo was that she might regret it for years afterwards, not that she might not live for more than a few minutes afterwards.

Toy waved to them off, 'Good luck to you, be happy, be well, be safe. See you soon in another life.'

Willow checked around, no helmets; *hopefully not too soon.*

Chapter 9

If it was unusual to travel three on a bike with no helmets, no-one they passed seemed in the least bit surprised, not even when they pulled up outside a five-star hotel.

Willow was convinced that there had been a mistake, but Lucia wriggled free from her frightened clutches and walked toward the entrance.

'What are you waiting for? This is where we are staying,' Lucia smirked, a glimmer in her eyes.

'This looks great!' Willow paid the boy with a large tip, making him whoop with glee, before he raced away.

Lucia shot up the polished marble steps, 'Sure does. Aaron has never made me stay in a bad place yet, but this is special.'

How many times had they travelled together? They seemed an unusual pairing. Willow wondered how Lucia and Aaron had come to be friends and was about to ask when she remembered the state of herself.

Her hand flew to her baseball hat, stifling against her scalp, she daren't remove it. Her hair was full of sweat and dust, her face bore tan lines like war paint, and her clothes were grubby from the day of riding in the searing heat. She wanted to stay on the pavement, but her bag was inside; perhaps she could shimmy up a fire escape, sneak in unnoticed?

Lucia strode through the doors confidently, as if in a channel suit. Willow took a deep breath, kept her head down and followed. They could check in quickly and freshen up before their odour offended anyone.

It was a wondrous mass of modern architecture, shining white floors and polished pillars, immaculate in contrast to the ruins outside. An impossibly elegant lady floated past in a satin dress, with perfect makeup and a designer handbag. Willow tugged at the edges of her denim shorts, which were far too short.

Where was the check-in desk?

She stopped, noticing an infinity pool nestled against the astonishing views of the ruined temples.

A porter in a smart canary yellow uniform approached them, 'Ladies do you have a reservation?'

'They are with me,' announced Aaron from across the lobby.

Willow turned slowly, wishing she didn't look like a scarecrow. He was wearing a blue shirt and tailored trousers, his hair pushed back from his clean-shaven face. She waved, unable to stop the smile creeping across her cheeks.

Lucia ran to him like an excited child. 'Aaron!' she yelled, leaping into his arms, 'This is a great place. I love it already.'

Aaron hugged her back, 'Hey, good to see you, but don't tell *them* how much you love it or they won't try to impress us!' he smiled.

Lucia disentangled herself and dropped to the ground, 'Thank you for having us,' she addressed the porter.

'It is a great pleasure for us to host your stay,' He said, bowing his head.

'Thank you, it's our pleasure to be here,' Willow chimed in, feeling as if she should say something.

'Hi Willow,' He waved, realising she was there, 'I wasn't sure I'd see you again. It's nice to see you survived Bangkok. This will be fun. I need a lady's point of view on all the facilities. I'll have you working while you are here,' Aaron screwed up his face, looking at Lucia, 'You smell rotten. *You* need to review the bath immediately.'

Lucia hit him playfully as they approached Willow, 'Did you hear that? You're a lady and I'm a stinker?'

Aaron recoiled, 'Wow you're red! You are really…' he paused, 'Really red!'

Willow laughed; what else could she do? 'I forgot my sunblock on the boat.'

He took in the patch on her shoulder, 'You can tell me about that later too,' he said, amused, then turning to the porter, 'These burnt, tattooed, beautiful scruffs are my companions. Can you help them to the room?'

Willow shuffled uncomfortably. *The room,* were they all sharing? She could hardly complain at a free stay in a luxury hotel, but she was capable of paying for a room of her own and wasn't comfortable sharing with him, no matter how gorgeous he was. She wasn't a teenager; group sleep overs were out of her comfort zone.

The porter scooped up their day bags and whisked them toward the lift. 'We have taken the liberty of arranging a table for dinner, for four people, at seven o clock. Is this acceptable for you sir?'

'That's perfect thank you….' he read the porters name badge 'Lee. That will be wonderful.'

Four; who else was there? A stunning woman, in a bikini with legs up to her armpits? Willow slowed her pace, the inevitable looming. Lee was informing them about the history of architecture, but she had grown deaf, her concerns reeling. They stopped.

'Room 206 is for you ladies.' Lee said, opening the door, walking inside to deposit their belongings.

'We're across the hall. 207,' Aaron flicked his head in the direction of his own room.

'I trust that you will have a wonderful stay. Please let us know if we can do anything to make you more comfortable,' Lee bowed and left them alone in the hall.

'Who else is staying?' Willow asked, more pointed then she intended.

'Che. He's rooming with me, always does,' Aaron said, his hand on his door handle.

She sighed too loudly, relieved.

'What?' Aaron looked confused.

'She thought that you had brought a woman.' Lucia muttered as she walked in to their room.

'That's not it at all,' Willow exclaimed unnecessarily loudly, burning to her ears, 'I thought…Che was staff. I thought you'd hired him? You know as a driver,' she bumbled, uselessly.

'I do pay him to drive, among other things, he's also a close friend, who has more business acumen then perhaps is apparent? His input to my work is invaluable, he's an integral part of the process.' Aaron stared at her, then smiled, letting her off the hook. 'Don't be so quick to assume.'

'Ok. I get it, he's your right-hand man and I'm an idiot? I didn't mean to be rude.' Willow backed away to her room before she could cause any more offense. 'We'll freshen up and see you at dinner. Thanks again for arranging this place. See you at seven.' Willow shut the door swearing under her breath.

'Enjoy your bath, you won't find another one easily in Thailand. You can even flush the toilet roll!' Aaron yelled from the hallway.

Obviously she smelled bad too.

'This is seriously lush!' Lucia exclaimed jumping on the colossal bed like a happy child, 'You can have the first bath if you like, I need to get out on that balcony for a bit,' she leapt from the mattress and raced out of the large double doors.

Willow laid a dress on the bed and smoothed down the creases, running her hand over the delicate nude, embellished silk, a flash of hand painted blue around the hem. From the moment she saw it at the weekend market, she had known she would feel incredible in it, suiting the curve of her hips and the nip of her waist.

She pulled underwear from her bag, her phone dropping to the ground with a thud. Her heart raced. She knew that she couldn't totally drop off the grid, she had to make sure that no emergencies were unfolding in London and she should let everyone know that she was ok; but who was there to tell? She reluctantly put it on to charge.

The bathroom was pristine, the marble floor and wall tiles a light stone that took her to the tropical sands of the coast. She stepped into the steaming bath, her aching muscles relaxing as she descended into the soapy lather. She marvelled at the amount of dirt and grime that swam away from her skin. When she finally wrapped herself in a jasmine scented fluffy white towel and left the bathroom, she was a new woman.

Lucia had emptied the contents of her makeup bag on the beauty dresser. 'I'm sure you've got plenty of your own, but I thought that you might like to borrow something to disguise those tan lines?' she smiled sympathetically, heading into the bathroom, 'How are the jacuzzi jets?'

'Blissful,' Willow confirmed, sitting at the counter, picking up each piece of makeup in turn. She had always enjoyed making herself up, feeling pretty, but it had lost all importance in the wake of her breakdown. She hadn't wanted to wear a mask. She had worn clothes with no thought, hair unwashed and face bare. She had wanted someone to look at her, to realise that she needed putting back together; people saw, nobody helped.

She coated her skin with cooling Aloe Vera, picked up a sheer shimmering eyeshadow and began. She followed by toning down her reddened skin with foundation and adding a subtle glistening highlight to her cheeks. A sweep of mascara, a slick of sheer lip gloss and she was done. She stared in the mirror, freeing her wet hair from the towel, letting it fall around her shoulders. She saw herself looking back, where for months there had been a stranger.

Willow broke away from the mirror, moving to the balcony and sinking onto the comfortable armchair, the evening heat drying her hair into soft waves. She gazed, transfixed, at the dusk sky glowing with sunset plumes. The buzzing of her phone shattered her peace. She darted inside, picked it up and pressed play for her voicemail:

'Where are you? Are you ok?' Claire sounded frantic. *'We need to talk, about the money and the fight. Are you ok? How can you be so selfish? None of us know where you are? I've called all the hospitals.'*

Willow waivered with a pang of guilt, but she couldn't help noticing that her sister's first concern had been about the money.

'....Sarah are you there?' Claire went on.

Willow turned off the phone, she didn't need to hear any more.

Lucia swung open the bathroom door, dramatically. 'It feels so good to be clean!' She sang, staring at Willow, taken aback, 'Wow you look amazing! I mean you're gorgeous, but I've never seen you dressed up.'

'Thanks,' Willow accepted, her great mood only mildly tarnished by her sister.

She stared at the odious phone in her hand. Every time she switched it on it brought nothing but sadness.

Lucia pulled on a backless, floral dress and a gaggle of glimmering bangles before rushing through her makeup and pulling her hair up in to a bun. 'Ta dah,' she pouted with glossy lips 'Let's go to dinner. I'm absolutely starving; aren't you?'

'Ravenous,' Willow agreed, smiling. 'I've never had such a gorgeous dinner date!'

As the lift approached Willow's phone was still in her hand. She glared at the screen, still nothing from James. She couldn't wait any longer for an apology that could never come, she took a deep breath and dropped it into the trash can before the doors shut.

Hearing the clank, Lucia turned, 'What was that?'

'Nothing important.' Willow said. Released.

There was a breeze as they walked by the pool side. Willow's dress skimmed against her body, floating behind as she swept towards the restaurant where Aaron and Che sat waiting.

Aaron stood to great them, 'Ladies welcome to dinner, you both look lovely.' He sat back in his seat, his eyes not leaving hers for a second.

Everything inside Willow froze. Something in the intensity of his look left her spellbound.

'Che, how are you?' Lucia asked, pulling him in for a hug, before he had time to decline.

Che nodded happily, 'All good for me. Willow you find cousin?'

It took her a few seconds to realise that he was talking to her. She pulled her eyes from Aaron and pulled herself together.

'No.' she said sadly, 'We showed the photos to lots of people. Nobody recognised the school, the hotel that was supposed to be here or Jay, but I could have tried harder. Rosa mentions the floating markets an awful lot, I will try there tomorrow.'

'Today we were busy having Sak Yant tattoos and riding bikes all over town.' Lucia nudged Willow, happy with their day.

'I'm glad you girls are getting on, I knew you would. Hopefully you'll have better luck tomorrow and less pain.' Aaron held a menu aloft, 'The Chef wants us to try the prestige selection. I have no idea what we are eating, but it will be here shortly. Apparently he's worked in Europe. Like that's supposed to improve his credentials for cooking Thai food?' He smiled, his gaze unashamedly, still, lying on Willow.

She started examining her nails, feeing uneasy with the attention. 'This is all very generous and really nice for me not to be eating alone from a stand on the street,' she said, twitching as Aaron squeezed her hand, a whisper of yearning burning her fingertips, awakened longing tickling though her body. She politely moved her hand away, concentrating on the view of the swimming pool.

Aaron didn't appear to notice, 'Where's the fun in being in a place like this alone? I wanted to share it with friends, old and new,' he tipped his glass to each of them at the table.

'Well said,' Lucia chirruped.

A small army of waiters dressed in gold and red suits arrived with a feast of glistening fat noodles, fluffy rice, fragrant curries and zesty scented soups.

Willow relaxed as they talked through the events of their days and the wonders of their surroundings. They dove into the various dishes enthusiastically. Every mouthful an explosion of tantalising flavour.

To Willow's pleasure, Aaron was impressed with their tattoos, even delicately peeling back the dressing, his strong fingers surprisingly gentle as they rested on her skin and caressed the raised design. Shivers ran through her body in defiance of the nights heat. She wanted him to touch her, she longed for it but when he did, she recoiled.

What was she so afraid of?

Through the fine fabric of his shirt she could see his torso. His own tattoos were everywhere, covering his chest and stomach, spreading up his neck and along his forearms. She longed to ask him about them, but he kept them all busy answering questions about themselves and educating them about the area, reluctant to share anything personal about himself at all. Infuriatingly it made him even more appealing. A mystery Willow hankered to unwrap.

When Willow had thought it was impossible to consume another bite, a platter brimming over with rich fruits and lashings of coconut cream arrived for the foursome.

'It's rude to not eat. You try everything,' Che responded to their rebuttals.

They dutifully tucked in. Each mouthful accompanied by more laughter and washed down with sweet non-alcoholic cocktails for Willow and whiskey for the others. She had plans for the following day, but more importantly she couldn't trust herself to make wise decisions when drunk.

As the meal came to an end, she sighed contented and forced herself to stand, 'I'm going to leave you to your drinks, I need to be up early.' she apologised, excited by the prospect, but reluctant to leave.

'Would you like me to walk you up?' Aaron offered.

She could feel Lucia's eyes on her, smiling like a Cheshire cat.

Thank God she wasn't drunk. She mustered her strength, struggling not to imagine the possibility of his naked body against hers. 'I'll be fine. Thanks again for the meal and this place, it's all been perfect,' she stood and made her way, not ready for what might have been.

Chapter 10

February 12th, 1991

Dear Caroline,

I am certain that you could not imagine what I am doing! I've been living here for nearly eight months now and all I have done is bounce from one beach to the next. I've loved every party and person I've met, but I've been lost if I'm honest, unsure exactly what it is I'm doing here, yet certain that I'm home. I cannot return to England, so please try to be happy for me that I have found a place for myself.

As a woman unable to have a family of my own it has been hard to build a home. I have no reason to put down roots, no-one relies on me or expects a thing from me. I can dress like an oddity and sing as I walk down the street; no one is embarrassed, nobody cares. I can get drunk every day and no one will be let down if I'm not up to make breakfast. Now I am finding my own path and meaning again.

My skin is now so brown I match the locals, my dark hair sun bleached and hanging in unruly dreadlocks down my back; yet I look in the mirror and I still see you looking back. I imagine you, your hair in a neat bun, your skin porcelain, but you are fading away from me.

I think we would only need to speak once and it would be like we had never been apart. If only you would take my calls, you would remember I am not the monster you imagine.

Everyone wants to learn or practice English here, but I am desperate to master Thai. It flows in the most beautiful singing loops; the locals hardly pause for breath between sentences. I want to be part of this world so I have found myself a language tutor. He found me really. He's incredible and I'm learning faster than I ever thought possible. After what happened at school, I had lost my taste for learning, but now it is as if my brain has been starving for information.

I was shopping, in the floating market, in Ayutthaya, bartering, using my embarrassing half phrases and he swept in, saving me from vastly overpaying for some duck and rice soup. I thanked him and he responded in English. We ate our lunch together and he explained that he is working in a school. His English was nearly as bad as my Thai, but we got by, somehow. We came to understand that we could help each other with our languages. I would have agreed to anything he suggested at that point. He has the most open and warm face I have ever seen; his eyes like tiger stones, mesmerising.

On that first meeting, after our lunch, we navigated the market for hours. He has a gentle patience with my poor pronunciation and clumsy wording. I believe he thinks I'm funny, but I don't mean to be, he laughs a lot though which can't be bad. It makes me feel great to make someone else happy. It's been a long time.

Since then we have met daily, for meals and haphazard lessons. His laughter seems to have rubbed off on me and I'm happier with him then I have ever been. He is here to spend time with an incredibly intriguing friend called Bic, a Swami who is teaching us how to meditate, but my English teacher is the only reason I've stayed on here in Ayutthaya for the past week. I can't imagine waking up and spending a whole day without seeing his face. He has lit up my life quite unexpectedly.

I know it is quick, but I know my heart and I know people. I will be leaving with him and heading to Phuket, where he works. He has got me a job at the school he works in. Yes I am set to be a teacher!

I will write and call again soon. I have kept the same PO Box in Bangkok and I will have it checked regularly for the next few months. When my lease on it expires I will not renew it. The school has no formal address yet, it is all very new and secretive. I will explain more another time.

How I long for any word from you, a snippet of news about Sarah or about life on the farm.

Love Always

Rosa

xx

P.S his name is Wan. What would Nana Maureen think of that! it's not exactly biblical, but we weren't all lucky enough to find a Peter.

Chapter 11

Lucia was sprawled on the bed, fully clothed on top of the blanket.

Willow dressed as quietly as possible and crept to the bathroom to clean her teeth. As soon as she opened the door the lights sprang on and the air-conditioning burred to life noisily.

Lucia sat up as if shot, hair sprouting in every direction, the previous night's makeup smudged around her eyes. She yawned, 'Urgh. Give me a few minutes I'll be right with you,' she began to move to the edge of her bed with evident effort, without opening her eyes.

Willow laughed, 'Please stay here and have a relaxing day. You don't need to hold my hand. I think I'd like to do this alone.' She was looking forward to taking her time at the floating markets, to walk the paths that Rosa walked when she was falling in love.

'Thank God,' Lucia groaned, collapsing back into the bed, 'I've already booked in a massage.'

Willow arrived at the floating market triumphant. She had taken a Tuk Tuk back to her bike, avoided being hit by the racing traffic, hadn't fainted in the heat or suffered a panic attack or got lost.

She dismounted the bike, her legs begging for a rest, she had conquered the roads. She would never be scared to ride again. She reached over her shoulder and patted her tattoo; maybe the magic was real?

The river was packed with longtail boats laden with food and souvenirs; mostly accessible by foot. Tourists and locals swarmed around the stalls and she felt far from alone.

A young woman with long dreadlocks and warm toned skin, the image of Rosa, sat on a bench. Willow watched as she bought spices, examined fruit and talked with stall owners. Then Willow jumped.

'You buy ticket for water theatre? Traditional Thai song and dance stories,' a teenage girl grinned, cheekily close to her face, holding a ticket out.

'Sure I'll take one.' Willow wanted to find out more about Rosa's life. What better way to do that than to immerse herself and try everything that was on offer? She followed the girl the few hundred yards to the water's edge and sat at a bulky crowded picnic table.

There was a large pond, encased on three sides by bamboo buildings on precarious looking stilts. The other patrons, all strangers, welcomed her and involved her in their conversations about their adventures in Asia.

Willow laughed when an older Australian couple recounted being *mugged* of their camera by a monkey on Koh Phi Phi and sympathized when a young Swiss man, dressing a knee wound, told of how he had come off his push bike that morning, but they all fell silent as the performers took to the stage.

The stage resided just below the water's surface, giving the actors the appearance of floating. They were dressed in traditional Thai robes, lavish head dresses and intricate theatrical makeup, set off by the wondrous backdrop of open fields and blue endless skies.

Pleasure surged as Willow lost herself in the captivating performances. The characters gracefully swept over the water playing out a fairy-tale, like that of sleeping beauty from what she could decipher.

The play ended to rapturous applause, the table heaving with a happy audience. She gathered her things, then stopped dead, catching her breath. A voice she knew was at her ear.

'It's quite indescribable isn't it?' Aaron squeezed down, next to her, raising a hand in greeting to her table companions.

Willow turned, looking straight into his eyes.

'It must have been something to marvel. Before it was burnt to the ground,' Aaron wondered, turning away from Willow and to the stage.

'What do you mean? Was there a fire?' she asked, not sure what he was doing there, but only having time for one question at a time.

'The Burmese invasion in 1767. They burnt the whole of Ayutthaya to the ground. Now the ravished remains hold a less grand and more simplistic beauty. I choked up the first time I saw it. This tumble of beautiful bricks was once the largest city in the world. It showcased all of Asia's greatest wealth and splendour, the palaces were gold laden. Can you imagine that?'

'Don't you ever stop working?' she teased. Wriggling in her seat, trying to create more space between them, her mind on the conversation and off his muscular arms.

'I'm off the clock now actually. I have one or two things to get here, but I was hoping to run in to you. I thought you could use a translator to help in your search. If we find you some answers quickly, we'll be free to enjoy the day together.'

'We'll see how things go. I really need to garner some facts to get me started, I haven't made much progress so far.'

'Good job I'm here to help then. Let me have those photos. I'm sure we can find that hotel without too much bother, someone must know where it is.' He stood up and took her hand.

They walked to the stalls, her fingers feeling strange between his, aching to caress the back of his hand, the sweep of his shoulders the ripples beneath his shirt. She stopped herself abruptly. 'How did you and Lucia meet?' she needed to talk about anything that took her thoughts away from sex.

He smiled at his memories, 'She walked into my bar one day, just another tourist.'

'I didn't know you had a bar?' She realised that she didn't know much about him, but there was more to him then she had initially thought.

Aaron shrugged dismissively, 'It's nothing too grand. Anyway, we got talking more and more each day. She had an aura that was pure pleasure. That's the only way I can explain it. She made me and everyone around happy, but she was a bit down on her luck. I encouraged her to push forward with her business, found her the property and some contacts. I'd spent years keeping my head down, concentrating only on myself. Helping her made me feel good and being around her made me feel something again. When I met you, you reminded me of her, lost, but your aura was...' he searched for the word, 'Warm. It was horrible to see such a beautiful young woman so sad.'

Willow stopped. She hadn't been called *beautiful* by anyone aside from her mother. Could he really see something in her that nobody had before?

'I wanted to help you, but there was only so much I could offer without being creepy. I was handing her on to you. Like a baton. I hoped that she could bring out the happiness in you, like she did in me.'

Willow recalled the time she had spent with Lucia, 'She certainly did for me too.' She couldn't imagine him needing anyone, 'So you didn't need her anymore?'

Aaron considered, as if deciding how much he wanted to give away, 'I've got a lot to be happy about these days. That wasn't always the case. I didn't want to let anyone too close, but she wasn't having any of it, kept turning up, smiling and eager for her life to begin. You know, she's like a kid, in all the best ways. Without trying she reminded me that there was so much more to come. When I met you, I thought to myself, *there's a girl who needs to remember that her whole life is still ahead of her.* I hope you don't mind me saying that?'

'Not at all,' she whispered. Who was this man who knew what she needed better than she did? Finally, someone had seen her and acted to help.

Claire and James seemed to actively *avoid* looking at her, as if her pain were a contagious fog that would cling to them if they were unlucky enough to stumble into its orbit.

Aaron was not afraid, he had made his way into it, deliberately.

'Come on, let's find this hotel.' He set off towards another stall owner, leaving Willow looking on, bemused. The man shook his head when Aaron handed him the photos, exchanging a few words but shrugging none the less. He called over a few of his friends. Nobody had any information to help.

They walked around for a while, admiring the small statues and other tourist fodder. Aaron bought a tiny, carved wooden replica of the reclining Buddha and slipped it into Willow's hand. 'I like an excuse to support the local salesman and you'll want something to remember this place by once you're back home.'

The mention of *home* filled her with dread. A home should be a place full of friends and family, work and social life, London had none of those things and the farm had been sold. Thailand had reawakened her soul in a way she had never expected. Drive, determination, excitement and even lust bubbled within.

Would returning to England once again leave her empty? Willow examined the mahogany figure in her palm, the serene face of the Buddha. 'Thank you. I will always remember Ayutthaya, there's something special about this place,' she placed the icon in her bag, not wanting it to be a parting gift.

Aaron contemplated the ruins. 'My wife often dreamt of this place. She had loved it here, but she feared its imagery in her dreams. Thai people can be very superstitious, she was no exception, she believed that it was the ultimate vision of life. It stood as a warning that all things, no matter how beautiful and strong, crumble and fade to nothing. It was as if she knew what was coming. A few weeks later she was dead,' he trailed off, 'Sorry I'm not sure why I said that. I haven't thought about that for years.'

Whatever she had consider had happened to Aaron's wife, death had not crossed her mind. She didn't know what to say, she didn't want to bring up her own problems to show empathy or ask to many questions for fear of upsetting him.

He appeared as if he would break if she touched him. She fell dumb. What was the right thing to say to a widower she had been lusting after moments before?

It struck her like lightening that she was experiencing the emotions that everyone did when she told them of her problems. Was that why everyone had avoided her? Was too hard to face her? She wouldn't be like them. She wrapped her arms around him, giving a supportive hug, 'I'm so sorry.' She whispered, empathy flooding her, all other feelings forgotten. They had to be.

She thought about the ruins, what they meant to her, 'This place has weathered many storms. It didn't fall to squalor, when attacked, it evolved into something different. It could not go back to what it was, but it went on. Like you, like me.'

Aaron pulled back and wiped his eyes, began to speak, stopped what he was about to say and started again, 'Come on, I'm distracting you, this day is not about me. You are on a deadline, let's get moving.' He wasn't ready.

They asked five more stall and three boat owners, then a frail old man took the photo and starred at it for a long time. Willow held her breath. Did he know where to find the hotel?

He addressed Aaron in Thai, Aaron's face showed relief, then disappointment, then finally satisfaction. He thanked the man and ushered Willow towards a bench.

'That man used to live on the same street as this hotel. The road was bought up by developers over ten years ago. It was largely torn down with the hotel being changed into a hostel and a bank. He didn't recognise your aunt or cousin. I'm sorry.'

Willows faith diminished, 'I hadn't expected finding Jay to be easy, but it's hopeless. The only clues I have led nowhere.' She blinked back tears of her own.

'Hey, don't give up so easily. The man did recognise something in this photo.' He held up a picture of Rosa stood outside of her school, the Dumbro sign looming over head.'

Willow nearly jumped with excitement 'What does it say? Where is it.'

'Calm down. He couldn't translate it, I told you it's a very rare dialect, but see these roof tops in the background.' He pointed out some specks in the distance. 'I should have seen it before, but the colours are so faded, I didn't realise the roof tops were gold, they look grey.'

Aaron stared into the photo, 'The buildings are quite something, I haven't been, you can only visit by invitation, but the way the white steps twist around the gold clad statues, see right there.'

Willow could just make out the shapes he was referring to.

'They are unique. This temple is up in Khao Lan Mountain, in Thap Put, Phuket. It's Wat Bang Riang, I'm certain. The school can't be more than a couple of kilometres from there, to the south by the looks of things.'

Finally she had something to go on. 'So I get an invitation to the temple and someone there can send me to the school.' Willow wanted to go immediately.

Aaron shook his head, 'Sorry but the chances of you being invited there are nil. Only the most spiritual of people can go. the monks who live there are notoriously reclusive. They have taken a vow of silence. What we can do is search online for schools in the vicinity, there must be some information out there.'

Aaron put his arm around her, 'Let's get back to the hotel. We can run some searches, take a swim and get ourselves packed. It looks like you are off to Phuket tomorrow.'

Chapter 12

The previous day she had run every google search imaginable and Che had called some friends in the area, but there was nothing. It was as if the school had never existed.

Without a better plan she had gratefully accepted Che's offer to meet her in Phuket. In two weeks he would be working in the area and could take a day or two off. He assured her that the locals were friendly, but in the more rural areas, would be more likely to trust a Thai person.

Until then she was going it alone, she would ask around about the school, but she had another idea. Find Bic. His sanctuary could be anywhere, but there were photos to investigate and Rosa's descriptions of the area to run past travel agents. People had to book their rooms there, somewhere.

Rosa had written about Bic and their time spent together so many times that he certainly had to have been a great friend to her, but more than that he was a Swami. If he didn't know where to find Jay maybe he could pull some strings, make it possible for her to visit with one of the monks at the temple? She doubted that was how things worked and there was no guarantee that he was still alive, but she had to try something.

Lucia was heading back to her café and Aaron was booked with work for the next month so, like it or not, it was goodbye. She would spend the day in Ayutthaya, alone, exploring the ruins, getting some money out and buying her coach and boat tickets. By the evening she would be in Phuket.

She entered the lobby with Lucia, walking slower than necessary, eking out their last moments together. Aaron was leaning against the front desk chatting with the manager, shaking hands like they were old friends. Che glanced up from his perch on top of their luggage and smiled.

'Are you sure you won't come with us?' Lucia, tried for the hundredth time, resting her head upon Willow's shoulder, looking up at her pleading.

Willow wished that her answer could be different, 'One day I will come and see you at your home I promise. Maybe I'll find Jay quickly and I'll be with you sooner than you think?'

'I hope so. Good luck with everything.' Lucia pouted, pulling her in for a tight embrace.

Aaron cleared his throat as he walked over to them, 'Where's my cuddle? I have to make do with his ugly mug,' he waved at Che.

Che pulled a face and got to his feet, 'Goodbye Willow. Good luck to you and your family,' he called. 'I get van now. Don't forget I in Phuket in couple of week, call if you need me.'

Her family, Willow liked the sound of that. 'Thank you Che. I'll do that.'

Lucia kissed her on the cheek. 'I'm going to go with him, keep in touch, I'm on Facebook everyday so no excuses!' she demanded, running after Che.

'And then there were two.' Aaron murmured, 'Let me know how your pilgrimage works out.' He leant forward and briefly kissed her on the mouth. 'You'll find whatever it is that you are really looking for, I'm sure of it.'

For a fleeting moment she knew exactly what she was looking for. She leant into the warmth of his breath, the softness of his lips, longing to pull him closer, grab onto his hair, feel his chest pressing against hers. Then a car horn rang out incessantly and he pulled away.

'My chariot has come,' he announced, sweeping up his belongings, 'Call me if you need anything.' He said, before running away toward the waiting van.

'Thanks, I will,' she spoke to his back. So that was that?

She returned to her room, dispirited. Where Lucia's bag and piles of things had been was only empty space. She was alone, with Rosa's letters; in the same position as when she had arrived the week before. Or was she? She felt different, some of her strength restored, there was no way she'd be wasting any more time hiding!

She bounced on the escaped spring in her bike seat, on her way to the ruins, beneath a cloud-filled sky. She quickly found a bank and with funds replenished checked her map, happy to find that she could go to the phone shop Aaron had recommended on her way back to the hotel.

A young man approached, asked directions to the floating market and she directed him, proud that she must be looking less like a tourist.

All around the shop and stall vendors were packing away their wares, the streets thinning of tourists. Was it a religious holiday?

She cycled on, relishing the space. Without people to dodge and animals throwing themselves into her path it was almost relaxing. Her confidence grew with each kilometre passed and she was reminded of how liberating exercise could feel.

The streets grew quieter, the skies darker and by the time the first fat drops of rain plopped down upon her, she was a long way from anything she recognised. A crack of thunder shook the ground and she found herself amid a torrential downpour, blurring her vision and making it treacherous to ride. Flashing lightening crept closer. She was afraid.

She turned her bike around and with some difficulty set off in what she hoped was the direction of town. More lightening split the sky. She screamed and wobbled into a bush, sliding from the sodden seat, scraping her calf on the rusted peddle. Her foot caught on the flimsy chain and snapped it. 'Shit!' she cursed, through gritted teeth, rolling forward, with no choice but to move on.

The rain swept in from all angles, the dusty path turning from arid to slick. She slipped along until the deserted quiet town came into view. She stopped at the first internet café she came to and limped off her bike, discarding it at a bike stand, thankful to be back in civilisation.

She peered into her bag, searching for the bicycle lock; as if anyone would steal the hopeless thing. Her front pocket was already open. Had she left it like that? A pang of alarm.

She dropped the bag to the floor straight into a dirty puddle and emptied the contents; a map, a bottle of water, a phrase book, sun block, a few business cards. No wallet! She double checked hopelessly, thinking back to when she had given the man directions. It would have been easy for anyone to have seen where she had put her wallet away and taken it.

The few people who were left on the streets darted about, hiding from the rain, no one pausing.

Feeling scared and very stupid, she sat on the floor, surrounded by the unruly contents of her bag. She longed to call her father, to hear his voice, calm and reassuring. He had always been poised, ready to sort everything out, no matter if it meant driving to pick her up from a pub when she was drunk or getting her to the hospital with broken fingers having fallen off Skyla. Her heart plummeted, there was no one to call, even if she had a phone.

Chapter 13

Willow's thoughts came in to order. Her hotel was booked until the following morning, her passport was in the safe and keys were with the hotel reception. She needed to find a bank, although she had no I.D; what could she do?

She could find her way back to the hotel. It would take hours but it could be done with a few directions, then she could collect her passport and arrange a western union money transfer. Surely someone would let her use a computer and phone once she'd explained her predicament?

She checked her short's pockets and, with relief, pulled out two hundred baht, about two pounds. She needed to cancel her cards immediately, before someone emptied her accounts and she really was in trouble.

Thrusting her things back into her bag, she stood with renewed drive and strode though the storm, arriving at a café just in time to stop a young man from locking up.

He held the door open for her and sat behind the desk, his eyes widening at her bedraggled appearance, 'Your leg is pretty gnarled up!' he grimaced, burying his head under the messy desk, snapping back up with a box of tissues.

'Thanks.' She accepted, heartened by the gesture. She dabbed the oozing wound, pleased to see that the rain had made it appear worse than it was.

'Go ahead, give a computer a shot, but the electric is fucked; keeps cutting out,' he explained, picking up a magazine.

Willow regarded the sea of black screens, taking a punt on the one furthest away, she didn't want to be overheard.

She switched the computer on. Nothing; she stared, willing it back to life.

A few long minutes later there was a bleep and a flicker of lights. Her fingers moved quickly over the keys as she prayed the power would not fail. She googled the phone number for her bank, but the connection was lost before she could write it down. Even if she did manage to Skype-call the bank she would never be able to wait for an operator.

When the power came back, she wasted no time. It had been a long time since she had used her passwords and she cringed typing JAMESLOVE1, into her skype account. James had set it up for her and she'd never contacted anyone else. She racked her memory for any other phone number but his. It was futile. Who memorized numbers anymore?

She took a breath, lifted the headset and pressed to connect. Each ring punctuating her growing proximity to the past she had strived to out-run.

'Hello,' James picked up, croaky with sleep.

Her heart stopped. She was transported; crawling into bed next to him, nestling her cheek against his chest, his arms holding her close. She had heard that *hello* a thousand times; she had longed to forget how much she had missed it.

'It's me,' she forced, unable to control the crack in her voice and desire to be back in the safety of their flat, before everything had changed.

'Sarah?'

Willow bristled, every emotion conflicting, her name dragging her back further.

'It's the middle of the night.' He complained, yawning.

She could picture him stretching, topless, in Calvin Klein's, the way he always slept. She had never known how to ask him for anything; not help, support, or even honesty.

He whispered apologies, to his girlfriend? Someone else was wrapped in his arms in *their* bed while she was lost, bleeding, robbed and alone. Her stomach tightened. She fought the urge to hang up. She had to get what she needed. He owed her after all.

'Sorry.' He said, the notes of sleep slipping away, replaced with irritation, 'Where the hell are you?'

What right did he have to be annoyed? he'd been trying to get rid of her for months, 'I'm in Thailand.' She said defiant.

For a satisfying moment he was silent.

He scoffed, 'What are you doing there? Jesus, Claire called the police and reported you missing. She's been worried sick!'

Willow didn't want to be cruel, but it was laughable. 'Why did she do that? I told her that I was leaving.'

'Sarah you haven't done a thing alone in a year and then you disappear in the middle of night! Nobody had heard from you in days, your phone went dead and you've not been on social media. We thought you might have done something to harm yourself again.'

'Whose fault would that be if I had?' She flared.

'Here we go again.'

She knew he would be rolling his eyes, dragging his fingers through his hair, exasperated.

She took a deep breath. He always made her feel out of control. 'If I want to come off social media that is my right, I'm not sixteen. I don't need to be posting selfies and fake smiling in photos to prove I'm ok and I was bloody sick of seeing you and your girlfriend at every party in London! I should be able go on holiday without intervention from the police. Claire is not my keeper and neither are you!' She stopped suddenly and then…'Why was she calling you? She hates you.'

He sighed again, 'She doesn't hate me Sarah, you're being ridiculous. She called me, thinking that I may have heard from you.'

Two people she had loved, talking about what a worry she was, what a burden. She needed to end the conversation. 'I don't have long to talk. I need you to call Claire and get her to check her emails immediately. You know she never checks them. I will send her some very important details which she needs to read and act on immediately. Most importantly she needs to cancel my bank cards straight away.' Willow, embarrassed, didn't want to go in to the details.

'Sarah what's the matter? You're not making any sense.' He pressed.

'Stop calling me Sarah.' She snapped, unable to bear hearing him say her name, it brought too much back.

'What is going on? Are you having an episode?' James sounded utterly confused.

She had worked so hard, reconstructing herself from the broken shards of *Sarah* and he was turning her back into the crushed mess of a woman he had before. 'James I don't want to talk to you!' she shouted, unable to hold her emotions in.

The Ozzy glanced up from behind the counter with vague interest.

Without warning she was crying, heaving pathetic painful breaths. 'James don't make this any harder than it needs to be.' She loathed the strain in her voice, the anger in her heart.

He pressed, 'Calm down. You don't have to get yourself in these states. Just tell me what you need.'

Her voice was ragged, 'Just call my sister! If she's that worried about me she will not mind hearing from you in the middle of the night. It's urgent.'

James hummed, 'It's not going to be a suicide note is it?'

The power cut.

Willow rattled the receiver in vain. If Claire cancelled her cards she could afford to wait until she was back at the hotel to find and send the details of where she could wire her the money.

Her two hundred baht got her half an hour on the computer, she had a few minutes to spare and didn't fancy going into the rain, embarking on the long walk back to the hotel before she had to.

The power came back on.

She rushed to sign into her new Facebook account and saw that she had been tagged in plenty of photos. Each made her smile as she remembered the pleasure of her trip so far, forgetting the present pain of her predicament.

She typed a message explaining her situation to Lucia as a message came through from Aaron:

How's your day going?

Her fingers lingered. She wasn't sure James would get in touch with her sister quickly. He was hardly Mr Reliable and she couldn't risk being stranded.

I've run into a bit of trouble. I've been pick-pocketed, I've got no phone, no card or cash. I'm a long way from the hotel and I'm not sure how to get back, my bike is broken. Oh and there's a storm. Can you help or advise?

She typed quickly, too worried to feel embarrassed.

Are you somewhere safe?

Quickly came his reply.

I'm in an internet café called....

She scanned the space for a sign and saw a pile of brochures on the counter.

Bow's Internet and Travel Centre.

She nervously waited for his response; how had she managed to mess up everything in just a few hours?

Ok don't....

Aaron began.

The computer screen went black.

The man behind the desk grumbled. 'I'm going to shut the place up, no point staying open in this.'

There was nothing left to do. She thrust her hands in her pockets and pulled out the precious 200 baht.

Maybe he could give her some directions and she could message Aaron from the hotel?

A phone was ringing somewhere. Willow's head shot up as the Ozzy pulled a handset from under the table.

'Hi Bow's Internet and Travel Centre. Jack speaking, how can I help?' he made a few *ummm* and *ahah* noises, scribbling notes on a pad. 'Can you say that again mate? Sorry did you say five-five or just five? Yep got it. Can do. No problem. What's the name on the card?' Jack was writing digits down, knitting his eyebrows, 'Koh Tao mate? Yah no problem, but it will be tomorrow. I'll sort it out and let her know. Ha! No worries. Hello? Hello?' Jack shrugged, putting the phone down.

Flickering hope kept Willow routed to the spot.

'Your mate Aaron said his battery was running out, he's been traveling all day or something.' Jack smiled, 'He's sorted everything.'

'What did he sort exactly?' she wondered, maybe he had sent a loan?

'He's paid for your boat ticket, to Koh Tao. He said that some dude called Che will pick you up at 8 a.m. from the hotel. He's still on the mainland, sorting some van repairs; I think he said something like that? I couldn't really hear.' Jack read his notes, 'He said the hotel will sort your dinner and breakfast and he'll meet you at the pier, work out how to get your cash.' Jack outlined the plan, victorious.

She thought of the beaches and the ocean in Koh Tao, her reservations floating away on the waves. That had to be better than waiting indefinitely for Claire to come through. She would speak to Aaron's friend Eric, show him all the photos and letters. If he gave her clear direction she could even take a day or two for herself. 'Thanks Jack.'

Out of the window Willow eyed the bursting skies. 'Can you help me with directions to the hotel Sala Ayutthaya? I need to take a route with pavements preferably. I've broken my bike and had my wallet stolen.'

Jack whistled slowly. 'You've had a blindingly crap day haven't you? You are either the unluckiest woman in the world or the luckiest one to still be standing. Your friend told me to get you a cab and charge his card.'

She laughed. What else was there to do? She was lucky.

Chapter 14

Che came careering around the corner, announcing his arrival with a cacophony of horn hooting and screaming brakes. His window was down, his face glowing with the happiest of smiles, 'Willow I see you sooner than I expect, but it nice surprise.'

She ran to the van, 'I think so too!' she wrenched the door open and lugged her things inside.

Che patted her shoulder, 'We are all happy to have you come to Koh Tao.' he nodded, swinging out into the road.

Willow checked her belt, recalling the journey from the plane. 'How long will this take?'

Che ignored a red light, 'Only five, six hour,' he shrugged, non-comital, flitting through the radio stations.

Willow scrutinised him. He was wearing his uniform of a Che Guevara t-shirt, short shorts and bandana head band. He would have looked at home driving a tank which possibly explained his driving style.

'The guidebook says it's eight hours to the pier and a further two on a boat to get to the island.' She hoped she was wrong, but feared she was correct.

Che shrugged, humming alone to the radio. 'Thai-time Willow, Thai-time. No need put a number on time. We get there when Buddha thinks we get there.'

She thought about the events of the past day and had to agree. None of her plans had come to fruition, but perhaps she was still going in the right direction?

Che took a call and she turned her attention to her phrase book, curling her tongue around the unusual chipped phonetics. She was falling in love with the way in which the punching words executed her meaning with fierce speed. The exaggerated vows made for an excited note to the most mundane of sentences.

Sometime later she exchanged tentative Thai phrases with Che, regarding their surroundings and weather. His pleasure at her progress encouraged her to venture into more complex observations. 'Wun tun tan rak gai.' She spoke with confidence, eager to compliment the chicken she had eaten for dinner the night before.

Che erupted, spitting out the soda he had been sipping. 'You say you love the cock last night. I think you dream of Aaron. Same word: cock, egg and chicken,' Che wiped tears from his eyes, 'Don't run before you can work. I teach you better Thai.' He was enjoying her mistake, oblivious to his own.

'It's: *Don't run before you can walk* not *work*,' Willow pointed out self-satisfied.

'Ahh, that make more sense,' he accepted before returning to his singing, accompanying Bon Jovi's *Living on a Prayer*.

After hours bouncing along, with sleep broken by Che's vocal gymnastics, Willow was surprised to find the pier full. The floors and filthy old benches packed with tired backpackers. She wanted to feel superior but her backpack and guidebook hardly set her apart.

She had listened to one of Aaron's blogs about Koh Tao on Che's phone and the unimpressive pier did not appear as the "*Gateway to utopia*" described. Luckily they weren't left waiting long.

They crammed onto the boat, with no chance of a seat. Willow was excited to see Aaron again and to finally have the chance to dip her toes in the South China sea, but she'd been hoping to do it in relative solitude.

'Many people, everyone go to Koh Tao before Koh Pang Nang for Full Moon in few days.' Che explained as they squeezed their way onto the deck and found a tiny spot, among their fellow passengers, to sit on.

'Great.' She was unable to keep the sarcasm from her voice. It seemed as if the world was chasing her piece of paradise.

Stories from the infamous party had not passed her by. It was the hot topic of conversation in Bangkok at the roof bar and Lucia's South African friends had been full of anecdotes from their night spent partying on the sands of Had Rin bay. She'd heard that anywhere from 10,000 to 30,000 people would attend each month. Just how good could a party be? She hadn't wanted to sound like an old fart when people told her about their experiences there, but a night spent without a seat, crushed on a beach listening to electronic music was not her idea of fun.

Che pulled his hat over his face and fell asleep almost immediately, leaving her to block out her discomfort with fantasies of the beautiful island waiting just across the water, but as they arrived under a bleak grey sky her spirits plummeted. The oasis Aaron had described was nowhere to be seen.

The sea was cloudy, a fine slick of petrol slipping on the surface, a few discarded plastic bottles and bags bobbing about. She stepped off and caught sight of Lucia, running.

'What a nightmare you've had! Little bastard thieves, you poor thing. Are you ok?' She shouted.

'I'm fine.' Willow brushed her off, mortified. Word of her ineptitude was out.

Lucia gave her a big hug, 'I for one am happy to have you here!'

Willow regarded her, animated with the pleasure of their reuniting, touched, but where was Aaron?

'You forget pains from travel when you go in sea,' Che assured her, taking her bag. 'I have things to do here, you go ahead, I bring bags in an hour OK?'

'Thanks Che, that'll be great,' she accepted, not expecting to see her things again for at least three. 'I owe you dinner as soon as my money is sorted.'

He grinned, 'Happy to help you.' Before heading off in the other direction.

Lucia caught Willow looking at an overflowing bin.

'The pier is not the island. I've seen the best that Thailand has to offer and I chose to make this place my home. It's incredibly special!' her pride was palpable.

Willow was ready to be convinced. She took Lucia's arm and raced to the beach hut hotel where she would be staying. Lucia explained that Aaron was in a meeting with a new hotelier and then, to her surprise, she left; having to return to work where there had been a *milk frother emergency*. Willow had almost forgotten that they weren't friends on a holiday, she was intruding on their lives. An inconvenience?

She was alone again and determined not to get into any more trouble. She knew exactly what she wanted to do.

She ran out of her hut, onto the beach; Che was right, every second of the journey was forgotten. The heavens parted and the sun warmed her skin as she stood in the shallows of Sairee Beach. It was impossibly beautiful; delicate white sand meeting turquoise sea, ephemeral lapping waves dancing on the surface, the beach edged by lush palm trees and scattered wooden huts. A postcard realised.

She had stepped into one of the images that her friends had flaunted on Instagram throughout their gap years while she had been stuck in London. Finally it was her turn.

Tourists dipped in and out of the ocean, adorned with snorkels and smiles. Simple hut-style restaurants emanated exquisite scents, mouth-watering dishes ferried to hungry divers, sitting on wooden tables, fins and tanks at their feet. Fruit sellers languidly strolled up and down the mile of flawless sand, resting from time to time beneath the shade offered by one of the many palms.

Willow peeled off her dress, threw it to the sand and skipped into the sea in her underwear. No time to waste waiting for Che to bring her bikini. She wasn't sure how long she was floating on her back, drifting with the current, but the sun had dropped in the sky. She moved to the shore and sat in the shallows, plunging her toes in and out of the sand, hugging her knees to her chest, audacious fish sauntering away from the depths to peck at her toes.

'I knew you were a water a baby at heart.' Aaron shouted across the beach, approaching with a smile.

Willow blushed, her underwear had turned sheer in the water but she couldn't stay sitting while Aaron stood. She got up nearly laughing at his befuddled expression. To her satisfaction he was embarrassed.

He smiled awkwardly, but didn't move to embrace her in welcome, 'It's a relief to see you safe and sound. We were all worried. One of us will get you to the Western union tomorrow and you will be good as new.'

Stuff the practicalities, she wrapped her arms around his neck before she knew what she was doing. His hard-muscular torso, warm next to her damp skin evoked a primal urge. Her nipples hardened, she ached for him.

'What's this for?' he chocked, stepping back. Keeping a safe distance?

She hesitated, unsure, 'Thank you for helping me out, look at all of this, I'm happy to be here.' She wrung the salt water from her waving tresses, busying her hands to stop them from shooting to her chest or his.

Aaron relaxed, 'Don't worry about it, it's happened to me before and someone was good enough to help me. Call it pilgrim's karma. I've taken out some cash for you, enough to last you through the night.'

Willow couldn't remember the last time she had taken money from a man, even a loan. She liked to be financially independent but was too relieved to quibble. 'Thanks, again, I'll make sure you get it back as soon as I have things sorted.'

'No problem. Do you fancy having dinner?'

Was he still shifting away from her? A dinner date in paradise sounded perfect. She beamed, delighted.

'Everyone is coming to this beach tonight. I thought you'd like to meet them, especially Eric, he's keen to help you. They'll be here soon actually. You have a few minutes to get dressed. I mean put some clothes on, I mean…you know?' he paused, reasserting his casual smile, 'Come on let's head to the huts.'

It wouldn't exactly be the date she had envisioned, but it was thoughtful for him to have arranged a night to welcome her and with Eric too. They walked in step and he let out a long breath. Was he stressed?

'I'll meet you there in twenty minutes.' He pointed to a bar down the beach. I'm going to check-in with a few people at *Senos Dive Shop*,' he waved, running away, as he had at the hotel.

He perplexed her, but he was the least of her concerns and she couldn't be in bad spirits. Her accommodation had sprung from a Flintstones cartoon, uneven stone walls, mottled in pastel shaded plaster and brick. A single bed took up most of the space, nestling safely beneath an enormous mosquito net, upon it her bag had been delivered. The floor was a continuation of the sand from the beach. A mirror hung on the wall and a bucket stood next to a cold tap where the shower should have been. The toilets, thankfully, were in a separate hut.

Willow washed the salt from her skin, invigorated by the cold blast from the bucket and dressed in a small dress, hardly more than a wisp of raw orange silk.

She walked to the bar and found that dinner was to be served at an enormous threadbare rug upon the sand. The veil of darkness had been fast to take hold, revealing a lavishly star-peppered sky.

A bonfire crackled, licking up into the night, illuminating Aaron's face next to her. He was talking with his friends, crowded onto the rug, while Lucia hastened to introduce her to the mass of strangers.

A few were divers; Gary, a young Welsh man worked as a plumber and general handyman for the hotels; Cassidy, a German girl was a hairdresser with unicorn coloured locks; Mary, an Irish girl in twenties with a buzz cut and tattoo of Marilyn Monroe over her arm, worked promoting her partner's tattoo parlour.

Ben, a fellow brit, did not seem too sure what he did, but Willow liked him immediately. He brought laughter to the group with a casual East London swagger as he sat down to her. He asked about her trip, teased about the mugging in way that made her long for a brother and joined her in watching the bonfire.

Not far away, two young Thai men danced expertly with staffs, blazing balls of fire on each end. The flames tore through the sky with a whoosh as the men, barefoot and topless, twisted their burning poles around their backs, flinging them into the air, weaving them in figure of eights and leaping to the American heavy metal music. Their hairless toned torsos glistening with gasoline and exertion as they weaved among their audience.

A small group of enamoured girls flirted and chatted with the fire dancers as they passed.

Willow could see how their fantasy of a holiday romance was embodied in those boys. She envied the naivety the girl's youth offered them. Their love filled summer would almost certainly fade away, perhaps leaving a sore scar, but they would pursue it regardless, living for the joy of the day, ignoring the pain of tomorrow.

She had hurt too much, too deeply to leave herself open to heartbreak again no matter how fun.

What was she doing pursuing Aaron, when she had no chance of building a future with him? If their relationship was to become any more physical she would not be able to hold her emotions back. She would be devasted when, inevitably she would have to leave. His knee brushed hers and she shrank back.

She had barely caught her breath since James and needed to care for her fragile heart. She had to focus on Jay, return to England and put the pieces of her life back together. Maybe then she would be ready to meet someone new?

'Poi Poi Poi,' Aaron shouted, quickly joined by the other members of the group. He turned to her, 'Poi, means *thrashing*, it's the name for those chains that the guys are dancing with.'

Che, in high spirits, had joined the fire performers, picking up what was presumably the poi.

Willow was surprised to see that they were metal chains with small cages full of wadding soaked gasoline at the ends. Che lit the cages, fire dripping to the sand like fluorescent magma. He bent, curled and bobbed beneath the flailing orbs, embers cascading in circles around him, burning up the sky.

He was a man transported, for a moment he was the boy that he had been. They cheered with vigour when the music faded and Che skipped back to them breathless and sweating.

'You are amazing. Do you do that a lot?' Willow was genuinely astounded.

He sat down, pulling his T-shirt back on, 'Used too. Not now. It give you cancer.'

'Can't argue with that.' Willow loved his candour.

A man approached, white hair swept back from his face and wearing beige trousers; fisherman pants, she had heard them called in Bangkok's markets. His smart white linin shirt made her think of *The Man from Del Monte* from childhood adverts. Eric.

Willow wanted to talk to him immediately, but he was speaking to Mary. Instead she settled back into her conversation with Ben, keen to fill her in on the dynamics of the group. His anecdotes cheeky and candid, making her laugh until her stomach hurt.

She learned that the group had a wide age range, from Mary, who was in her early twenty's to Eric who was in his sixties. There was so much palpable affection that Willow could see them for what they were. Family. They had chosen each other as such, bonded as tightly as those who were by blood - she could feel it in the way they enquired after each other's health, finances, romances and business ventures. Nothing was off limits, so when Ben asked, *"So what brings you to Koh Tao Willow? Except for the handsome men of course."* The group fell quiet and she had to be truthful, with them and herself.

Ben beamed encouragingly, 'Everyone arrives with a story, but not everyone is ready to tell it.' He leant back on his elbows offering her an easy get out, 'But if you don't tell us you will have to buy the next round,' he rose his glass with a cheeky grin.

Lucia patted her hand, stood up and announced, 'I am a high school dropout, far too stubborn to re-sit exams, too proud to ask my dad for a job and no-one else would give me one so I made my life here, where no-one cares about qualifications.' She sat down, whispering in Willows ear, 'We do this when new people join our group it's an indoctrination not interrogation. Say as little or as much as you like.'

Eric stood next, 'I'm Eric and I'm a bankrupt divorcee!' Everyone made the relevant sympathy noises until Eric put his hands up, looking at Willow. 'All my own fault, turned out my secretary was not worth the alimony cheques and the business didn't run too well once she did a runner with the yearly takings.'

The group switched to pantomime boos and jeers and Eric continued, 'I've been here eighteen years, never going back. Even if I wanted to, no-one would have me.' He raised his glass, toasting the group.

Mary stood as Eric sat, 'I'm a lesbian and I haven't told my family. This is my first year, but I have found my love so will be staying if possible, because I'm twenty-four and I'm still scared of my parents!' she put her hand on her girlfriend Diana's knee and kissed her.

Everyone applauded.

Gary was up next. 'I'm Gary. Got out of prison four years ago and couldn't get a job in Wales. Been in and out of care my whole life, no family to go back to. This is the best home and family I've ever had. Looking after luxury properties beats robbing them in the rain back home for sure!'

There were heckles of love and warmth as he sat, his freckled cheeks burning red.

Ben stood next, 'I'm Ben. The London stock market nearly destroyed me. Working eighteen-hour days left me burnt out, single and with a serious drug and drink problem. I only came here for a holiday, but I never went home, that was six years ago. I sometimes wonder what happened to all the things? Maybe there's still an empty seat in a dark office waiting for me to return?'

In the fire light Willow noticed that his arms were covered in large black tattoos and faded fierce scars. His jean shorts hung low on his waist and his tired looking t-shirt made him look far removed from corporate life. It was impossible to picture him in the standard issue Tom Ford trench and made to measure suit of canary wharf.

Che got up and patted his chest, 'Born here, can't get away. Nowhere to go' he shrugged, 'Thai passport, much use as tissue paper without visa.'

'Cry me a river, you've never wanted to come to America or England with me,' Aaron shouted at him across the rug, 'I've been asking you for years.'

'Not go with you. Want to go with pretty lady,' Che winked, lifting his bottle of beer to his friend.

Aaron scowled as he got up, 'I came travelling with university lads, to drink and party. Instead I ended up with a pregnant bar girl and a wedding band within three months. They're gone, as you all know, but I could never leave them here so I will always stay.'

The group's jovial buoyancy ebbed. What did he mean *they're gone*? Had his wife's family taken Phoenix away when she died? He was floundering following his confession.

Willow stood up, not knowing what else to do to relieve him of the attention. 'I guess it must be my turn?'

He hurried to sit down.

'My name is Willow. My parents died last year, I didn't cope with it very well and my fiancé dumped me, leaving with a younger infinitely more beautiful model and over thirty thousand pounds of my savings.' Saying it aloud stung, but she wanted to continue, 'She really was a model and my subsequent breakdown was very minor - hardly humiliating at all.'

Everyone joined her laughing, not so much in sympathy, but empathy. They all had reasons for running away but somehow none of it seemed to matter as they sat in paradise, laughing at their mistakes.

When she failed to say more, Aaron prompted, 'Tell them about your Aunt and your pilgrimage.'

'I've bored you all long enough,' she sat down, not wanting to dominate the evening, keen to hear from the others who hadn't had a chance to share their stories.

Eric exclaimed, 'You're the woman Aaron has told me about!' Excitement was written all over his face, 'I do love a quest, it's a nomads' driver. We've all been a nomad before we found our little spot in this world to call home! We'd love to hear all about your adventure Willow.' He prompted.

Encouragement fluttered from around the rug. Willow took in their eager faces, hungry for new stories. They must have heard each other's many times. She took a swig of beer and filled them in on the details of the Will and the sketchy leads she was using to find Jay.

'Were they identical twins, your mother and Rosa?' Ben asked.

'Yes they were, although from the pictures I've seen they did everything they possibly could to look different.' Willow pictured her aunt's dreadlocks and her mother's short sensible crop, worn the same way for over twenty-five years.

'So this cousin is biologically a half-brother?' Ben mused, 'That's cool.'

'No, Rosa could not have children of her own, Jay was adopted. That's why my mum knew it would have meant so much to Rosa that Jay and I would find each other in the eventuality of losing them. From Rosa's letters it was clear that her biggest fear was that Jay would be left alone again, she wrote about it time and time again. So you see I had to come. For him, for me, for our mothers.'

Eric nodded, 'Aaron mentioned that I might be able to help you with some translations? I've been around here for a pretty long time and worked with a lot of schools. I'm confident I can at least give you some pointers.'

Willows heart lifted. This could be the man to help her. 'Eric I would love that. When are you free?'

'I'm leading a trek tomorrow, but I'll be back by the next day. Give me what you have, I will try to get through it by the time I am back. Come to my shop in the morning and we can work out what you need to do next.' He grinned with unveiled enthusiasm.

It was unsettling to be parted from Rosa's letters, allowing someone else to read them felt as if she was betraying a confidence, but she trusted Eric. If anyone could help her he could. 'Wonderful. Thank you so much. Walk me to my hut later and I'll give you the box.'

With Eric on the case she acknowledged that she had been given permission to enjoy herself for the next twenty-four hours.

Chapter 15

As a teenager Willow had risen early, nearly every day, with the animals on the farm. She would sneak out, careful not to wake anyone and run across the fields, basking in the solitude.

Her favourite month had been June, when the rapeseed crops glowed in luminous yellow brilliance. She would run through the boastful flowers with no direction or agenda. Running for the love of freedom, collapsing only when her breath ran out, upon the earth. She would take in the wonder of her small world, while an irrepressible yearning burnt in her stomach. She needed to see what was beyond the horizon.

She dreamt of foreign skies and flowers, beaches and temples, flavours and scents. She was too young to travel alone and her parents never left Europe so she brought the world to her, through language, spending every moment perfecting her dialects and watching foreign films.

When her classmates were branching out to university she went along with the crowd, it was not the exotic leap she was dreaming of, but it was a step. She was happy to be studying linguistics and moved to London without thinking about whether she would like it.

The first time that she realised she may have made a mistake was when she ran through the morning streets. There were beggars, drunks and stern commuters to side-step. Pounding against the concrete hurt her shins, there was nothing to calm her soul, no fresh air to breath, nor grass to rest upon.

The city was intimidating and instead of enjoying the parties and the sports clubs she found herself in her room; Alone with her dreams and her books.

By the time graduation was looming, talk in halls had moved to gap year travels. She pictured herself in Japan riding the bullet train from Tokyo, walking the Inca trail to Machu Picchu, laying her hands upon Aires rock, but at the forefront of all her fantasies had always been Thailand. Maybe it was the large books crammed with photos of the beaches and exotic temples which inexplicably filled her parent's book shelves or the Asian food her mother cooked that ignited her desire?

Without malice she had been left out of the planning between the closer friends. She had set herself too far apart.

Staying in London had never been her plan, but she invested in a flat that summer and the market dropped, then she met James and life seemed to *happen.* She loved him with every ounce of her being and the promise of becoming a wife and mother to his children was a wonderful gift. They could see the world together, later, it was not going anywhere.

James wanted stability in his home life, his career was erratic and she was his constant. He too brought something to her life, being in love with him gave her confidence, having a partner to explore London with gave it a new appeal. She could not let him go, not even for her dreams.

Finally she was in Thailand. Willow smiled, stretched her sleep-heavy limbs and wished she knew some yoga to alleviate her morning aches. Out on the beach the sea lay beneath the perpetually clear sky. Koh Tao was waking while the people were sleeping and she was alone with the earth as she had been as a girl. A time worn urge returned. To run. She pulled on her trainers, not wanting to waste another minute and she set off in her pyjamas.

She kept to the beach path, her stride opening as she found a familiar rhythm. The sand flew up, her feet tearing through the powder, lungs straining, she kept going. She wasn't waiting for her dream any longer she was living it!

She kept going for nearly an hour, then stopped in her tracks. Her blood ran cold. Her heart began to race. There was nowhere to sit and nothing to steady herself against. She crumpled to the ground, shock taking over. She counted to ten, slowed her breathing and continued to sixty. She stared at the man. He was sat outside a huge hotel, in the restaurant. Looking relaxed, reading a British newspaper was James.

She sat on the beach gaping in disbelief.

He stood up, flawlessly handsome against the island backdrop, Ray Bans resting on his chiselled cheekbones. He wore a checked shirt, the one she had bought him for his last birthday, sleeves rolled up, buttons undone showing his chest and collection of beads. His denim shorts were patched and frayed by a designer hand. He was the illusion of perfection, exactly as she remembered.

Paralysed with fear, she prayed that the anger from their previous conversation would return; but as tears rolled down her checks she knew it was pointless. She could not deny that she had loved him and when he turned and noticed her, it was as it always had been.

Her heart continued to thump, her mouth dry, words caught in her throat. He smiled and held his arms open. She remembered how it had been to fall into his embrace. She stood, trembling, her head screaming at her to run away. Her disobedient legs took her to him and her broken heart threw her into his arms. She nestled her face against his chest and breathed him in.

He squeezed her tight and picked up off the floor. 'Hi stranger. What on earth are you doing in your Pyjamas. Were you jogging?' his eyebrows raised, slightly laughing, 'Since when do you jog?'

Was he shocked or mocking? He had a way of making her feel uncertain, as if her decisions were stupid; perhaps they were? She stepped back, reminded with a sting that the man she had loved was a fantasy. The reality of James was different, selfish and cruel.

She nodded, trying to look confident, 'I thought this was a good place for it.' She wanted to scream *"What the fuck are you doing here?"* instead she gawped, helplessly confused.

'Good for you, if you're into that kind of thing?' James placed his hand on her shoulder and gave it a slight squeeze. 'It's great to see you. Such a relief, despite the crazy hair.' He teased, ruffling it with his palm.

She tried to pat her salty unbrushed hair flat and wiped the sweat from her face. If he had come all that way to see her maybe he wasn't all the awful things she had thought he was? Maybe he had really loved her, maybe he still did? She shook herself, urging the tears to stop, were they of weakness, relief or happiness? He embodied so much hurt and loss that she found it hard to look at his face without crying.

She stepped back, bewildered.

'You're happy to see me, right?' he took her hands in his, 'It's good to see you, even if you are in your Pjs, you silly thing.' He laughed softly, peering into her eyes.

She looked away, staring at the sand. He hadn't held her in over a year. At one point all she wished for was his touch, dreamt of it, believed that she could not live without it, in reality it felt foreign. She wriggled her hands free and he moved his confidently onto her hips, his eyes boring into hers.

Her mouth was so dry she struggled to get her lips around the words, 'What made you think that I would be happy to see you?' she wanted to run back to the safety of her hut. Was she dreaming? She shook her head. He was still there.

He put his hand to her cheek. 'It was only a few months ago you were sending me emails every day, begging me to come and see you, now I've come all this way don't argue. I dropped everything after you called and It wasn't easy. I turned down a big acting job and sent at least ten emails. This is pretty bloody far from our home, it took me ages to get here. So yes, I thought you'd be pleased.'

He put his sunglasses on top of his head and gazed quizzically out to sea, the same expression she had seen him use in a chewing gum commercial years before.

Home. England had been crumbling from her consciousness which each passing day, but with James in front of her, it all came back. Their flat, the lounge and the sofa they had chosen together, the sleek metallic coasters and place mats, the wall clock from her parents as a house warming gift. The reality was that she did have a *home*, whether she wanted it was a different question. Could she be like Ben, abandon it all; was it all just *stuff* or was she just on a holiday?

She caught his eye, 'I didn't want to be found James; I was nearly happy. How did you find me?'

He ruffled his hair squinting, but refusing to put his sunglasses on, his eyes were his best feature after-all. All his usual tricks were transparent.

'I didn't mean to upset you. I know how fragile you are. It's been one hell of a year for us, but I think I could help you now. I'm ready. When you called and I realised that you were out here on your own, in trouble, I was shocked by how much I felt for you. Terrified you would hurt yourself. This time I had to stop you, save you from yourself.' He shrugged, playing the role of bashful saviour badly, reaching for her hand.

She shook with….what was it? Longing or fury, desire or repulsion?

He turned her hand over and brought her palm to his lips, 'You don't need to be alone anymore, I'm here.'

Willow scrutinized his face, there was nothing beneath the surface. 'You've never cared about me. Not properly. You came all this way, but you weren't terrified for my wellbeing, you thought that your meal ticket might have finally expired.' She could go back to her old life, but she didn't want to, 'What about your girlfriend. Isn't Emily her name?' she snapped.

'She's gone. I never stopped loving you but couldn't get close to you, physically or emotionally. You said that you wanted me back but you tried to change me and I couldn't take it. I didn't break us by myself.' he whispered.

After everything that she had changed about herself, her dreams, her life, he wasn't prepared to even get a job that paid his bills! Then she thought about Emily, 'So she left you? You didn't leave her for me?'

James played the look of a wounded puppy, reached out and stroked the chain around her neck, taking their engagement ring in his palm, 'I'm telling you that I still love you, I want to give things another go. You're still wearing your ring. Be honest with yourself, you're not ready to give up on us either.'

She took another step back, out of reach. The burn from his touch lingered, spreading up her arm and encasing her heart in a cold vice. The joy for life, which had delicately begun to bloom was being crushed with each moment that she was near him. 'You need to leave!' she managed. She didn't want him. She could hardly believe it herself.

He flinched, a little off balance, 'Sarah we need to talk. Your sister's having problems and I have news on the flat. There's a lot to say.

'The bills must really be mounting up without me.' She sniped, not caring for any further polite conversation. He narrowed his eyes and took a deep breath. To her surprise there was no rebuttal, he was always quick to put her down. What was going on?

He composed himself, 'I didn't come all this way to watch you run off. Not to mention that we owe it to ourselves to talk about us. Don't you think? We should have been getting married in a couple of days-time; We could still make the family that we dreamed of.' His eyebrows raised, his head nodding, prompting her to agree.

He'd played his trump card. Willow was thirty years old. She and Claire had been born when their mother was in her early twenties and Claire was married at twenty-three. Willow had always feared that she would miss her window. She was without a family and he was offering her one on a plate. What if this was it, the only chance she would get, could she turn him down? He hadn't been perfect, but as he had pointed out, neither had she.

James sensed weakness and stepped forward, taking her in his arms and kissing her with a hunger that she could not reciprocate. Everything was wrong, they no longer fit. She pulled away. She'd rather be alone than with the wrong man.

When she had found Rosa's letters she had been given Jay and the chance for a family. Since that day she had pushed thoughts of James and their wedding from her mind, filling her empty heart with adventures, people and experiences. Without realising she had been moving on. She was over him.

'I need to go back to my place.' She muttered.

'I thought you might have been staying here?' James motioned to the grand hotel behind him.

'Why would you think I would stay in this soulless, European monstrosity? There are plenty of other places on the island.' Willow asked, saddened. In all their time together he had failed to get to know her at all. The hotel was as far from her tastes as he was from home.

'It's the best on the island,' he pointed at the grandiose spectacle that was the *Four Suns Horizon Beach Paradiso*. 'After you inherited all that money I figured; why would you stay anywhere else?'

'Claire told you about the money? She told you I was here?' Willow was relieved of any guilt she had for denying him a reconciliation.

James raced for words, 'Well I knew the farm must have been worth a bit, but I had no idea the land would go for so much and then you came over here intent on giving a third of it away to a total stranger. Anyway, forget the money! Claire sent me the banks address, where you requested the transfer. I knew you had to be here somewhere. You've not been well, this is crazy, we are both worried that you are being rash. You might end up doing something that you'll regret later. Giving away that much money is insane. Spend the day with me. We are in paradise, let's enjoy it together. We can talk everything through.'

Willow could hear it in the way that he spoke to her, see it in the way that he looked at her. He didn't even like her. She had nothing left to say. She turned away.

James snorted, amused, 'Bloody hell, you've had a tattoo! It's very....' He searched, 'Big!' Willow's hand flew to her beloved etching as he grabbed her other wrist, desperate, 'Come home Willow, come with me, let me take care of you. Our relationship freaked me out before. It was the intensity of our love I think. You were the strong stable one. I didn't know what to do when you stopped being able to take care of yourself. You were always putting me down. You even started doubting my acting talent!'

The intensity of their love? What a moron! She laughed. 'I had faith in you, but you kept letting me down!'

James groaned, 'And you didn't let me forget it. You started asking me to pay for things, to sort the shopping and the bills when if you had thought for a moment, you would have realised how humiliating that was. I didn't have the money. Every day you made me feel like a loser. I opened a few cards in your name, but that money was for us, for the flat. I didn't tell you because I didn't want you to worry, I was going to pay you back as we had discussed a thousand times. It was like you forgot who I was and expected me to be *Mr Reliable nine-to-five*. Then you made out like I'd stolen the money!'

Willow scowled, 'I trusted you and you broke my heart! Be satisfied with the damage you have already done and let me go. Whose paying for this Asian jolly James?' it wasn't her. All the cards had been cancelled which left the possibility that he was working. Unlikely. 'It was Claire wasn't it?'

She knew the answer before it came.

James pouted, 'Well she wanted to come herself but we thought it was best if I came, with the kids and everything…'

He knew about the inheritance and had manipulated Claire into sending him on a posh holiday. 'So you did her a favour by taking her money and coming here to get more out of me? A long time ago I needed you to be a man, to step up and support me while I was struggling, but you failed. You are a failure not me.' She punctuated every word.

He groaned theatrically, 'How can you speak to me this way? You need to come home and get professional help. You can't keep spouting nonsense, running about in your underwear and getting crazy tattoos on your own. You're not well.'

He just wasn't getting it.

'You do not know what is best for me, I *was* unwell and now I am fine or I was until you turned up. I love to run in my PJs, my tattoo is fabulous. I am not on my own anymore, I have friends here.' With everything said that needed to be Willow turned to leave.

James was incredulous, 'So where are these imaginary friends of yours?'

She could stay and argue with him all day but what was the point? His grip on her wrist tightened.

'I'm not leaving without you.'

Willow tugged her arm away, his grip loosened and she fell onto the sand with a thud.

'Hey,' Ben shouted from down the beach, running over and offering his hand to help her up. 'Are you ok? Is this guy bothering you?' he shot James a warning look.

She brushed the sand from her bottom, 'I'm fine thanks Ben. This is my ex, James. We've had some things to talk through, but there is nothing left to say. He is leaving now.'

'Oh I see. You've got yourself a new guy. Well good luck with her mate, she's a nut case!' James spat the words at Ben.

Willow knew it was his ego that was broken and not his heart. She fumed, 'Ben is my friend. It may be impossible for you to believe but I would rather be alone than with you. In fact I am perfectly happy alone.' To her surprise and, evidently his, she meant it.

'You're not alone.' Ben murmured, leading her away.

'You'll be begging me back before the end of the year! By then I'll be living in LA and you will be too late. You need to think seriously about this. Don't be rash!' James called after her pathetically.

Ben whispered, as she rested her head on his shoulder, 'What a delusional idiot!'

She laughed, grateful for the confirmation, 'How did it only take you a minute to realise, while it took me nearly five years?'

'I don't know much but I know people.' He assured her.

They walked in silence until they approached a stretch of road with a few restaurants and morning crowds.

Willow turned to him, 'Thank you Ben, I don't feel like anyone has fought my corner in long time.'

Ben shrugged, 'Happy to help a lady. Fancy a drink or would you rather I walk you back to your place?'

'I'd love a drink, but I haven't had breakfast yet and I'm in my PJ's!' she realised she was having a very weird day.

Ben pulled off his t-shirt and handed it to her. 'It's thirty-five degrees, wear this as a dress and I'll go topless. I haven't been to bed yet so really it's a night cap. All sorted!'

She looked at him properly, noticing the dark circles around his eyes. 'Don't you want to get to bed?'

Ben quickly shot her down, 'And miss you telling me what exactly happened between the pair of you? No chance.'

There was something in his eager manner that told Willow he wanted to be alone as much as she did.

She accepted the T-shirt and followed him into a bar, where she selected a table with a view of the ocean and didn't breathe a sigh of relief until she put down her first empty beer bottle.

'God I really loved him once. Ben do you think I'm crazy?'

Ben scrutinised her, 'Love is a form of madness. It's not the actions of a sane man to leave a flat in Mayfair fully furnished and packed with designer clothes. Love has a lot to answer for!'

Chapter 16

Willow had grown up attending private schools, living on the farm, surrounded by acres of beautiful land. She turned her back on more prestigious careers to become a teacher. Ben had been raised in a council estate in Croydon, beating all the odds to become a successful stockbroker.

Despite their differences, they had both ended up in the same place, without direction.

Ben was vague on the details of his past, but a great listener. Whether it had been the beer or finding a kindred spirit, they had talked until the day turned to night, then they had danced and drank until the early hours.

She was unburdened, free of James and hungover.

The sea was a vibrant turquoise to match the morning sky. Not one cloud dimpled the heavens perfection nor person the sand. Aside from a few dive boats on the horizon Willow was alone, by choice and she wouldn't have wanted it any other way.

Her mind was whirling, she had so much to go over with Eric, she couldn't sleep another minute. She removed her PJ's, dressed in clothes actually suitable for running and set off.

Her legs ached from the previous morning's exertion, but she pushed on lengthening her stride, breathing in the fresh ocean air. She ran past the enormous palm trees and rows of huts, feeling free. She swept along the sand until a mile down the Beach she found Eric's shop, *Longecrang Tours*.

She took it in and had to admit that, much as she had enjoyed her work, looking out to a lecture hall full of eager faces, the view of a Thai beach trumped any workplace she had been in.

There was a commotion from inside and the shutter sprang up.

Eric was dressed in another smart linin get-up, his hair and white beard immaculate. 'Good morning. You're bright and early. Have you been waiting long?' He smiled cheerfully.

'Just arrived.' Willow assured, 'I'm dying to know your findings.'

'Come on in, let's get started.' He ushered her into the modest open-fronted hut.

A large sofa was on one side next to a desk buried in files, four rows of computers were dotted around the space on tables and photos of the numerous trips on offer adorned the walls.

'I'll just pop out to get us breakfast. We've got lots to talk about. An army marches on its stomach!' He was making his way out before she could offer help.

'Make yourself comfortable' He waved over his shoulder, 'Back in five.'

Willow inspected the photos on the wall. There was one of Eric hanging off the side of a limestone mountain by a rope, others of him kayaking, tubing, cycling, fishing, camping and riding elephants. She was as impressed as she was jealous. He had been to every corner of Thailand and *lived* each moment to the fullest.

Eric reappeared wielding two large cups and a bunch of fruit Willow had never seen before.

'Breakfast is served.' He handed her a cup.

'Wonderful!' she gushed between swigs of mango smoothie. 'Thank you. What are they?' She peered at the small deep purple alien fruits.

'I don't normally get to have breakfast with a beautiful lady, so I thought I would spoil you; these are mangosteens, they are like lychees in consistency, but orange-like in taste.'

He pulled one from its stem and ripped the hard skin away, revealing a fleshy white fruit inside. 'I like them the way that I like people. You expect one thing and get quite something else. I first bought them on a whim thinking that they were a type of small aubergine. That made for a very interesting ratatouille!' He shuddered, passing her one.

Willow cautiously put it in her mouth and chewed. 'Wow, it's delicious.'

He nodded knowingly, tucking in to his own.

She pointed to a photo of him on a zip wire, dangling hundreds of feet above a jungle. 'They're like you. I had no idea that you were such an adrenaline junky! You've seen and done so much.'

He smirked, looking boyish, 'Still got a lot left to do!'

'I spent most of last year trapped in my sister's house and before that living a life that I wasn't in control of.' Willow didn't want to talk about her time in hospital, but she was ready to admit one thing, 'I haven't done enough.'

He put a paternal hand on her shoulder. 'We are not the sum of what we do. We are the sum of what we do for others. You've got plenty of time, while I, alas, have far less. You are a young woman, fill your life with love, adrenaline-fuelled stupidity, laughter and adventure and you'll never be sorry. It is all out there waiting to be taken; whenever you are ready to snatch it!'

He made her jump as he threw his arm in the air with a grabbing motion.

'Forgive me I am a sentimental man and perhaps this is too early for my ponderings?'

Willow shook her head, warming to him immensely, 'Absolutely not! You have called me young and beautiful before 9 A.M, I may come back every day!'

She considered what she had been missing out on. 'I would like to go on some of your excursions one day.'

'We need to locate your cousin fast if you are going to find time to jump off a cliff or two before heading home.'

He beckoned her to a desk. 'Enough about my photos, let's talk about yours.' He pushed the files to one side and lay Rosa's photos and letters out.

Willow caught her breath, so full of hope and nerves she couldn't speak.

'Firstly; I need to tell you that I can't give you a phone number or direct contact for Jay, but I can give you some options for how to proceed.'

Eric removed a huge long-haired cat from Willow's chair, 'Be off now Milo.' Milo glared with distain, before flouncing away. 'Don't mind him, he thinks he owns the shop and me, not the other way around.'

Eric examined Rosa's correspondence, 'What a beautiful woman.' He held up a photo of Rosa, at her hip was Jay, 'With a good heart. You can see it in her eyes.' He pointed out, then picked up a letter, 'She had good bit of grit too!'

Willow surged with pride, 'It's hard to imagine what it must have been like for her to have arrived in Thailand with nothing. She sculpted a life that was not just OK, but full and rich with love, family and a career.'

'Maybe you'll find your happiness here. It's happened before,' Eric waved the letter at her. 'Who's this Peter? Was he your father?'

Willow was caught by surprise, hearing his name again. 'Yes, but how is he relevant to my search? Did he know something. The letters hardly mention him.'

Eric raised his eyebrows, 'You really have no idea why your mother and your aunt fell out?'

Willow took the letter from him, absent minded, 'I have no clue. It must have been huge; my mother was an incredibly calm and gentle lady. She never yelled at us or fought with my father. She was content, serene even. She would never have left

Jay all this money if she hadn't cared and wanted to put things right. I can't imagine why she didn't do it sooner?'

Willow had asked herself *why?* a thousand times and found no answers, but she knew from her own experience how easy it was to find your sister was a stranger.

Eric put his hand on hers, 'Humans are survivalists by nature. Something must have happened that challenged her stability. Read this letter again. The part about your father.'

'OK' she agreed, uncomfortable with the turn their conversation had taken. What exactly could be getting at? She'd read the letters over and over and found nothing.

Eric took her empty cup, handing her a napkin and holding a chair out for her. A gentleman.

'Do your kids come to visit much?' It was easy to picture him as the head of a large family. Fun, exciting, caring.

Eric closed his eyes for such a long time she began to worry.

'No.' he stated, organising her letters into piles, with no apparent system, growing flustered.

'I made mistakes, drank too much, cheated, failed in my business and ran away. I left my kind wife to raise our beautiful babies alone. I just couldn't stay. It hurt too much to see what I had lost. I always planned to go back, but as the days turned to weeks, months to years, I imagined their resentment growing. I was a coward. I would like to say sorry to them, but I would be apologising for a man I no longer am. I understand how Rosa must have suffered, begging for forgiveness that was never granted. In the end I hope she forgave herself, that's all that any of us can do when we truly leave a mess in our wake.'

Willow didn't like to imagine Eric as the man he had been, she could see how much he had changed. Perhaps Rosa hadn't been all the wonderful things she had been imagining either? 'I think your children would be very proud of you if they met you now. It's not too late.'

Eric turned his face to the heavens and kissed a crucifix, that hung around his neck. 'As they grew older I hoped that they would travel. I prayed they would come to find me, but they were not the types. When I started my company it was just a hut with a few computers. I kept up with their lives on social media. By all accounts, they had a fabulous stepfather and for that I will always be gratefully. I have watched my grand-children's first birthdays, steps and days at school. They have been a part of my life even though I am no-longer a part of theirs.'

Willow took his hand, 'They could be waiting for you to make the first move?'

Eric waved his free hand. 'I do not want to push into their lives and upset their balance. I send them Christmas and Birthday cards, they know I think of them. I show them I love them by staying away. God will guide us together again when the time is right.'

Willow patted his hand, 'I'm envious that you have God for reassurance.'

'You believe he has taken too much from you? Take a breath of this air, look around this beautiful island.' Eric pointed to a blooming tropical flower, on the veranda, 'Look at that. It's exquisite! God gives a great deal.' He held up his bowl of mangosteens, 'Eating this; aren't you thankful to a God? It is delicious!'

She pondered, finishing her fruit. 'I'll be even more thankful if you can tell me where that school is from Rosa's photos. Aaron told me that you do a lot with schools for under privileged children and you may be familiar with it?'

Eric stared at the photos, 'I do what I can. A free day trip here, an activity weekend there when I can spare them. This sign, it means *Place for Boys, at the feet of God. Live, Work, Prosper.*' Eric translated the Dumbro, 'I believe that you know the rough area and you've checked for schools but found nothing? I took the liberty of searching for the school by name, as well as searching for the moto, but I found nothing. It's unlikely that the school is still in operation. The building could be a hotel or perhaps it's fallen to decay? Thai people have not been good at keeping paperwork over the years.'

He went back to looking at the desk, selecting a letter from the pile.

Willow had read them all, he wouldn't find anything useful there. 'I guess that's it then? She stood to leave, her heart heavy.

Eric thrust the page towards her, 'Hang on! There's more. Yinga.'

Willow perked up, 'Who's Yinga?'

'Not who, where? It's the sanctuary Rosa speaks of, it's not in the photos but that's not surprising, many of these places do not allow cameras. She was heavily involved with establishing this health and wellness centre. It's a hugely respected and successful sanctuary of sorts. I've tracked it down to Koh Pang Nang. I actually know a few agents who specialize in those kind of holiday bookings. Once they heard Bic's name it was straight forward.' Eric sat back proud of his work.

Willow didn't understand, 'But I googled his name, I searched for everyone that she spoke of, I found nothing.'

He shook his head, 'You won't find Yinga in guide books, they don't need to advertise, fully booked for months in advance and he's not exactly media savvy from the sound of things. You have to know the right people to ask.' He said, his eyes sparkling. 'I have the address for you.'

Willow grinned, 'Are you kidding?' That's great!' She picked up a photo of Bic with Rosa in Ayutthaya, 'This photo must be twenty-five years old at least.' Bic was already a very old man. 'Is he still alive?'

Eric shrugged, 'I doubt it. No-one I've spoken to has seen or heard from him directly, but let's concentrate on the positives. Yinga is still in operation. Bic may no longer be there, but there will be a spiritual leader. They may have known Rosa or might even be in touch with Jay? If they are a Swami they could put you in touch with Wat Bang Riang temple and those monks would be sure to know more about what happened to the school. There are lots of options. I've already emailed Yinga. They don't have phones or computers onsite, but they'll check their emails once a week apparently. I can't book you in, but I have let them know to expect a visit from you. You'll have to wait until after the full moon party to travel to Koh Pang Nang, the accommodation is all booked. It'll be chaos if you arrive without anywhere to stay. Wait here for three to four days and I'll make all the arrangements for you. Chances are that my email will have reached Yinga by then and we can make more concrete arrangements.'

'I don't know about thanking God but thank you Eric!' Willow gasped. She loved Rosa's letters about the sanctuary, the idea of going there filled her with glee, but it all sounded a bit cloak-and-dagger, 'Why does everything need to be so clandestine? Could there be something about the school people wanted to keep a secret? Why's nothing straightforward?'

'It's Thailand.' Came Eric's definitive response.

Willow left Eric to his work. She had a plan for her next step but felt more confused than ever. What had he seen in the letters, about her father, that she had not? She sat on the beach and unfolded the crumpled paper.

Dear Caroline,

The school I'm working at is part of an orphanage, but it's not like an institution, it's more like a huge home. The building itself is falling apart, but once it must have been something very beautiful, we are renovating where-ever and whenever we can.

147

Luckily the government don't want the orphanages to be close to the tourists, so we are in a bit of a no mans' land, far away from town in a stunning spot deep in the forest. It feels like our fabulous secret. I am earning a wage and I have a permanent roof over my head, now I've no reason to return to England, I feel richer than ever.

I have fast become, not only an English teacher and part time builder, but a soccer coach, playground monitor and mathematician to boot!

I had worked twenty-seven straight days when I had my first day off. I went for a walk and collapsed into a blissful sleep on the bank of a mangrove. The sun was high and there was no one to be seen in any direction. I used to be afraid of solitude, but now it's such a rarity I enjoy it.

I woke with a start when a boy from school curled up next to me. Jay is a tiny skinny thing with black hair that sticks out in every direction; it makes him look wild but he is a wise, meek soul. He is around six or seven, he doesn't know exactly and we have no way of telling. He was still in his pyjamas and had black rings around his eyes, but when I put my arm around him, he immediately fell asleep. I didn't have the heart to wake him, to find out what was going on so we stayed like that until the sun began to drop and he jumped awake. We walked back home together, he wouldn't talk to me but seemed happy enough when I returned him to his dorm with his friends.

His behaviour had rattled me. I called in on Wan straight away and he told me Jay's background. Wan had found him begging on the streets, during the monsoon, soaked to the skin and riddled with lice, a run- away from a child sex trafficking ring. Thankfully a local lady had alerted Wan to his situation and we'd been able to take him in. The places are limited, heartbreakingly not every boy can be offered a home.

Jay spent the first few weeks of his stay getting in and out of bed, walking the hallways, sleeping in cupboards or *under tables, anywhere he could safely hide. He had never slept properly. Wan had tried reading to him, even sleeping by the door of the dorm to reassure him, but Jay was terrified of all men and who could blame him?*

I'd been aware of him before, he had been feeling me out since I arrived, hovering around me but never brave enough to talk. I've found it's best to let the boys come to me when they are ready and not to force my way in to their lives. That day was the day he decided that I was to be trusted.

When you held your babies for the first time, I'm sure you felt as if their eyes searched, their fingers reached, just for you? Without you they were utterly defenceless and vulnerable in a world that's full with danger. Did you wonder if you could just love them enough and hold them tight enough you could keep them safe, make them happy on their life's journey? That's how I felt when Jay looked up at me, that day, he was mine and I was his.

Jay had been abandoned in the worst place on earth, his chances in life had evaporated. I don't believe any God would have had a part in putting him in that place, but something was at work when life brought us together. He needed me to take care of him as much as I need to do it.

Sadly or fortunately for me, the authorities do not care much what happens to these children. Wan and I decided to marry to make it all run more smoothly. We have only known each other a couple of months, but we are grown and we know our hearts. We had no problems being granted custody of Jay. When we asked him if he would like us to be his parents he cried with happiness. In this tropical oasis we have become a family.

Finally I understand why you've never spoken to me about what happened. I've always imagined that if you did I could make you understand, but as a mother now, I can see that you are protecting your family. Despite everything you must believe that I never meant any harm to Peter, Sarah or you.

You don't want to hear the details and I respect that, but you need to know that I was largely alone when we were teenagers, you were in and out of hospital with your breathing issues, Dad was always with you and mother was long passed. I needed a companion, someone to witness my life was actually happening, I was disappearing before that summer. He was everything but I didn't need a man, I needed you, I needed a family, I was just too blind to see it.

Love
Rosa
Xxx

Willow read and reread the last paragraph, it wasn't clear, but the truth was rising to the surface.

Chapter 17

It was the morning that Willow was to have been a bride. She should have been celebrating the promise of a wonderful future with her family.

She observed in the mirror that her face was clean and growing tanned, her hair the usual unruly mess.

Months before, flicking through the glossy pages of the bridal magazines she had known immediately which hairstyle was for her, looking at it, her mother had gushed, *'You will make the most beautiful bride.'* While pushing Willows hair up, to resemble the elegant shape in the image.

Her mother would never see her wedding day. Maybe she would never have a wedding?

Leaving the hut, she pulled on her trainers. The beach was deserted; the only sound the jungle dawn chorus. When a monkey chuckled from within the jungle canopy behind, she set off in its direction.

She Kept to a path which lead up the hill until she was unable to take another stride. She stood surrounded by the splendour of the forest in every direction, took one deep long breath and screamed.

She screamed for the loss of her certain life. She screamed because she had nothing left to say about any of it. The birds granted her the dignity of a moments silence before going back to their chirrups and calls.

Willow walked back to the beach with a lighter soul, eager to freshen up with a swim. It was 9 A.M. by the time she towelled herself dry and went to Aarons hut. She'd hardly seen him over the past two days and was looking forward to finding out what he had planned for her.

He swung open the door, in his shorts, the sun catching on his bare torso. He squinted and smiled, 'Morning. How does a gentle trek, kayaking, snorkelling and a picnic looking out to sea sound?'

'Like exactly what I need,' she admitted.

She filled Aaron in on the plans that she had made with Eric as they walked high into the hills, the looming canopy masking them from the worst of the sun's rays.

She hadn't realised they were nearing the top until Aaron stopped and she bumped into him with a jolt. Her hands shot to his back, where they lingered, palms pressed against naked flesh.

She peered over his shoulders and her eyes widened at the panoramic view. 'Oh my God,' was all she could say as she took in the miles of azure ocean, dappled with patches of electric coloured corals and scattered dive boats.

'I knew you would like it. This is my favourite place on the whole of the island.' Aaron turned around, facing her.

She closed her eyes, longing for him to take her in his arms and forget all the reasons they shouldn't be together. She opened her eyes urging him to make it happen.

'Every time I'm here it feels as if I'm looking at it for the first time,' he said looking straight at her.

She remained still, hardly daring to breath.

He softly moved her aside with his strong hands, 'Sorry you're stood on my bag,' he motioned down to the ground.

She jumped, realising she was trampling his things, grateful that her blushes could be written off as exertion from the walk.

He wrapped his arm around her shoulders, pulled his phone from his pocket and thrust it in front of them. 'Come on, smile! We need a photo. Something to remember all of this by when you are back in London. Moments like this need to be captured.'

She smiled for the snap but felt increasingly unhappy. All around was tropical rainforest, above her a sun filled sky, ribboned with flitting birds. She didn't want to imagine leaving it for a London sky filled with grumpy pigeons and rain clouds.

Aaron stepped away, his phone vibrating, 'I've got to take this call. Excuse me.'

Mesmerised by the ocean she didn't turn to see where he was going. She could have been stood in church saying vows, instead standing there, she had never felt closer to a God.

She grabbed her engagement ring, pulling it hard, the fragile chain snapping. She ran her fingers over the dainty gold band for one last time and flung it over the cliff edge, sending it spiralling into the depths.

Aaron reappeared, thankfully oblivious to the poignancy of the moment. 'I can't wait to get into that water! You ready to move on?'

I am, she thought. 'What are we waiting for?'

She edged past him, running down the narrow jungle pathway towards the awaiting sea.

They laughed as they skipped around roots and rocks. Finally collapsing on the white sand of the bay to catch their breath.

Willow composed herself and propped herself up, shaking the sand from her hair while Aaron jumped to his feet.

'Let's grab a boat. I must show you the underwater gardens, oh and the turtles and the coral! You've got to see it all!' he glanced around the shore and called out, 'Joe!'

A man with a boat turned and waved.

Before Willow could worry about the waiting depths Aaron had pulled her to her feet and dragged her over to Joe's longtail boat.

He hopped in self-assured.

Clearly Aaron had travelled in these boats hundreds of times. She clambered in awkwardly behind, falling onto his lap when a small wave sent her flying.

'Sorry I haven't found my sea legs.' she apologised, mortified as she realised that her hand was on his groin. She leapt off him and settled herself in the seat by his side feeling like a school girl on a first date; why couldn't she behave like a lady?

She hid her red cheeks, looking around the Longtail. It was long like a canoe and illogically balanced. When Joe took up his position, at the back, to steer the rudder, the nose flicked up into the air sending her backward with a jolt.

Aaron's firm hand caught her, keeping her in her seat.

'If you want to hold on again warn me.' He jibed, cupping his crotch, evidently enjoying her ill-ease.

Willow scowled but was unable to keep the smile from her lips.

The engine hummed to life, hypnotically burring as they cut through the glassy water, the sea growing darker in patches as they moved away from the shore.

It was quicker then she had expected. Their gentle bounce upon the water's surface relaxing. She raised her hands to the sky, not caring if she looked silly, her worries blowing away.

They slowed when one large hill and two smaller mounds connected by sand bars came into view. Lush green forest appeared to sprout up from the white sands that peaked from the surrounding waters.

'They are part of a national park, uninhabited, at least mostly.' Aaron explained as the boat's engine cut out; Joe continuing to guide them in on momentum.

'There are a couple of restaurants to cater for the inevitable sightseers. How can any of us resist our shot at spending a day in Eden, but we'll all be damned if we want to do it without a cold beer and a decent toilet!' He goofed in a terrible colloquial British accent.

How did he manage to be sexy, playing the fool, while she tried to be sexy and ended up foolish?

She laughed with him and tore her eyes from his chest, noticing a smattering of longtails were anchored along the shore and the faint moving shapes of a few people moving on the beaches. Amongst the Palms and the beach ferns were the tell-tale outlines of makeshift roofing panels.

Joe navigated them around a few small granite islands which dotted the sea, until they approached a looming rock and Aaron pointed out a small gap in its face.

'In there. They're called *Nang Yuan* caves.' He announced, pulling on his fins.

Where the hell was he going?

'Aren't we taking the boat to the shore? I thought we would be snorkelling in the shallows?' Willow asked, fearing the answer.

'The boat's far too big to get through the caves and they're amazing, you can't miss them. We'll swim through and make our own way to the beach. It's less than 300 hundred metres. Joe will meet us there later.' Aaron said, pulling on his mask, oblivious to her discomfort.

So, she was expected to swim through a tiny black hole in the middle of the deep ocean putting herself in a dark cavernous toom, full of water, where God only knew what animals could be lurking? Her stomach flipped.

Noticing that she wasn't moving, Aaron stopped preparing himself, 'We can snorkel in one of the bays if you're not up for this? It's a once in a life time experience though.'

She couldn't turn him down.

She pulled on her fins and positioned her hugely unattractive goggles with shaking hands, 'I am absolutely up for this!' she lied, giving him a thumbs up and immediately regretting the boyish gesture.

Really, what the hell was she doing?

Aaron appeared happy to have won, quickly getting into position for the off. 'Let's go!' He waved from the edge of the boat as he tipped backward, plopping in to the ocean.

Willow wobbled after him and half leapt, half flopped from the boat, hitting the surface sideways, water knocking the snorkel from her mouth.

She inhaled the salty water, spluttering, 'Did I mention that I'm not much of a swimmer?' she tried to wipe the liquid that was streaming from her nose away, without drowning, unsure if she was terrified or having a good time. Maybe both?

Aaron took her hand gallantly ignoring her mishap. 'Come on, the fins will make it easy. Trust me, you'll be perfectly safe.'

At the entrance to the caves the temperature dropped and the impending darkness crept towards them. Joe's engine roared to life and he began to move, leaving them behind.

Willow swallowed hard.

'Trust me this will be something you will tell your grandkids about.' Aaron tugged gently on her hand.

If she lived long enough to have them?

Willow took a jagged breath, thinking of Eric and all the things he had done. She pushed forward, lifting her head out of the water, reaching up and feeling the walls around her, the water beneath.

The darkness was absolute, the smell stagnant. The light from the entrance had disappeared and there was no space to turn.

Her heart was thumping, breathing strained, chest tight. She clung to Aarons hand, focusing on the swoosh of her fins through the water and it wasn't long before the inky blackness softened with light.

Moments later she pulled the snorkel from her face.

Where there had been only darkness stood glittering splendour. The vast walls and ceiling glistened with sun sparkled ocean residue. The sun's rays poured in through breaks in the granite, reflecting up from the waters crystalline surface.

'This is magical.' She observed.

Aaron pulled off his mask & snorkel. 'It was worth the journey wasn't it?' His face was illuminated with the magical light.

Everything that had led her to that spot had been worth it.

They languidly trod water in their small world. They were encased by walls glinting like diamonds.

She shifted under the intensity of his gaze.

He pulled her closer and kissed her, his bare skin pressing against hers as he held her up in the water.

There was no-one else in the world but them.

Aaron pulled away first, brushing her wet hair from her face, smiling, 'We need to go somewhere that I can put my feet on the ground,' he kissed her neck then spluttered as his mouth dipped under the water.

They had become so entwined, her arms around his neck, leg wrapped around his waist, that he was struggling to keep them afloat. She had to move away from him for fear that she would drown him with her hunger.

'How quick can you swim?' she laughed, suddenly keen to get out of the place she had, moments before, been so happy to be in.

'You'd be astonished how fast I can move when I have my eyes on the prize.' He teased, caressing her bottom lightly before his fingers came to linger on the lip of her bikini. He groaned frustrated, pulling his hand away, 'We have to get to the beach!'

He didn't have to tell her twice; she was already yanking her snorkel mask back on.

Once they were ready he led her through to the cave's exit. Her palm firmly in his as they swam, their heads bowed into the waters.

Fish were everywhere; electric and skittering around in the deep whilst others came closer, prying. She was so taken-in by the abundance of beauty that she forgot about the dangers until Aaron came to a sudden halt.

She stopped dead, fear flaring, there was a disturbance in the water far beneath, coming closer.

A dark shadow swept through the fish causing a chaotic flurry of activity. Her immediate thoughts were of sharks and rays.

She pointlessly pulled her legs close to herself, frightened and floundering on the surface. Then a turtle, well over a metre in length, came out of the depths. Despite its bulk it moved with incredible grace. Willow had to resist the urge to touch it as it circled their legs and slipped away.

She wondered what it was doing there, then remembered that she was an intruder in its world and not the other way around. What was *she* doing there? What was she doing in Thailand at all? If she wasn't actively searching for Jay was she holding out for Aaron? Hadn't she learnt her lesson?

Willow let go of Aaron's hand when they swam on.

She tried to concentrate on the lush coral forests waving rhythmically, luminous streamers in the current below, but every kick brought the shore and possibilities with Aaron closer. Her worries would not cease.

Needing a moment to think she paused, her feet coming to rest upon the sea bed and she was hit with a searing stinging. 'Shit!' she exclaimed, instinctively pulling her foot up, struggling to tread water as she was dealt another pulse of excruciating pain. Her fins sent her off balance and plummeting face first in to the sea.

Aaron positioned himself behind her, leaning her body against his, 'Lie back. I'm going to get you to the beach.' he reassured her as he began to swim.

Willow concentrated on breathing slowly, 'What happened to me?'

Aaron was breathing heavily, but moved quickly, 'I don't know, maybe a jelly fish? I'll look just as soon as I can.'

When finally he lifted her from the water and lurched toward dry land, she peered at her foot, alarmed to see that her diving fin had been pierced at least ten times, her heel riddled with thick black spines.

Aaron walked on, holding her protectively close, his face contorted as he saw the damage, 'You've stood on a sea urchin. I should have warned you to keep your feet up. I wasn't thinking.' He berated himself as he lay her on the sand.

Willow hated seeing the guilt on his face. 'How were you to know some idiot novice would stamp all over the precious coral?'

Aaron took her foot in his hands and frowned, 'You can't leave the spines in. I've got to remove them.'

She closed her eyes and fought the urge to writhe with the throbbing, 'I don't care what you do just make the pain stop!'

He firmly gripped the first spine and yanked it out with one quick swipe.

The relief was instantaneous. A few minutes later and her tender inflamed foot was free from the evil spines. She removed her fins and slumped back onto the sand with a moan.

'I'm not used to taking beginners out. I just wasn't thinking,' Aaron raked his fingers through his hair and jumped up, 'Wait right here. I'll be back in one second.'

She half-laughed, looking at her swelling foot, 'Where am I going to go?'

'Sure, right.' He shrugged by means of apology, ran toward a bar a few hundred yards away and returned with a glass of ice water, napkin and a bottle of vinegar.

Joe joined them with their day bags, exchanging words with Aaron in Thai and laughing at something Willow could not understand.

Was it really a time for jokes?

'He says you're an idiot,' Aaron explained with a nervous laugh.

Willow couldn't help but find the Thai honesty amusing, 'He might be right.'

Aaron's shoulders dropped, clearly relieved to hear her joking, 'He's seen this many times; if it makes you feel any better?'

It didn't, but when Aaron cradled her foot and gently dabbed it with the cloth, sodden with the ice and vinegar, the relief was immense.

Having seen that she was ok, Joe was happy to re-join the other skippers further down the beach with their boats.

Willow kept breathing deeply until the pain lessened. She basked in the sun, recovering from the adrenaline high, her skin growing tight with salt as the sun baked the sea water away.

Lying by Aaron's side made it nearly impossible to keep a clear head. How was she supposed to think sensibly when every part of her longed for him to lean over and kiss her, to take her right there on the beach? She tensed feeling him sit up.

She opened her eyes behind her sunglasses and watched as, unaware of her knowledge, he looked over her body.

'You are going to fry in this sun. You need some lotion. You don't want a repeat of Ayutthaya!' He teased putting a gentle hand on her shoulder as she moved to sit up, 'Stay there sleeping beauty. It's the least I can do. I just wanted to warn you before woke up to find some creepy American rubbing you down in oil.'

A cool dollop of lotion splodged onto her flat stomach. She squealed but shut her eyes. He was too close for her to risk looking. She would stand no chance of resisting.

His hands moved quickly at first, getting the job done, then his motions became slower, more lingering. His fingers worked across her ribs and beneath the rim of her bikini top, her nipples froze as he got dangerously close. She caught her breath with the anticipation of his touch as his palms glided across her shoulders. His fingers caressing her throat and up to her face. Every inch of her tingled. His breath on her lips. So close. Then Joe Yelled.

'Aaron! Aaron!' He shouted running doing the beach.

Willow's eyes sprang open. Was there never any peace from Aaron's drivers?

Aaron turned toward Joe, stood behind him. 'Yes Joe; What can I do for you?'

They had a brief exchange before Aaron turned back to Willow.

'He's going to lend us his motor bike when we get back to the main land. He thought you might struggle with a long walk. We have to leave now so he can get a lift with his friend at the other end.'

He got up, whisking her into his arms, carrying her like a bride toward the boat. 'Sorry our day has been such a disaster.'

Willow rested her head on his shoulder, her defences depleted. 'It's not been all bad.'

They travelled back across the sea, silently wrapped in each-other's arms, Joe's longtail skimming over the waves.

When they were back on Koh Tao Joe showed them to his motorbike and went on his way with his friend.

Aaron jumped on, smiling from his seat 'Are you coming?'

For a moment she saw clearly that she was playing with fire, then she got on and pressed herself against his warm body, parted her legs behind him and ignored all caution.

'Hold on tight,' he shouted over the roar from the engine.

She clung on around his naked waist, fingers resting on his taught stomach, her cheek turned to rest against the Phoenix tattoo on his back and she breathed in his sweet scent.

They were on the other side of the island quicker than she would have liked. She swung her legs over the bike, jumping off exhilarated, licking her salt laced lips, a reminder of their day in the ocean.

Aaron's eyes shone as he edged towards a mini mart, 'I definitely owe you a beer, after what you've been through today. Wait here.'

Willow did as instructed. She plonked herself on to the sand, sorry he wasn't whisking her away but pleased that the day was not over.

The sun was dropping, its rays splintering across the water.

Aaron returned and they sat in silence sipping their drinks, her head on his shoulder as if it were the most normal thing in the world, not moving until the sun had become a memory and the moon had taken its place.

She turned to Aaron, 'How do you ever leave? I have never seen anything so effortlessly beautiful.' She'd been asking herself the same question for the past hour.

He leant back on his elbows, looking around, 'I never take it for granted but my home is elsewhere. Be careful you don't get lost here. There's so much more to see and places to go.'

She'd thought the same thing. She could be doing more to find Jay. She should be out there looking for him at that moment rather than waiting for Eric to do the work or the full moon party to pass. If she was honest, there was something about Aaron that made her find excuses to stay.

She didn't want to talk about it, the thought was making her uncomfortable.

'What's your house like? Is it a hut on the beach or a penthouse in Bangkok? Where does a man like you lay roots?'

Aaron drank his beer, examined the sand with his toes and eyes, shifted in his seat, appeared to ponder the fingers of his left hand. Finally he cleared his throat, 'It's a place close to my son, Phoenix. *The Lost Sole's Club*, it's a house and some huts for tourists, a bar, that type of thing.' His gaze was firmly on the sea.

'Soul's? That sounds a bit bleak.' Willow mused.

He shrugged 'Not really. It's named after shoe sole's, not spirits, well not entirely. I don't want to talk about it. It's just the place I live. I can't be too far from my boy.' He coughed.

In the half-light Willow make out tears gathering in his eyes. 'You must really miss him when you are working away?'

A parent's pain in missing a child was not something she could fully comprehend. Perhaps that was why Aaron didn't talk about him? Phoenix was in, or was referenced in every one of Aaron's guides but he avoided questions about him like the plague. She knew the gentle colour of Phoenix's skin, the curls of his hair, the edge to his smile and the silvery scar that broke his left brow from when he had fallen off his bike in Ayutthaya. Aaron had described him in loving detail while never sharing a word about him in reality.

She was eager to learn more. 'Who looks after him when you are away?' she prayed he didn't have wife number two stashed away

Aaron didn't look at her. 'God and his mother, in heaven, I hope.' He wrung his hands, tears racing to his eyes and dropping onto the sand. 'He drowned in the sea along with her. From my house I can see where their boat went down. It brings me a peace to be there.'

A sadness reached her core. The child who had been so full of life in her mind was a ghost.

Aaron had possessed the dream that she had dreamt of, a marriage, a child, a family and he had lost it.

'I'm so sorry, when you said Phoenix was *gone,* I thought you meant to live with relatives after his mother's death. I had no idea.'

She knew all too well why he had kept it a secret. The questions that follow the truth are too painful to answer. She took his hand, letting him know that she was there when he wanted to say more but didn't probe.

A small group of tourists in high spirits bustled by, disturbing the moment.

Aaron wiped his face dry. 'I was away working. I don't know why I say that? That's a lie. I used work as an excuse to go and get wasted in Bangkok. I was with some old friends who were in town for a Stag. Phoenix contracted Denghi fever, he was severely dehydrated, hallucinating and losing consciousness. Pat, my wife, was desperate. She took him to a boat in the middle of the night. I imagine she was in such a panic that she didn't realise the driver was drunk. He crashed into a dive boat that was anchored far out. There was a fire, they never stood a chance.'

Willow jumped, caught off guard when he quickly bounced to his feet.

'There's nothing you or I can do to change the past. I try not to let it ruin too many days; let's not let it ruin this one.' He brushed the sand from his shorts and held his hand out to her.

There was so much more to say. She could see him brimming over with the words, struggling to keep them in. She contemplated coaxing him to share his torment, but when she looked in his eyes she could see that what he needed most was for her to take his hand and pretend that life was not cruel.

Chapter 18

The sand-pressed paths evolved to concrete, the beach huts to shops illuminated with neon signs. Advertising boards and posters for boat trips, rock climbing and promises of outings to paradise were everywhere; as if they hadn't already arrived.

People offered greetings; Thai and English for Aaron, smiles for her. Willow's hand remained in his, her fingers warming under his touch, burning with the fire of possibility.

She traced the line of his neck and shoulders with her eyes, longing to tap him on the back, turn him round and kiss him right there. She wanted to take away his pain, to offer him the chance of a future.

Her life certainly did not need any complications, but, and there was a *but* which kept her from dismissing her desire. He trusted her, enough to share his deepest secrets and the way he had looked at her in the caves gave her hope that it was far more than friendship between them.

Despite everything, they could be exactly what they had never realised they needed.

To Willow's relief they left the town behind and found themselves by a series of beach front venues. She had been limping slightly and longed to take the weight off her feet.

'My friend Matseuse owns this place.' Aaron told her as they walked into a lively open-air restaurant, looking for his friend.

By Thai standards it was a sprawling set up, tables packed with a nearly a hundred people. Clearly he was searching for fun as a distraction.

Willow's stomach growled loudly. They hadn't eaten since a few snacks on their walk that morning.

Aaron grinned, 'I'm glad you're hungry, I'm starving. They have a great chef. I am going to introduce you to the finest pad thai and grilled fish in the whole of Asia and you haven't lived until you've tried fried quail eggs. You know I've never seen a quail in Thailand, but I've sure eaten a lot of their eggs.'

He was buoyant in a way that made it hard for Willow to follow. He had been keeping their conversation so packed she couldn't ask any questions. He was running scared when there was no need.

She tried to join in with his excitement and clapped her hands, 'Perfect! Where do we order?'

She looked for a waiter among the delicate, carved lanterns lighting each low table and the candles dotting the sand where walls should have stood. A couple of men sat on the beach, playing bongos against the backdrop of the ocean while numerous staff buzzed about with trays of beverages and high piled plates.

'Let's wait for my friend he'll be here somewhere.' Aaron looked around unaware of a man, so muscular he resembled a cartoon, running up behind him. Clumsily he knocked into customers, exchanging apologises and smiles as he continued his path of destruction.

'My ears are burning!' He boomed with a Swedish accent, sweeping Aaron into a bear hug and lifting him off his feet. 'You've been back on this island for days and this is the first time you come to see me! Too busy for your old friend hey? Is it your beautiful friend who is to blame?' he enquired more softly turning his attention to Willow, 'Welcome to Sunrise bar! I am Matseuse and this is my place.' He waved his hand with a surprisingly flamboyant flourish.

Aaron rolled his eyes, 'Hold on big guy. This is my friend Willow. Work has kept me busy nothing else.'

'Well hello Willow,' He enveloped her, squashing her face against that of Kylie Minogue's which was emblazoned across his T-shirt, squeezing the air from her.

'Nice to meet you too.' She smiled once he had put her back on the ground, smarting from Aarons dismissal, *My friend.*

He addressed Aaron congenially, 'Did you know that Marc got back today?'

Aaron's eye-brows knitted, his eyes twitched around as if looking for them, 'Uhh, no, I didn't know that was happening. I'm sure we'll catch up at some point though, there's no rush.'

Aaron flipped the conversation in a different direction, 'What the hell has a man got to do to get a drink in this place?' His pitch a little too loud, tense, cutting the conversation dead.

Matseuse rolled his eyes melodramatically but took the hint and moved things along pointing them to a tiny table with a view of the ocean. 'I'll bring you some drinks; you want the usual food?' He was already heading toward the bar, knocking in to yet more patrons.

Aaron yelled to his retreating friend, 'Of course!' then spoke to her. 'You're in for a treat; did I mention that the food is Great? What's been your favourite dish so far in Thailand?'

She was happy to leave questions about Phoenix unanswered but this she had to ask, 'Who's Marc?' the exchange had left her feeling out of the loop. Clearly there was an issue. What could it be? Aaron was everybody's friend. She watched, suspicious as he fiddled with the melting wax from the tables candle in a bottle.

'No one special. A season diver.' He answered, sounding bored.

Willow was no wiser, 'Do you like Marc?' she didn't appreciate the speed at which she had gone from being his closest confident to in the dark.

Aaron was concentrating on the men playing the bongos 'I love these guys!' he informed her without looking away from them.

'Do you like Marc?' She tried again, louder, struggling to keep her tone light to mask her insistence.

'Sure.' Aaron nodded, composed. 'Who cares about Marc? Let's talk about you.'

She didn't want to spend the night talking about this man if Aaron didn't want to, she was hoping to cheer him up not drag up more issues. 'What about me?' she gave in.

Aaron's posture loosened, his held breath escaped, 'If you find Jay; what next?'

She was momentarily distracted from his question as Matseuse raced past, dropping off a tray full of whiskey and soda, Pad Thai noodles with charred, succulent BBQed fish and skewers packed with quail eggs, wrapped in filo and deep fried.

Aaron mercifully dove straight in, motioning for her to do the same, she couldn't have resisted for a minute.

'So what's next for you?' he asked again once they had had their fill.

The amazing food, the breath-taking scenery, the friends, family, Aaron. She didn't want to think about leaving any of it.

'To tell the truth, the longer that I'm here, the more I want to stay. I find it impossible to see myself going back to England, but I don't know that this is my home either. I just know that it makes me happy; that's got to be worth keeping hold of right?'

All he needed to do was agree and she would stay for him, the rest could be worked out later.

Aaron raised his glass, 'I'll drink to that,' they clinked their glasses.

Were they toasting their possible future or her leaving? She was tipsy and not thinking as clearly as she would have liked to have been for that conversation, it could wait. She leaned closer, hoping to be kissed.

He popped a quail egg in his mouth, ate quickly and downed a full glass of whiskey, 'Eat up, we should be getting going soon.'

Was he keen to get her back to his hut or drop her off at her own? Willow had no idea what was going on but she could hardly argue about calling the night over, it was late and they'd had a lot to drink.

She joined him in thanking Matseuse and ambled back in the direction of their huts.

He didn't take her hand as he had earlier but he didn't run away as he had in Ayutthaya. He engaged her in conversation, akin to a lecture about the history of the island and continued to swig from a bottle of beer with lustre. With each step they took towards their beds Willow feared that the invitation for a nightcap would not come; did she even want one?

With many of the island's visitors heading to Koh Pang Nang's Full moon party the next day, the bars and restaurants had fallen quiet earlier than normal. They hardly saw anyone until they were nearing their huts and two girls came into view.

They were laughing and tripping over one another, drinking out of straws from a shared bucket.

Willow thought how nice it was to see girls enjoying their friendship. One was shorter with enviable curves, shown off in a bikini top and tiny shorts, the other tall and svelte like a model. Both were impossibly blonde, Nordic.

As they came closer Willow could see that the taller one had exquisite blue eyes, gloss glistening plump full lips and enviable long-tanned legs.

'There you are!' the taller one called happily when she noticed them.

Willow tucked her baggy t-shirt into her shorts to give her a little shape.

Aaron stiffened. A deer in head lights, 'Shit!'

The girl walked directly to him, throwing her arms around his neck and kissing him on the mouth. He averted his eyes from Willows.

No matter how much Willow willed him to step away from the girl, he stayed firmly in place.

A discomfort grew with every second that passed.

Finally he turned to her. The modelesque girl's lithe arm hanging around his waist, her head leant towards him. He at least had the decency to look uneasy.

'Willow,' he enunciated slowly, 'This is Marcella and her friend Annie. Marcella this is my friend, Willow from England.'

Marcella flashed a smile, teeth white, perfectly straight, showing off adorable dimples on flawless cheeks, 'Hello,' she half waved, bored. 'Please don't call me Marcella, only my parents call me that.' She pouted at Aaron, telling him off, 'Everyone calls me Marc.'

Willow's stomach tensed, the warmth of the day draining away, hoping that it was some sort of joke. She didn't trust herself to talk for fear of crying. She remembered how she had managed when anyone had offered sympathy in the wake of her breakdown, she pulled out the same mask, forcing an over-used rehearsed smile.

Marc addressed Annie, without her grip on Aaron dropping. She spoke in Swedish, *'Of course he's not sleeping with her, just look at her, she must be forty. He will have been waiting for me like every year. You're losing your mind!'* She guffawed.

Aaron, oblivious to what they were saying appeared to grow more tense with every passing second.

Willow's Swedish was rusty, but passable, her insecurities were realised. Aaron hadn't been falling for her, he had been playing with her until Marc came back. As soon as Matseuse had told him about Marc being on the island he had changed towards her.

A lump of total humiliation formed in her stomach, she had to get away.

'Goodnight girls it was nice to meet you.' She rushed to say, praying that no one would see she was shaking.

She didn't wait for a response, muttering to Aaron as she walked away, 'Thanks for getting me this far. I'll be fine from here on my own.'

She would have run if her injured foot had allowed it, instead she limped away, without looking back.

Chapter 19

Willow had hardly slept, every emotion on alert battling for position. She had been up with the sun, packed her things, ran to Eric's shop and bought a ticket for Koh Pang Nang. Eric, miraculously, had managed to find her a bed for the night, it wasn't at anywhere he would recommend, or would personally go near, but she was desperate and grateful.

She had to leave.

Eric hugged her goodbye, insisting she call him when she got there safely, the way her father used to. She surged with affection. She would not crumble. She had been through far worse.

She walked back toward her hut taking in the cleansing beauty of the island, giving Aarons hut as-wide-a-birth as possible, but turned when she heard a noise from within. His door swung open and Marc emerged wearing one of his t-shirts and her pants, exposing her beautiful long legs. Aaron appeared behind her, she turned and wrapped her arms around him.

Willow hated to see it but couldn't pull her eyes away. Adrenaline surged, she couldn't let him see her. She darted behind a tree, then on to another, hiding all the way down the beach until she was well out of view.

What the hell was she doing?

She straightened herself up. There was one more place to go before she left.

She skulked along until, at the end of a remote track, which had taken her up past the headland and on to a secluded bay, she saw what she was looking for.

A solitary building, adorned with a large hand-crafted sign, *"Smiling Beans"*. It was covered in exotic flowers and forest foliage. There was a small square bar in the centre, jars of coffee beans tumbling over one another at its heart. Driftwood tables rested on the floor, worn ornate cushions acted as chairs. The whole place rested beneath the canopy of an enormous leafy costal tree.

Willow spotted Lucia floating around her café, conversing with customers, her ivory hair shimmering in the sun, her feet bare, the hem of her purple trousers skittering across the compacted sand floor.

Willow ran down the hill towards her flooded with relief, pausing in the doorway trying to catch her attention.

The drinks smelled delicious, the view resplendent. It was worth the treacherous journey, as the many customers stood to prove.

Lucia spotted her and she skipped over. 'Hey what's this for?' she choked when Willow grabbed her in a hug. 'Welcome to my anchor, the place that holds me still in this world.' She waved around the beautiful cafe.

Willow produced a smile from her memories of a time when she was happy, not wanting Aaron to ruin her last hour on the island, 'So this is what it's like to be in one of your dreams?'

Lucia smiled, bursting with pride, 'Welcome to my home, my heart!' her face dropped, she tilted her head this way then that and ushered Willow quickly to a table. 'Ann look after things for a while darling; I'm going to grab a break.' She shouted to a waitress. 'Tell me; why are you are really here?' She fixed her with her gaze, immovable until she was dealt the truth.

Willow slumped onto a floor cushion, shame-faced, 'I'm so sorry, I feel like I'm always coming to you to moan. I don't know what's wrong with me?' she rubbed her sore eyes, shattered, 'I'm leaving today and I think my emotions have caught up with me.'

Lucia raised her eye-brows, 'You do not always moan! Why are you leaving? I thought we had you for a few more days, I thought we were having a picnic today? I'm a bit behind, what's been going on? Have you found Jay?' she bounced hopefully.

'No. I wish it was that simple.'

Lucia stared at her, baffled, 'You ran away to Thailand, you can't run away in Thailand honey! Does this have something to do with Marcella?' she asked carefully.

Willow nodded. Could it only be the previous day that she had been running around the island trying to avoid her thoughts of James. It made no sense that she could launch from being upset over one man straight to the next. She knew that she had no right to feel hurt, but she did. 'Why didn't you tell me he had a girlfriend?' Willow bristled, *girlfriend*. Was she the last to know?

Lucia fervently shook her head, 'He doesn't! I wasn't sure if she was ever coming back, but I heard something on the island grapevine yesterday. I would have said something if I thought that they were going to carry on whatever happened last year. Have you met her yet?'

Willow nodded, defeated, 'Yep, yesterday when I was coming back from a night out with Aaron. He left with her and then I saw them kissing outside his place this morning,' Technically it had been her that left them to it, but that was semantics.

Lucia looked suitably surprised and unimpressed, 'Had something been going between you and Aaron?'

Tears involuntarily began to fall down her cheeks. Willow thought about their day in the ocean, their kiss in the cave, the romance before she stamped on that stupid urchin. 'Is Marcella a really good diver?' she sniffed. Marc was probably good at all the same things as Aaron.

Lucia tittered, 'Firstly, I'm going to take the look on your face as a yes, and I need to say that he is a pig! Secondly, I'd have more important things to ask than her credentials, but if that's what you want to know, she's a professional underwater camera woman.'

Willow was crushed, she could picture them in *their* cave, spending days together exploring the corals, evenings on the sand making love not dressing wounded feet with vinegar. 'I can't even snorkel without killing the vegetation, or fish or whatever the hell an urchin is.' She sulked, holding her foot in the air to show off her wounds.

Lucia scoffed at Willows red foot, then hugged her and looked into her eyes, 'You've not had the best few days have you?'

'You have no idea!' Willow laughed, relieved she'd stopped crying.

Ann arrived with Chai-scented iced lattes, offering a delicious distraction.

Lucia huffed out her cheeks, thinking, 'Marcella will stay here for a few months each year, she's just got back from Mexico, god knows where she'll be off to next. She'll return for as long as it suits her. She's no more than a European seasonnaire. There are thousands of them in Thailand. She could set up a life here if she wanted, but there's nothing and nobody here for her to settle for.'

Willow's eyes widened, 'There are thousands of hot girls like that running around Asia? I may as well give up and go home now before my ego evaporates.' She grumbled, sipping her coffee. It had been a long time since she had been on the dating scene, things were worse that she had feared. Chris in Bangkok must have been a fabulous fluke.

Lucia threw her tea towel at her, exasperated, 'You're not getting it! One day the summer will have slipped past and the rains will start. I will realise I haven't seen Marc in a while and she will be gone. She doesn't see this place as home and she doesn't see Aaron as forever. Simple.'

Willow wasn't sure how any of that was supposed to make her feel better? 'So she will leave soon and I should just wait around for my turn?' She scoffed, she wasn't desperate or even in the market. The whole thing was a mess, exactly what she had been hoping to avoid.

Lucia's playful rebuttals had stopped and her face grown serious, 'No. He wants her because he doesn't have to keep her. There's no pressure. You weren't imagining it, I saw him flirting with you, the first time I saw you together and the way he spoke about you. When he asked me to go and find this *intriguing woman from the plane*.' She mocked his accent, 'I came to find you because I knew you mattered to him and he matters to me, I thought he deserved a chance. In another time I think you guys could have had something, sorry, I didn't realise that he wasn't ready.'

'Ready for what? We were just getting to know each-other.' Willow protested, but she knew that she had wanted more than that, she had already been thinking into the future. Had he been turned off, could he tell she was too keen to be loved again?

'He couldn't save his wife and Phoenix so he's a bit of a *fair-weather saviour*. He likes to pick up people who are broken and put them back on the shelf. I don't just mean women for romance, he's helped me, Ben, Eric, most of us in one way or another. He could give you a holiday romance to shake your world, do wonders for your confidence and send you home bursting with love, but if you were to stick around you could see beneath the surface. He's got nothing to offer you, his life is basically in ruins.' Lucia told her with certainty, seeming to have all the answers.

It didn't excuse his actions but Willow softened at the mention of Phoenix. She had looked to Aaron to have all the answers since they first met, but it turned out that he was just as clueless as her. 'If he wanted me in the beginning what changed?' she asked Lucia, certain she would never ask him.

Lucia took her by the shoulders, 'You were vulnerable, you needed him, but you're not broken anymore and you may be sticking around a lot longer than planned. Am I right?' she probed, hopefully.

Willow paused. Lucia was right, she wasn't broken anymore, but she didn't know what she wanted either, 'Who knows? I don't know what I'd do if I stayed.' she admitted. Had it been Thailand that had seduced her or Aaron? She had to separate her feelings for the two before she could think straight.

Lucia smiled, 'So where are you off to next?'

'Koh Pang Nang. I was going to wait, but now I need a change of scene. Besides it's the full moon party tonight.' Partying was the last thing on her mind, but she didn't want to admit that she was planning on hiding out until the whole thing was over and she could go in search of Ying sanctuary.

'You want some company?' Lucia asked, always ready to follow the fun.

'I'd love you to come but I think I need to go on alone but don't worry. You turned a light on in me and I'll be damned if I'm going to let a man snuff it out. What I do need is to find my own strength, the way that you found yours. I'll come back to see you once all this over and I'm complete.'

'Hang on a minute.' Lucia jumped up, disappearing behind the counter, returning with a phone and charger, 'Sometimes it's good to go it alone, but don't cut yourself off or get stuck again! It's my old phone, it still has my numbers in it, a few you might want to keep, Ben, Che, Eric; others delete!' She instructed handing the bundle over.

Willow took it gratefully, 'I'm not planning on getting mugged this time, but you never know!' she admired Lucia, such a perfect fit in her surroundings. 'Thank you for everything. You've found your place. It's time I find mine.'

Chapter 20

When the boat docked in Koh Pang Nang there were hundreds of touts racing around, collecting people for their hotels, waving fliers for free buckets and shots. Jovial visitors bumped into her as they walked in a zombie herd, following the lights of the town and lure of Hat Rin beach.

Willow didn't lose heart, thankfully Eric had assured her that it was an island of two halves: the crazy half and the quiet beautiful hills on the other. She would be firmly in the hills by the following afternoon, she just had to wait get there.

She took a motorbike the short distance to the hotel, never fully escaping the crowds. The full moon party sounded fun, if you had friends to go with. Alone amongst the revellers she felt vulnerable, overwhelmed.

There were a lot of police, carrying guns and batons. Stories of back packers being arrested and thrown in jail on false drug offences rattled her.

She would have gone straight to Yinga for some peace and quiet, it was only a short drive and then a mild trek, but she could hardly do that in the dark and night was approaching.

She was grateful, walking into the small dormitory to find she was alone. She hadn't slept on a bunk bed since Brownies and had forgotten how tiny they were. She lay back and closed her eyes.

Seconds later the door sprung open and three bouncing Northern English girls came toppling through, in a cloud of laughter and high spirits.

One was tall and thin with a boyish short peroxide hair-cut, one short and round with bouncing red curls and a lip ring nestling against her bright pink lips, the other had a dark skin tone and wore waist length braids.

'Oh hello.' The red head cried out in a friendly Brummie tone. 'You must be Lucy's replacement?'

Willow sat up, pleased that they seemed friendly, even if loud. They must have mistaken her for someone else. 'Who's Lucy?' she asked.

'She was traveling with us for a bit, a month ago. We made it all around the north islands, then she met a guy and went off with him to Lanta. We'd arranged to meet up here.' The girl with braids humphed, dumping her bag on the floor.

The blonde tutted her disapproval, 'Seems like she had a change of heart cos this morning I got an email, saying she had just arrived in New Zealand with this Tim guy. Apparently he's the love of her life or some shit.' she perked up. 'Lucky we cancelled her booking and now you are here. Means we'll get her money back!'

'I'm pleased it's all worked out ok.' Willow smiled, enjoying their energy.

The girl with braids yelled, 'Woohoo first round of buckets on Lucy!' her spirits quick to lift,

'I'm Rachel and this is Karen and Abi'. She presented, pointing first to the blonde and then the redhead.

The girls turned to Willow, smiling in unison. Their energy revived her, but their fervour made her feel very old. They had to be younger than the students she taught.

'Nice to meet you,' she smiled back, feeling like an imposter.

'Are you here on your own?' Abi asked, looking around the tiny room.

Willow nodded a bit embarrassed, 'Yep I am,' she felt like the new kid at school with no friends.

Karen stared agog, 'Wow that's so cool.' She gasped in awe, 'I wish I was as brave as you!'

'Hey.' Shouted Rachel 'What's wrong with traveling with us.' She stuck her tongue out, slapping her friend on the arm.

Karen scoffed, turning back to Willow, 'We've not had a holiday without each other since college.'

The girls were so in-sync, it was like having a conversation with one person, Willow wasn't sure which face to address. She found it easier to look in their vague direction then to single any one out in particular.

She wished that she had gone to the parties of Pang Nang when she was younger, she could have made friends with girls like them and had a wonderful time; but it was too late.

Rachel rolled her eyes, 'I can hardly take a piss without one of these bitches coming in the cubicle for a chat.'

'Are you on your gap year after university?' Willow guessed.

'Is it that obvious?' Abi raised her eyebrows, looking at her friends.

Willow took in their surf style hoodies, skimpy vest tops and fresh matching tattoos on their midriffs. 'Just a bit.' She smiled.

They began calling dibs on beds, jumping upon them and throwing their things into drawers, Rachel put on Abi's shoes without asking and Karen started painting her nails with a polish she had lifted from Abi's bag.

With a jolt Willow remembered weekends she and Claire would dress up together and go out into town, in search of cocktails and boys. She rejected her memories and concentrated on the girls.

Rachel was taking up the mirror, turning this way and that, 'You're coming to the party aren't you Willow?'

Willow had no desire for more alcohol, but her intrigue was growing, 'I might pop out later and take a quick look.'

Rachel incredulously yelled, 'Fuck off! You're coming with us! This is the best party in the world. I've been working double shifts in McDonalds for two years to fund this trip. This party is what I've kept in my mind when I've been cleaning vomit off the walls on Friday nights and dealing with kids throwing food on Saturday mornings. If you are on Koh Pang Nang and it's full Moon you sure as hell do not stay in a dorm by yourself!'

Abi shook her head, her face contorted dramatically, 'Yeah has to be disrespectful or some shit. You are coming with us!'

What would Eric do? Despite being at least twice her age she knew that he would say yes, so would Rosa, so would Lucia. What was she waiting for? Did she really want to sit in while one of the best parties in the world was unfolding down the street?

'I can't argue with that. Count me in!' she accepted.

A few minutes later and they had fallen in with the crowds, wielding glow sticks like weapons, blowing whistles like battle trumpets, slathering their faces and bodies in illuminous paints at the road side stalls. They made their way toward the pumping music on the shore of Had Rin; Willow wondering if she had made a mistake with every step.

Abi was ahead, nearly running, 'There are going to be somewhere between ten and twenty thousand people at this beach party. That's a fuck load of men,' she squealed, unable to contain her anticipation.

Willow had to laugh, if she was trying to avoid men she in the wrong place.

Karen gasped, 'Do you think those Danish guys we met on Samui will be here?'

Rachel squealed, pointing at a shirtless man dancing down the street wearing a unicorn mask. 'OMG look at that one!'

The electric energy grew as they neared the beach, Willow relaxing into the fun.

Abi was the first to run to a roadside stand and to return, slopping the sticky mixture from four whiskey buckets, 'Let's down the first one to get warmed up!'

Willow didn't want it at all, her body longed for a healthy smoothie and an early night, but she was bored of spending her life as a bystander. She grabbed a bucket, sucking on the straws until it ran dry.

'Woooooo,' screamed Karen. 'Down it down it you legend!'

Willow coughed and hiccupped when she finished, glimpsing what she had been missing in the student union all those years ago.

A small group of Spanish men stopped to chat, putting an end to her moment of glory, as the other girls downed their drinks.

'Hi girls you going to the party?' one asked.

Where else would they be going? No chance of the young guys impressing her with their chat, Willow smiled, longing to talk to Aaron then scolding herself for being such an idiot.

'We are,' Abi screamed joyfully, 'Carry me to more drinks!' she demanded, jumping into the arms of one of the larger men, giggling as he sprinted down the road.

'Come back with our friend!' Rachel creased up, setting off in pursuit.

Willow was enjoying playing at being twenty-one again as Karen grabbed her hand and dragged her down the road. They caught up with the rest of the group, buying more drinks and having their faces painted with the arbitrary party paints.

Sod it, thought Willow, having glitter and gems glued to her forehead; *why not*?

They approached the beach, the ground vibrating with base, clashing music thumping from every direction. Willow's head was already beginning to spin by the time they reached the first bar, another bucket of whiskey in her hand.

The coastline was crammed with people, undulating to the music, she couldn't even see the sand underfoot. Fire jugglers and dancers were out in force, tourists jumping flaming skipping ropes and hurling themselves through hula hoops of fire. Willow threw her arms up in to the air and let herself be swung around, dancing with a screaming Abi.

The next few hours passed in a blur of laughter, dancing, drinking and frolicking in the sea along the sandbar, beneath the star filled sky. No deep conversations, no self-analysis, just fun.

Willows t-shirt clung to her, see-through with sea water, her shorts soaked. Her cheeks hurt from smiling and her throat burnt with the exertion of talking over the music to all the new friends she seemed to be making at every turn. She had acquired some glow sticks and was actually enjoying dancing.

Abi appeared with a muddy, milky looking drink.

'What the hell is that?' Willow turned her nose up. Could it be blended insects or something else from the realms of travel horror stories?

Abi smirked, pupils dilated, 'It's a magic mushroom milkshake.'

'Are you ok?'

Willow was relieved as Abi nodded happily, jumping about laughing.

The peculiar drink, the alcohol, the infectious atmosphere of the evening; all were leading her to be inquisitive. 'Where did you get that?'

'A guy from Amsterdam. I can't remember his name, he was so cute, he's over there somewhere. He got them from up a mountain down the beach. It's called *Mushroom Mountain.* Isn't that a hoot?! You want one?'

Abi watched her own hand as she waved it in front of her face, 'This is amazing. The lights are so wild.'

Willow had never taken drugs before; then again she was doing a lot of things that she had never done before. Surely people from Amsterdam knew good drugs? James was not there to judge, Aaron wouldn't give a damn if she was reckless or mature, no-one would care if she died. That didn't have to be a bad thing.

Fuck them all.

'Yes I want a mushroom shake, of course I do!'

Her last memories had something to do with jumping through a burning hula hoop and diving into the sea, some hazy images of kissing a man or was it two? It could have been a woman? Then lots of irrepressible laughter and more dancing.

There was a hammering on the dormitory door. Willow peeled her eyes open, groaning. How had she found her way back?

Across the room she saw Karen had made it to her bed, cuddled up to a random man, the two other girls were missing.

Willow's mouth was an arid desert, cigarettes plagued her breath. She hadn't smoked in years. In the crook of her arm was a warm, half-drunk whiskey bucket, the only fluid in the place. She was desperate for water.

'Willow Brady. You get out now. Check out ten o clock, island fully booked. You go!' A Thai lady screamed from the hall like a drill-Sergeant.

This was evidently not her first time clearing up the *waste* the morning-after-the-night-before.

So much for Thai hospitality, Willow suspected it had dried up after to many run-ins with hungover tourists.

She garbled some type of reply, hoping that Karen wouldn't be woken and subjected to the pain that she was in. It seemed to placate the woman.

'Five minute.' Came the voice from the hallway at a more conversations volume.

There had been no need to shout the first time, the doors were paper thin.

Willow dragged herself from her bunk, still wearing her clothes from the night before, wrote a quick note thanking the girls and left the dorm utterly in pieces and unable to fully lift her head.

The world was swaying, unbearably bright. What time was it? Where was she going? She needed fresh air and a drink before she passed out.

Her room mates were booked into the hostel for three days. Lucky buggers. She knew from Eric's warnings that she would struggle to find a bed anywhere so there was no sense in searching.

She had to go on to the sanctuary, ready or not.

The streets were near deserted. A wave of irrepressible nausea sent her dashing for an over flowing bin. She vomited.

A stray dog stopped eating from a filthy burger wrapper on the floor long enough to give her a disgusted glance. She wiped her mouth on the back of her hand, grateful that most of the islanders were sleeping off their hangovers.

She walked, unstable on her feet, until she found the only restaurant open. It proclaimed to be *All British*, which on any other day would have be madly unappealing; however it was all she wanted or at least all her stomach wanted that morning.

After nursing a large strong coffee, she slowly sipped her way through a bottle of water and, feeling better, devoured full English breakfast, cleaning the plate with her toast.

She wasn't sure why she had woken up wearing and Australian army hat, but was grateful for its protection from the sun, she pulled it down to cover her face.

How the hell was she supposed to get up a mountain to find Yinga? Aaron would not have stayed up most of the night drinking mushrooms and behaving like a bloody idiot. Of course he wouldn't. She smarted, he would have been curled up in bed, wrapped in Marc's arms.

She huffed as she sat down at the roadside, picking glitter gems off her face with sick breath.

'You want lift to the boat?' A motorbike taxi man yelled, his endearing Thai smile brightening up Willows morning mood.

It was as good a time as any to get going.

'Do you know where Yinga sanctuary is?' she asked, without holding out much hope.

He turned his nose up and shook his head.

She staggered to her feet and handed him the piece of paper that Eric had scrawled the name on in Thai.

'Ah yes. Very nice.' The driver nodded. 'I take you now?'

Did he actually know where she wanted to go? She weighed up her options: even though she was unsure if she was ready to keep the contents of her stomach in place, she couldn't bare another moment sitting on the street.

'Yes please.' She nodded, clambering on the back of the bike like a pro.

As they rushed from the tight streets to open roads, it seemed she was the only person on the island to be venturing north. It did cross her mind that she could be being abducted but the town had given way to an entirely different island and she was captivated. Hills lined with tropical jungle and views of deserted beaches formed a panoramic backdrop. As they sped along the wind woke her senses and cleared her head.

When they came to the edge of a rainforest and the driver informed her that he could take her no further, she knew they were in the right place. She couldn't see the retreat but she felt it. The small hill that Eric had alluded to was nowhere in sight. In its place stood a looming mountain.

'You be ok.' Assured the driver, handing over his phone number on a scrap of paper. 'I drive people here before. They leave happier than when they come. You will cheer up.'

Willow wanted to scream for him not to leave her, but she had to watch as he drove away, forcing the unease from her heart.

She pulled herself tall and, with feigned gusto, set off toward the only path. No point in hanging around.

She had to walk to the top of the hill with her bags, from there, allegedly, she couldn't go wrong.

Looking at the mountain she cursed her ill planning and indulgences from the night before; why hadn't she bought hiking scandals instead of sparkly thong flip flops in Bangkok?

The trees brought welcomed shade, but the darkness left Willow jumping at the slightest crack of a twig. If it was the sheer amount of people in Bangkok that had frightened her it was the lack of them there that left her cold.

Doubt rose; she could get lost or attacked by a wild beast, no one would come looking for her, she could die from dehydration! She could go back to the road and call for the Taxi-man, but she wouldn't find anything to lead her to Jay on the road.

After the longest ten-minute walk of her life Willow nearly cried when the path widened. A couple of food and drink stalls by the edge of a tiny village came in to view. Relative civilisation! She hobbled towards them as quickly as she could manage, finding the usual bounty of coconuts for sale alongside warm cans of coke.

She stocked up on water and exchanged morning greetings with the few locals who wandered about, unphased by her arrival. Just another tourist. One pointed down the path, knowing exactly where she was headed. Thank God someone did.

It was only a few hundred yards until the path faded away and she was stood alone in a glen. The sunlight pirouetted across a swirling fresh water splash pool, born from by a looming waterfall.

'Oh my God,' Willow gasped, smiling as she took it in.

'It's quite something.' A male voice, seemingly, came from nowhere.

Her heart leapt, she swung around, her back pack sending her toppling off balance, crashing to the ground.

Chapter 21

'Bloody hell!' yelled the man, leaning over her on the floor.

Willow blinked hard, seeing stars, winded. A freckled face and shaved head came into focus, then the smile that warmed her heart.

'Ben, what the hell?' she spluttered.

Ben helped her to sit, removing her bag from her shoulders, 'I'm so sorry. I didn't mean to startle you. Are you alright?'

Willow took some deep breaths, absorbing his voice, a tonic. 'I'm fine. What on earth are you doing here?' Was she still hallucinating?

He shrugged, looking into the natural pool in front of them, 'Probably the same as you?'

There was that London accent, familiar. She was flooded with relief, 'You're going to Yinga? Don't you ever work?' this part of her journey was supposed to be for her alone, but she crossed her fingers and hoped.

He took a long drag on the spliff he was holding, 'I think I may have mentioned that I have a weakness for narcotics and crazy women, less so for work.' He raised his hands, defenceless, 'I'm not a perfect man but Yinga brings out the good. I've been once before.'

She took his hand and got to her feet, catching the scent of alcohol emanating from his skin and noticing his bloodshot eyes. Ben always made her feel that being herself was ok, there was no need to apologise for her own bedraggled appearance, 'I take it you were at the full moon?' she placed a safe bet.

'Yep. I'd planned to come straight here; or maybe I hadn't? I booked my boat ticket for the day of the party which was a mistake in hindsight. Like I said I have a weakness, nothing a couple of weeks of meditation, yoga and cleansing won't cure.'

Willow smiled, 'You don't have to explain yourself to me. I was there too. I was introduced to mushroom shakes.'

They exchanged a knowingly look.

'I don't know what's come over me recently?' she confessed, 'I don't know this person I'm becoming and I'm not sure if I like her yet.' It was not like her to go about the place kissing men she hardly knew or more; having sex, taking drugs and drinking. Maybe she wasn't finding herself so much as burying herself under the facade of somebody else?

Ben stubbed his spliff out on the bottom of his shoe, 'Don't beat yourself up. No one likes themselves all the time, unless you're Gwyneth Paltrow and then no one likes you.' He kicked off his sandals. 'Eric said I might find see you. What a coincidence. I've never stayed there with anyone I know before. It'll be fun, a journey,' he inverted his fingers around the word *journey* and rolled his eyes at the cliché.

Something occurred to her, 'Have you met or heard of Swami Bic?'

Her heart fell when Ben shook his head.

'I'm only going to Yinga to speak to him, or someone that knew him, then I'll be back on the ferry this evening to the mainland. From there it depends on what information I get. I'm not staying. They're booked up for months. How did you get a room?' Willow sighed, taking time at a sanctuary that could bring out the best in her and having a restful day. That would have been amazing.

Ben winked, 'I have my contacts, the rooms a huge, stay with me if you like?'

Willows eyes widened. It was exactly what she would like. 'I'd love to, but if they tell me how to find Jay I must go immediately. I don't have much time left and I keep being waylaid.'

Ben didn't look convinced, 'The sanctuary has a way of drawing you in and not letting you go until it is done with you, not when you choose. Wait and see. The offer is there if you want it.' He pulled his t-shirt off, exposing his slim torso, decorated with the standard party paints and a medley of badly executed tattoos. 'It seems that we are both in need of some cleansing. Come on let's take a swim before we walk. I need to wash away the sins of last night.'

He dove into the water with an enormous splash.

'Come on in. How can you resist this?' he yelled at the top of his lungs.

Willow imagined crocodiles and Jurassic sized malaria ridden mosquitos, 'Is it safe?'

Ben shook his head, pulling a non-committal face, 'You've survived magic mushrooms, a mugging, a visit from your ex and a night drinking with me. I'm sure you can survive a swim.'

'I was pick-pocketed not mugged.' she corrected, being deliberately pedantic.

She slipped off her dress and leapt in. Resurfacing with a huge grin on her face, 'Hmmmm, this is the best hangover cure I have ever had!' Forget about the mosquitos and to hell with the crocodiles.

'You said it!' Ben dipped in and out, an excitable puppy.

'I'm so glad you're here,' Willow yelped, surprised at the intensity of her gratitude. Maybe just one night at Yinga would be ok?

Ben insisted on carrying her back pack, she was thankful but couldn't help laughing at his intermittent groans of pain along the way. She offered help many times, but male pride or perhaps decency stopped him accepting. The Jungle grew dense, the foliage, a jumble of palms and prodigious ferns. Their passage was tranquil, an hour passing in comfortable silence as they enjoyed their surroundings, recovering from the night before. Then there was a subtle change in the line of the trees in the distance. Were her eyes were playing tricks? There were straight structured branches, woven palm thatch roofing and glassless windows.

Ben stopped in his tracks. 'It's crazy to think that we are over 600 meters above sea level and some crazy bastards decided to build a sanctuary here. Every single piece has been constructed by hand, from what the forest can provide. That's what I was told anyway.'

Willow was astonished at what had been achieved, 'It's true. My aunt was one of those crazy bastards, she was here at the beginning. She wrote to my mother about the building work. What about water and toilets, food and washing?' Willow wondered. The toilets in Thailand were a ceaseless horror.

They moved forward quickly, excited

'Compost drop in the forest over there, there's a small reservoir for showers and washing, drinking water is in bottles.' He explained, dumping their bags under a tree and leading the way to a ladder.

They climbed hundreds of rickety wooden stairs, until they popped up into a huge tree house. A hut supported by numerous stilts and trees, sitting at the centre of the complex, thirty to forty smaller huts in the sky surrounding them.

A few voices travelled on the wind, but no one appeared. Were the residents in hiding, like the monkeys that chattered and skittered around the roof tops in Koh Tao, always watching from afar?

Willow surveyed the enormous, spacious, cylindrical building made entirely from wood. Despite the glassless open window frames, shutters flung back, the space was full with the scent of lemongrass and the humidity of imminent rain.

There were open doorways in every direction, leading to a large balcony and to various rope bridges, she was in the body of the spider. She bounced lightly trying the floor boards, they held firm, but her head swarm with vertigo.

Ben steadied her arm. 'There'll be someone around here to help us soon. Just look out for a dude in a dress type of thing.'

He wandered off towards the veranda, looking at home in the serene abyss despite his rough exterior.

A man sat on a bony wooden chair drinking an unappealing green liquid, his eyes closed in meditation, unroused by their intrusion. Two ladies entered silently, wearing pristine white flowing trousers and billowing tops. Another about the same age as Willow was reading a book about enlightenment on a hanging chair in the corner.

No-one appeared to be in charge. They were all so impossibly serene, she didn't want to approach them, for fear of breaking the spell.

Willow was thrilled that they had taken a swim and hadn't arrived in a cloud of stale booze and glitter. She rubbed at her under-eyes in a bid to rid them of any of lingering mascara, turning as she heard footsteps.

'Can I help you?' a monk wearing red and orange robes, with the most perfect sphere-shaped head Willow had ever seen, appeared behind her. His face welcoming.

'Hello. I'm looking for Bic, the Swami. I've heard he might be able to help me or somebody who knew him perhaps? I'm not sure if he is alive or still living here?' She was tripping over her words in a race to find her first solid lead to Jay.

The Monk nodded, 'Bic live here. Bic helps us all.'

Her heart could have burst! 'Can you find him for me?' she asked, struggling to contain her joy. She looked around again but couldn't see the elderly man from the photos.

The monk smiled, shaking his head, 'No, not possible.'

Was he messing with her? She couldn't read him, 'Why not?' it seemed like the logical thing to ask but the monk just stared at her smiling, inane.

195

'Bic not here.' He finally replied without elaborating.

'So Bic is not here but he does come here? He is alive right?' either she was being played with, he was being stupid or rude or she was an idiot. She cursed her bleary brain.

The monk nodded, starring as if she was not grasping something very clear, 'Yes he is here, but he is not here, you see?'

No she did not.

'Yes he is here or yes he is not here?' Where was Ben when she needed him? She resisted the urge to yell for him amid everyone's peace.

'Bic is Swami' the monk said, closing his eyes, as if that explained everything.

Willow nearly jumped with eager energy. They were getting somewhere. 'That's the man I am looking for, Bic the Swami. I'm looking for someone he knew once. He can help me find them?'

The monk nodded encouragingly, waving his hand in front of her eyes, 'Close your eyes. Bic is all around you,' he hummed, searching her face for understanding.

She closed her eyes to avoid his scrutiny. When he said nothing more she impatiently opened one and found his face inches from hers. Both eyes sprang open and she screamed before she could gather her poise. Everyone turned to stare, even Ben, who had returned, raised an amused eye brow.

Willow dropped her voice, stepping back, regaining personal space. 'That's not what I meant.' She clarified, 'I really need to have a conversation with him.' It was her turn to search his face for understanding. There was none. Her desperation was growing, 'I need to have a real-life conversation with him. I was told he could help me find a lost friend. They are very precious to me.'

The monk took her hand in his small, dry palms. 'Maybe you are lost, not your friend? If your friend knows Bic they are exactly where they should be, you can be sure of that. I am Jin' he patted her hand. His smile spread, exposing his crooked teeth and deep-set dimples, 'You should take more care of your precious things. Don't lose them so easily again,' he wagged a finger at her.

Willow was about to launch into a short-tempered reiteration of what she had already said twice, when Ben joined them, putting a hand on her shoulder, as if to say, leave this with me.

'Jin it is wonderful to see you again pal,' Ben acknowledged the peculiar monk with a bow of his head.

Jin's face lit up like a vibrant bulb, 'My Ben has returned!'

Willows exasperation melted away, as she thanked God for Ben, yet again.

'Where is Bic now?' Ben asked Jin, turning to Willow, 'You need to ask the right questions.' He winked, making her laugh.

'I tell your friend, Bic is in meditation.' Jin explained as if he was the only one who had been talking sense.

Ben overstated each word, picking them carefully, 'When will he be returning to teaching?'

Jin continued, 'Six days. Then he leave on pilgrimage for six weeks.'

Willow was rattled, she only had thirteen days left to find Jay. If she continued making progress at such a slow rate she would stand no chance.

She thought again of talking to her sister Claire. It would be possible to give the money to Jay after the deadline if she agreed to it, but Claire would be pleased if she failed. She was nothing if not greedy.

'Is there any way we can reach Bic before that?' Willow asked, desperation sneaking into her voice.

'No. No way at all,' Jin almost sang, still grinning, oblivious to her distress.

Her mind reeled, exhausted, every way she turned she was getting it wrong. 'So I can leave and come back in six days?' She was crest fallen, where was she supposed to go?

'No you cannot leave. You come here for a reason, so you stay. Bic would want this.' Jin starred, as if reading her mind and saying *there I've made the decision for you.*

'I came to see Bic. I can come back when he is here.' Willow contemplated, the thought of clamouring back down the hill and returning to the unknown, no nearer to the goal, brought tears to her eyes. Ben had offered to share his room, but she didn't want to impose upon him. As much as she liked him, they hardly knew one another.

Jin pointed out of a window, confused by her lack of understanding, 'There he is. You can see now, but you cannot talk. Bic meditating.'

Willow raced to the window and saw the wild haired man from Rosa's photos. He was sat in the lotus position, his eyes looking into space.

'He's here!' She yelped, kerbing the urge to high-five Jin and bound straight to Bic.

'You've got to hand it to Jin, he speaks literally.' Ben told her, putting a firm restful hand back on her shoulder, 'He will not break meditation to speak to you. He won't even acknowledge you. You will have to wait.'

She stayed still, resigned to the reality.

Was she seeing things? Were the magic mushrooms playing havoc with her eyes? She stepped forward, her mouth aghast. Sat by Bic's side was an enormous wild cat, it shook its head and she drew back, having considered that it could have been stuffed. 'Bloody hell!' she gasped looking at Jin, 'I'm so sorry, it's just, wow!' she giggled with a nervous energy, transfixed by its ethereal beauty.

It was at least three times the size of a domestic cat, heavy set and sturdy, with poised muscle. Its fur was cinnamon and laced with paler sun splashes; rather like her own, she noted. It had large white spots and stripes that crept across its nose and out over its head with stark black ears, oscillating this way and that. Despite its resting posture, it was fully alert. 'Is it chained up?' she could see no evidence of restraints.

Jin shook his head, 'Poi Tierake has no chains. She is not wild, but she is free, like all of us. This was her home before ours, we are her guest.' He said clearly.

Ben put his arm around her shoulders, equally mesmerised, 'She is very old now. She was found here right on this spot. Her mother must have been taken by poachers, or something, they're extremely rare, worth a lot of money on the black market. Jin told me before that his Swami saw Poi Tierake as a sign that he needed to build the studios here. That must have been Bic. It's a place that Buddha led him to and the cat showed him it could be a place for those who need to love and be loved in return. She may look alarming but she won't bother you, just like me really. She is as tame as a tabby. Cool right?'

'Very,' Willow breathed, longing to lose her fingers in its plush fur.

Jin was grinning like the proverbial cat, 'Poi Tierake kill nothing, but snakes.'

'Hang on a moment, just how many snakes does she catch around here?' a wild cat she could deal with, snakes she was not so sure.

'Many. Come rest before classes.' Jin shuffled away, indicating that they should follow.

Willow's desire to stay was overwhelming, but she had to clear things with Ben. 'Jin I'm sorry I have not booked.'

'You know Aaron yes? He say you coming. All taken care of. You share with Ben.' Jin instructed her, already walking away toward a rope bridge.

Willow was stunned to hear his name. 'Don't worry I'll find something else.' She didn't want Aaron's help ever again.

Ben was following Jin, 'Come on these rooms cost a fortune, please share with me, you'll be doing me a favour, I don't like to spend too much time in introspective thought and nights alone in the jungle, it sends me a bit crazy. I'm happy for the company and I don't snore, I promise.'

Behind his reassuring smile was a hint of a look that she recognised all too well. Fear. She wasn't the only one who found being alone a scary prospect.

'Ok, but I'm staying for you not for Aaron.'

'Great.' Ben grinned.

As they made their way to a rope-bridge she tried to picture Jay there as a child. It was hardly held to any health & safety standards she could contemplate.

The bridge wobbled underfoot; aging timber planks groaned in complaint with each step, but she hardly noticed the hammering of her heart straining to remind her to be scared.

How could she feel afraid when she was walking above Eden?

They reached their tree house and Willow had to ask, 'Jin do people bring children here?'

Jin shook his head quickly. 'No. Children are enlightened. We lose our way from the path when we grow older. No place for children here.'

Willow pulled Rosa's photo from her pocket, the only one she had on her and handed it to Jin. It was a picture of Rosa and Jay, he could have been no older than six, sitting with a younger looking Bic on a beach, 'What about this child, or woman?'

'No. I have never seen either of them.'

She thought of the letters. 'I was told that they spent many months here with Bic.'

'Then this child, this lady must have been very special to Swami Bic. They must have come in Swami's personal time. Like family visiting.'

'This boy is now a man. He's the one who I am looking for. Could you have met him as a man or heard Bic speak of a man called Jay?'

'No. I been here twelve years, I have not heard that name. This photo old, taken before I come. Maybe you talk to Bic.' He stated without a hint of irony, thrusting his hand from under his robes, holding his palm out, 'I take your watches, phones, computers now. No cameras or technology.'

Ben handed over his contraband, 'You're mugging us my friend, you're a smiling assassin.'

Jin shook his head with good humour, took Willows things and turned to walk away.

'Wait,' Willow called, 'Can you at least give the photo to Bic please?' she held it out to him, sensing that he was on the brink of protesting, 'Please, they were clearly very close. You do not have to say anything just give him the photo. It may stop him leaving on his pilgrimage before we have a chance to talk?'

Jin nodded, silently taking the photo, accepting his mission.

Their room was a fantasy come to life. The walls bamboo panels, the roof thatched with reeds. Twin beds lay under huge mosquito nets. There was a large open window overlooking the forest below and in the distance the pristine shores of a beach were just visible. There was a large balcony with only a flimsy wooden banister to stop them falling to their death. A hessian Hammock swung in the breeze, on one side, on the other were two yoga matts and pillows.

Willow buzzed in the bliss, 'I didn't think places like this existed. It's a tree house made from a spiritual fantasy. It's like being inside my aunt's mind. This is all *her*.'

Ben expertly hopped into the hammock, pulling another pre-rolled spliff from his pocket and lit it, 'Your aunt must have been one cool lady.'

Willow was amused to see that her bag was already waiting on a bed. It must have been taken there before she had agreed to stay.

Something else was more pressing: 'That cat...' She began.

Ben blew out a plume of smoke, 'She's an Asian Golden. You should see her when she's in the water. She loves the plunge pool, where we were today, goes crazy chasing fish and flickers of light. That's how she got her name.'

Willow searched her memory to recall the meanings behind that words she'd heard the men using when referring to the majestic animal. *Poi Tierake*, she turned the words around smiling as she interpreted, '*My Thrashing Darling*. That's lovely.'

She thought about Bic, the man who had saved a kitten and built a sanctuary for her, himself and now for all the lucky patrons. She longed to talk to him but was delighted for the excuse to stay for a few days.

'You've been swimming with a wild cat?' she couldn't believe it, 'Ben you are full of surprises!'

Ben held out his spliff toward her, she politely declined.

He took another puff, 'It wasn't something I did regularly in the London office, but she's no wilder than us. I'm sure she has her moments like we did last night but mostly she's under control.' His eyes shone with mischief.

Willow rolled her eyes preferring to forget about her more feral behaviour.

She slumped on to her bed, yawned and closed her eyes, listening to the creak of Ben's swaying hammock, the bird song from the trees and swoosh of the fan over-head. Before she knew what was happening she had fallen in to a deep contented sleep.

Chapter 22

Willow woke to a loud knock at the door. It was sometime in the late afternoon, judging by the descent of the sun in the sky.

She was officially off grid for the first time in her adult life; she didn't need to know what time it was, she had slept because she was tired. She had no fear of being found or reached by Claire, James or Aaron, life had become simple.

'Come in.' Ben yelled.

Jin entered, 'Classes begin now in main studio. Please change and join us,' he dropped some beige linin clothing bundles onto a chair and left.

Willow splashed her face with lukewarm rain water from the tap and dressed quickly, rushing Ben out of the door. He laughed at her skipping along the treacherous rope bridges, Willow pausing only to look longingly toward Bic's hut.

When they arrived, the studio was fizzing with people, all dressed in the same outfits.

Her fears of new social encounters had deserted her and she longed to dive in. Who were these people who had found their way to such a unique place?

There was a mixture of men and women from early twenties to perhaps eighties? The atmosphere was relaxed and the interactions light. Many were new arrivals, others were embarking on their second week, all eager for the lessons to start.

Ben made his own introductions with very *un-British* hugs and kisses on both cheeks to the delight of the older ladies and confusion of some of the men.

He came back to her with a grin, 'Be prepared for an emotional rollercoaster. Lots of the teaching here is centred around loss and healing.'

Willow shifted, she was stronger, but she had buried much of her pain and secrets in places she wasn't sure she wanted to go. Her doctors had tried to make her talk for months; what was the point, who would it help?

She set herself down, next to Ben in a quiet corner, resisting the temptation of holding his hand for support. A beautiful lady, long white hair, swept into a bun and pale skin etched with soft expression lines, entered the room. All eyes turned.

'Welcome,' she spoke from the front of the class, 'I am Madame Sophie and I am here to help you find your inner happiness and calm. Once you have found your pleasure place you can visit whenever you need, even when you are back in your hectic lives. Sounds good?' she spread her soothing words like a blanket over them.

Her strong French accent crooned of Brittany and Willow was pleased that she was in charge of finding her happy place. If this sublime lady couldn't find it, nobody could.

Sophie ran her finger around the top of a brass bowl, half-full of water, it sang with each rotation and the group fell silent. 'Let us start.'

She ushered them into a circle, 'Please remove your shoes and sit facing the forest. You do not want to look at my face when you have all of this beauty to take in.'

Nobody was immune to the magnificent view.

Willow engaged with the cleansing breathing exercises, feeling silly to begin with, but soon losing herself in them. It reminded her of praying, but she asked forgiveness guidance and strength from herself and no deity. It was a concept she relished.

Sophie offered suggestive guidance, her loose trousers whispering over the wooden floor as she sewed her way between them. Her words drew them together on their journeys.

'What are you thinking Willow?' she questioned, from behind, just loud enough for the group to hear.

Willow blushed, guilty, 'That I wish I could have my phone.' She answered honestly; relieved when hummed agreement floated all around.

'Ahh' Sophie acknowledged; 'Why?'

Willow had no wish to be reached, but she longed to reach everyone, to show them how much better she was; better than them sat at home? At last she was doing something amazing, but nobody knew.

She stared at a vibrant pandemonium of parakites flittering amongst the branches of a tree, 'I want to take photos of everything! To capture all of this, to share it, to show everyone what I am doing. To bottle and revisit this moment forever.'

Sophie patted Willows shoulder, 'Take time. Breath in the scent, feel the sun on your skin. A photo cannot do that for you or the people you seek to impress. They cannot be here. This is for you only. Enjoy it'

Willow floated away on the waves of Sophie's words. Why did she care what people thought of her? She had been depressed and no one had cared, they had no right to share in her happiness. Immersing herself in the view and the moment, her desire to gloat evaporated.

Sophie continued, her voice and padding steps as much a part of the jungle symphony as the songs of the birds and baritones of the frogs. 'Never click a photo and walk away. One day you will leave this earth. You will close your eyes for the last time. Close your eyes now. When you close your eyes in your final moments the last thing you have will be your mind, not a phone, a computer or a photo. Hold what matters in your minds-eye, in your heart. Some of life's greatest moments cannot be shared and why would you want to? Why does someone else's opinion on your life's achievements and experiences hold more merit then your own?'

Sophie chuckled, 'Is your mother or lover, Jon from Illinois or Lilly from Beijing liking your Instagram post more important than you are enjoying the moment for yourself?'

As evening fell Willow, still high from Sophie's positive session, embarked on her first ever yoga lesson. Her neglected muscles were not as supple as many of her advanced classmates. Yoga was not as easy as she had hoped, but it was fun despite her unstable core and lack of balance.

Afterwards Willow walked with her fellow students to dinner in the main round-house. They were friendly and chatty but her thoughts were with Ben. He had left Sophie's class in silence with a dark look on his face, then skipped yoga. Had something happened?

The sun had left the sky a velvet starry drape and the mosquito blinds were down in every hut as they ate a fresh fish and noodle supper, but there was still no sign of Ben. She was beginning to worry that he could have been savaged by the wild cat or he had done a runner back to civilization when he turned up.

Willow tried to position herself next to him, but he was fast becoming the most popular man there. She watched as he asked person after person how their day had been with genuine fascination. He sympathised and laughed in all the right places before excusing himself and moving on to the next.

He could hardly stay still for five minutes between his interactions, appearing in high spirits; but she was concerned. There was a falseness to his jollity that, as someone who had faked it, she recognised.

'Ben are you ok?' she managed to ask in a hurry before he ran away again. Was he avoiding her?

He turned, a confused expression, worn to mask his true feelings, 'I'm fine, how are you? Is there something wrong with you?'

Willow couldn't put her finger what was bothering her, 'No. I'm good. I was worried, after Sophie's class you seemed a bit...' she didn't get to finish.

'Honestly I'm great. Couldn't be better. Just got to nip to the loo. Back in a sec.' He was gone before Willow could say anything more and she was quickly swept back into the group conversations.

Candles lit their chat, the jungle buzzing with life all around. Everyone shared their stories, but Ben never returned.

It had been a long day, maybe his full moon had left him more hung over than she realised? She tried not to worry; they would have plenty of time in the morning.

Three days later and Willow was increasingly troubled by Ben's behaviour. He playfully interacted with her and everyone else while dodging her concerns or offers to talk. He appeared to be immersed in the sessions and larked about arranging fun cricket tournaments in the breaks between classes. He recited humorous, self-penned poems over dinner and played cards with a Swedish couple for hours at a time; but in their room he was quiet.

He spent his time on the balcony smoking weed, writing in his diary and staring at the jungle. He insisted that he was perfectly happy and, on the surface, he seemed fine.

His eyes gave him away.

Willow was beginning to suspect that she was bothering him with her incessant concerns for his state of mind and she was aware it was not any of her business. He had warned her that Yinga made you think. Perhaps he was working through some personal things that he wasn't ready to share?

Willow returned from Dinner and found Ben was in his usual spot, an ashtray full at his feet, having ducked out hours earlier. His hand was shaking, his eyes red.

She had promised herself that she wouldn't push him, but she had to try one more time.

'Ben what's going on. Why won't you talk to me?'

'I don't know what you mean. I'm ok.' He didn't meet her eyes, 'How are you doing? You seem to be enjoying your time?'

She removed the spliff from between his fingers, stubbed it out and held his hand. Unwilling to be fobbed off, waiting until he was ready to talk.

His eyes didn't leave the view. 'The first time I came here I was in a bad way. I'd been through months of living to excess to bury my shame. Prior to that it had been years of drug abuse to have *fun*. I could hardly look at myself in the mirror let alone face anyone I knew. I've done some awful things, let people down, cheated. I thought it would be easy, that coming here for a few days would *cure* me,' he rolled his eyes, 'I thought I might feel strong enough to go home. I wanted to put things right. I thought a push in the right direction was all I needed. You know what? All the hippy nonsense worked. For a while. I left with dreams of getting on a plane, returning home, sober and repentant. The prodigal son returned.'

Willow remembered how she had fantasized of going back to James for a long time. 'Sometimes there's no going back to the way things were, but you need to revisit before you can move on to something else. That doesn't mean it's worse.'

Ben nodded but stayed quiet.

'So what happened?' she prompted, not wanting him to clam up again when she was getting somewhere.

Ben got another joint from his box, lighting it as he spoke. 'I woke up. I'd been rich and successful, had a beautiful fiancé. Why would I go home? I'd lost it all. Problem was and still is, I don't know what to do here either. I did what I always do, I went back to the drugs and drinking. That worked for a while too.'

Willow frowned, she had found a path to give her life meaning again. What would she do once it was all over?

'What now?' she asked, hoping he could answer for both of them.

He took a long drag, exhaled and turned to face her. 'Now nothing works. I don't know what the point is anymore.'

His words alarmed her. From the moment she met him he had been enraptured by other people stories, their pasts, fears, problems, what he could do to help them. His interest in her had been flattering but he had given precious little of himself away in return.

How on earth did he and Aaron hold down a conversation? They were both so guarded but where Aaron was confident and comfortable with who he was, Ben didn't know much about himself. What he wanted his career to be, where he wanted to live and what he did know he didn't like.

She could see her old self in him, someone who believed themselves to be worthless, a burden for everyone around them. Was Aaron out there feeling the same? That was for Marc to be concerned about she reminded herself. She couldn't help him, but maybe she could help Ben?

'Ben I've met a lot of people who care about you. I think a lot of you. You do good things for others all the time, you don't even realise it, that's a good person I say and there is always a place for a good person in this world.'

'Tell that to Jesus.' Ben scoffed, rubbing his eyes, climbing back into his hammock and placing a towel over his face. Conversation finished.

Willow remembered the nights that Claire had sat by her bed side in silence, her presence enough to bring comfort in the darkness.

Sometimes there's nothing to be said.

She sat on the floor next to Ben as he swayed back and forth, holding his hand, thinking of her sister; leaving only once he had fallen asleep.

Willow woke up to find that Ben was already up, fresh from the shower and tidying his things.

He smiled when he saw her sitting up, 'Thanks for the chat last night. I'm feeling much better now.'

To her relief he looked it, 'That's great. Why's that?' she couldn't recall their conversation having a positive outcome. Perhaps he needed to know he was not alone?

He clapped his hands, decisive, 'I have a plan now. I know what I want.' His eyes were wide.

Was he excited or manic?

She sat up, 'Slow down. Are you sure you're ok? What's the plan?' She was struggling to keep up.

'I couldn't be better, but I'm not ready to talk about it. Honestly you don't need to worry.' He stopped and grinned at her. 'You coming to class?'

The next few days followed a routine of communal breakfast, taken with the rising sun, group meditation for an hour or two, some free time followed by Yoga and then communal lunch. One to one self-enlightenment therapy sessions then communal dinner.

Ben was genuinely happier. He still liked to be alone, but the black rings around his eyes had softened and he was happy to talk more openly than before. They conversed about their parents, happy childhood memories of school and pets, about their impressions of Thailand, the other guests, but never the future. Neither wanted to acknowledge how lost they were.

Then one-night Ben sighed, looking at the forest, 'I wish I could stay here forever. I think I'd be happy with that.'

'Me too.' Willow agreed, resting her head on his shoulder. It wasn't real life, but it sure was *a* life.

The following morning Ben was gone. Damn. Willow longed for his distraction. It was the fifth day. Her desire to talk with Bic was insatiable.

She tried to meditate, but the temptation nagged like an ever-growing swarm of flies. She went onto her balcony, where she could see Bic sitting on his own balcony. She stared intently and waved. He was no more than thirty feet away. He could have been miles. He was in the same transient state that he held each day. His face never twitched a smile, frown or nod.

After a long time Bic shuffled back into his hut with *Poi Tierake* by his side. Willow got to her feet, scowling with failure; did he even see her?

Mercifully Ben returned, making her jump, 'Fancy a walk?'

Willow shoved her feet into her shoes. 'Hell yes!'

It was another glorious day in the jungle, they talked about the previous day's class, in which they had been in search of their spirit animal. Willow had been unable to take being a rabbit seriously and Ben had nodded off. She was enjoying it all so much she didn't like to think of leaving; was he?

'Are you looking forward to being back on Koh Tao Ben?'

He shrugged, 'No not really. I'm never looking forward too much babe. You must be pretty excited to get some answers and to move on to God knows where?'

Deflecting again.

Willow thought of what could be waiting for her next, 'Do you want to come with me? It might be fun?' she didn't want to leave him.

'No thanks. I told you I have plans of my own. We'll meet again one day, when all of this is done.' He pledged earnestly.

She didn't understand exactly what he meant, but when he threw his arm around her shoulder she knew that things would work out.

They enjoyed their last day partaking in some bad yoga and healing massage. The evening passed much as the preceding ones, in good company, with good stories and humour.

Ben was present and relaxed.

'Today has been a really good day.' he acknowledged as they made their way to back to their hut.

Willow marvelled at the curative powers of the sanctuary, 'Yes it has. I wish I had come here a long time ago.'

She stopped talking.

A worn wooden box, no bigger than a shoe box was on their doorstep. The last time she had seen a box like that the direction of her life had changed forever.

Ben picked it up and opened the door, looking puzzled, 'Maybe it's a gift or challenge?' he found a wooden pegged lock and pulled it.

Willow snatched it, holding the lid shut. 'Stop! Don't!' She was gripped by a fear that she couldn't articulate.

'What you are doing?' he yelped, letting her have it, already walking away to the hammock, his interest in the box replaced by desire for a spliff.

Willow sat down at the table, took some meditative breaths and pulled at the top. The lid creaked open, sealed closed by years of dust and rusted hinges. Inside sat a faded, yellowed, envelope. Emblazoned on it, written in Rosa's familiar hand was one word. *Caroline.*

Chapter 23

Wan had insisted Rosa join him to see his Swami and friend, Bic. The two men had been born in the same village, thirty years apart. For Wan, Bic was a religious teacher, a father figure, an inspiration. He had left the village without money or direction and made a difference, with nothing to offer but his mind and teachings.

Without Bic laying the path Wan may never have left or gone on to become a teacher, he may never have heard his calling to dedicate his life to helping the boys. Bic was to thank for every part of Rosa's happiness, her husband and her son.

It was the school holidays and Rosa, Wan and Jay were taking their first trip together as a family. They had arrived as the rains were beginning and two weeks later there was no way up or down the hill, which had become a mud slide. What had been billed as a holiday was turning out to be much more.

Bic had constructed three of the proposed twenty buildings that he envisioned for the space. A young eager monk and a yoga teacher from Deli had arrived three weeks before Rosa. They had ensured that Rosa's family had an adorable and, more importantly, water-tight treehouse to stay in.

Rosa huddled with Jay and Wan, in a soft bed at night, comrades against the elements, happy despite the hostile conditions. Jay naturally thought it was the greatest of adventures. Up in the hills with his parents, two holy men, a middle-aged female fitness guru and a wild cat for a guard dog. He was hidden from the world that had sought to harm him, safe, nestled at the centre of those who loved him.

At times Jay would run around and play like any normal child with a kitten, then he would fall into philosophical conversations with the adults. He had lived far beyond his years, seen things that could not be unseen, but he was still Rosa's baby and she loved both the baby and the man she could see him becoming.

They adapted quickly to the days, carrying timber and hand-weaving rugs and mats.

The sanctuary was growing up around them as if the ground was willing it on. They had water, some dry stores and tinned goods, enough to keep them going. The gardens needed regular tending in the fight against the elements, they sheltered the seedlings and nurtured their crops as if they were children. They bathed in the rainwater which channelled from numerous collection vessels, flowing through makeshift pipes to a hand operated shower.

Every part of each day bonded them to the land, until they were part of the very ecosystem. Bic said that they were growing closer to God by doing his work in his world. For the first time in her life Rosa had a spiritual awakening.

From the moment they arrived Rosa had seen the look in Wan's eyes. He was planning something. Then, one night as they settled into bed, he told her. He wanted to set up a sanctuary of his own. Rosa snuggled under his arm, holding on to Jay's sleeping body and nodded. She had been dreaming of the same thing.

Wan painted a vivid picture, of an island, an oasis of spiritual calm and rehabilitation, offering a place for the poorest most forgotten members of society. People like the boys from their orphanage, people who deserved to have somewhere to rejuvenate their tortured souls. It was the most beautiful dream, they had no idea how to make it a reality, but she knew that it was fated to be.

It's a strange thing to befriend a Swami. He was always a teacher, sat by the side of God, offering his guidance, desired or not. He unearthed emotions in Rosa, leading her to consider a past she thought she was free from.

She would go to sleep happy and wake weighed heavy with sorrow. Caroline's tear stained face would step from her memory into her life, shattering her happiness. She had to be free from her.

One night a storm swept through the forest, winds throwing the rain, errant branches and debris against the huts. The treehouse shook in the sky so ferociously they were forced to take refuge in the more solidly built stone store room.

Jay gently snored, wrapped in a blanket, in his father's arms and Rosa was left with her thoughts. She knew what she had to do.

The following day, the rains departed, the forest steamed with warmth and fragrance of a hinting sun and Rosa held her pen and paper, Poi Tierake resting her large head on her lap. She rolled on her back, staring expectantly, pressing for a tummy rub. Rosa indulged the ever-growing kitten until she wriggled free, sauntered in a circle, sniffed the discarded pen and walked away.

Rosa had put it off long enough. She started writing.

Dear Caroline,

I hope that you have been given this letter by my dear friend, Bic. He is the guardian of Yinga Sanctuary and of all of those who visit. If he can't convince you to exonerate me, for your own happiness as much as mine, then no one can. Grant him a chance, he will pull all the darkness out of your soul and cleanse you of its residue. Give in to his teachings and your life will be fuller than you can imagine.

Under his instruction I have been thinking about the letters I have sent to you. With shame I know that I have never acknowledged what I did. I have said sorry over and over, but never what for. I have always been too ashamed to put it in writing, maybe I've dodged the facts or perhaps it hurt too much to acknowledge them. However I think that you've needed me to own up to my wrongs, you deserve to know what really happened; perhaps then you will accept my apology?

Bic asked me to consider how you could ever forgive me if I couldn't forgive myself? Yes I told a holy man about the greatest sins of my life! He held my hand and we meditated. My thoughts took me back to the farm, where I could see you and your family, as if I could reach out and touch you.

That awful Christmas Eve just after Daddy had died, when you over-heard my conversation with Peter, was the worst of life. I should never have said anything to him, I was drunk and lonely, angry and jealous. I had spent the day playing with Sarah and even managed it with a smile on face. That was until you had started to press me about finding a partner, pushing me to admit that I too would like a baby. I could have swallowed it, but to see Peter nodding in agreement when he knew the truth was too much to bare.

I will never forget the look on your face when you walked into the kitchen. I knew instantly that my voice had been too loud, my venom to close to the surface, you had listened too long.

We may not have been close growing up, but your emotions were clear on your face. I had destroyed your life. I could not bear to see it. So, yes, I ran away. I was the worst kind of coward, giving you no chance to hear the truth, or to show me your anger, which you had every right to do.

I need you to hear the truth from me, as I remember it and not have a version of events that you've had to invent.

When we were kids Peter was the only boy we knew for miles around. I guess it was natural to be drawn to him, all those teenage hormones and nowhere to focus them. I was lonely. You were away in the hospital with your chest problems, sometimes for months at a time.

With Mum passed and Daddy by your side more than he was ever at the home, I had nobody and was expected to keep the farm running. Someone had to feed the animals and tend the fields, but I wanted love, fun, adventure, I wanted to be a teenager. I had no-one else but Peter over those years. He was my friend, my family and in the end my boyfriend. It should have been no more than a crush, but the intensity grew, filling all the empty spaces in my life.

I had been sent away to boarding school while you were ill and when I came home for the holidays you were gone into the hospital. It was the longest time that we had ever been apart and that Summer was a blissful sun filled one, ripe for fun. I longed to enjoy the days with someone. Peter and I were kids really, only sixteen. We'd finish the chores and spend the days swimming in the pond, stealing Daddy's home brew. With no supervision you can imagine how things escalated.

I wanted to tell you at the time, I was bubbling over with excitement, but when I came to visit you were so frail. You were missing so much, it would have been cruel to gloat; but I can't lie it was exhilarating. I was having the summer of my life. I was turning into a woman. I was just Rosa and not "one of the twins". I was Peters' girl, I was someone's special one and not 'one of two'.

We were reckless, as kids are. When I discovered that I was pregnant, I was terrified, but it was the seventies and I had options. I feared my life closing when it was just beginning to open. All my opportunities and dreams disappearing in a pile of diapers and bottles. Then there was Daddy, the stress of it would have killed him. I couldn't do it to him or to myself. I had an abortion without thinking clearly. I was in such shock, I wanted to pretend it had never happened. I was unforgivably naive.

I thought Peter and I would have plenty of time for marriage and babies later, but you know how religious he is, abortion not even a consideration for him. I lied and told him that I had suffered a miscarriage, but a week later I got a terrible fever.

Peter had to drive me to the hospital, in his mother's stolen car. He refused to leave my side when the doctor came, holding my hand tight. They told me that I had contracted an infection from the abortion. He dropped my hand immediately and never took it again.

He believed that we were being punished by god for my decision and told me so. He didn't speak to me for what was left of the holidays, or when I went back to school. I wrote to him many times, but I only received one reply, asking me to stop.

I wanted to talk to you, but you were just on the mend from your own battles and I didn't want to burden you. Then I collapsed during netball and woke up in hospital. The infection had never fully cleared, in fact it had spread, causing irreparable damage. The doctor told me in moments that I would never bear children and I was packed off back to boarding school.

Do you remember when I came home for Easter one year? I was miserable and awful towards you and Peter and even poor Daddy at times. I hardly spoke at all, if I had opened my mouth the truth would have spilt out. Peter was there every damn day, trying to build a bridge of friendship, but I wouldn't hear a word. He was a constant reminder of what I had lost. Every invitation he extended, I shot him down and you went without me. Seeing the lights in town, films at the cinema.

My anger was not only driving you both away, it was pushing you together. You two were so alike, I didn't want inclusion, but begrudged the exclusion.

I saw it first when Daddy forced me to sit with you both for the longest dinner. You had the same sense of humour, raved about the same music, had grand ideas for the farm and ways to improve the yield of certain crops. You were like an old married couple at seventeen.

I was so jealous, not only of the affection growing, but he seemed to understand you in a way that I never had. I hated him. He had robbed me of my future children and stolen my sister. That sounds crazy now, but it was what I believed at the time.

I was never a threat to your life, marriage or family, I just didn't know how to bear witness to it when mine was so empty. I didn't want your husband, but I didn't want to see him either, he was a reminder of everything that I could never have. If I had thought for one minute that you would be engaged by the following year; I would have told you everything, but you were so young I didn't see it coming. It seemed that if I could just forget all about that summer no one would need to be hurt by it.

I am so sorry for all the hurt that I caused but accepting all the blame has made me feel a guilt that was not warranted.

As the sun rose this morning a raging storm faded away and Bic asked me to decide what, if anything remains to be done – either let my storm continue to rage within or let it pass by.

Whether you can forgive me, I need to forgive myself.

If you can love me, find me; I will be waiting for you in the place that was born here. I will be waiting on Koh Khrabkhraw.

Love Always
Rosa
 x

Chapter 24

Willow clutched the letter, leaning her head on Ben's shoulder, who had returned, having finished his smoke. He put his arm around her as tears fell down her cheeks, crying for Rosa, her mother and all that they had lost as well as gained, their mistakes leading them to happy lives in the end.

'Today has been a really good day,' she echoed his earlier sentiment, laying back on her bed with him.

For the first time she had a man in her life who didn't want a thing from her, not sex or money, her friendship was enough. She was enough.

When Willow woke the room was empty, it was time, day six.

She would be taking so much away but leaving a part of herself behind. For the rest of her life, when she meditated, it would be to Yinga her mind would return.

She packed and paced, watching Bic's hut for any sign of life.

Later, as sun cascaded though the blinds, she was still waiting. Ben turned his key in the lock.

'Morning.' she called, from her watch point on the hammock.

Ben was breathless, 'Morning. How you doing? I was worried I'd come back and find you gone. I lost track of time at the dawn meditation class.'

She closed her eyes, enjoying the warmth of the sun on her face, 'I'm waiting for Bic to get up, then I'll be off.' Her stomach fluttered.

'Can I help you with your bag?' Ben called.

'No thanks, I'll take it myself.' She replied, her eyes not leaving Bic's hut, Ben joining her.

'I've been thinking and I have to tell you something.'

He sounded worried; She panicked, 'What is it?' what could possibly have happened overnight?

He started uncertainly, 'Some things in life are purely coincidence and some are fate. My meeting you here. It was fate, but not coincidence.'

Even he didn't seem sure what he was saying.

She was unnerved by the serious look on his face. 'Have you been smoking too much pot?'

'Yes, but that's not the point.' He shuffled picking his words carefully. 'Aaron met me for lunch, the day that you left. He was a mess.'

'Yes.' She muttered, her instincts on high alert at the sound of his name.

'He knew that I was struggling in my own way. I've had a lot on my mind. I wasn't exactly coping.' Ben said, tapping his head. 'He had royally fucked up with you. He was worried about you coming here alone. He thought that being here could help me too.' Ben bit on his lower lip.

Willow's eyes narrowed. Claire had kept her knowledge of Jay from her, James had lied, her doctors had tried to keep her medicated. She was sick of being manipulated, a puppet in someone else's play. She was not anyone's responsibility, especially not Aaron's. He had made that perfectly clear when he had ditched her for Marc and there he was interfering in her life.

'If he was so worried then why didn't he come after me?' despite her anger, she yearned to hear his apology, for him to at least try to convince her.

Ben rolled up a spliff. 'He's afraid of some things, of you and being here, he's not ready to face his torment.' Ben sat by the hammock, seemingly unburdened by his confession.

Willow wanted to give up. Why did men have to be so complicated? 'Why's he scared of me? I was disposable to him. He replaced me with a better model the second he got the chance.'

Ben raised his eye brows, 'He knew how to hurt you the most, how to push you away when you got close. Once he'd done it he felt like total crap and couldn't see how to undo it. That's what I think anyway. Have you even seen the way that he looks at you? It's as if he's seeing you for the first time, every time. It's how I used to look at my ex. I should know that's what love looks like. That doesn't come along to often. It would be a shame to let it go.' He stared at her hopefully.

Willow smiled at the possibilities, then got a hold of herself. Aaron had humiliated her. Her life was full with choices that she finally had the power to make and she didn't want to forgive him, she was better than that! Who did he think he was, summoning her back to him because he had changed his mind? She had to change the subject. 'So you weren't really here for the full moon party?'

Ben was acting as if he'd forgotten about his part in it all. 'Oh I was always coming to Pang Nang for the party, but I was planning on debauchery rather than detox. Don't get me wrong I love it here, but this place isn't cheap. If Aaron hadn't offered to pay then I wouldn't have come. You have no idea of my relief when I saw you by the pool! I would have hated to have let him down, but it was more than that. I saw what a prick your ex was and I thought that you deserved the chance to be happy again. You deserved to come here, to heal and then to see if you could move forward with or without Aaron. I personally think you should give the guy a chance, but who am I to give relationship advice?'

She had to admit that Aaron, once again, had known what she needed. She stared at Ben for a moment, 'I was so happy to see you, you made me feel safe; my own little piece of home.'

'Then I was successful. That was what Aaron asked me to do, keep you safe, not to drag you back to him or do a PR act. He cares for you is all I'm saying.' Ben held his hands up. 'Is there any chance you will come back to Koh Tao? See Aaron, give him another shot. Maybe after you've found Jay?' he asked hopefully.

Willow closed her eyes and pictured Aaron's crazy unkempt hair and icy ocean eyes, his riddles of tattoos and that smile that lit her up from inside. Then she remembered Marcella wrapped around him and knew her answer.

'He will always mess up or run away when things get scary. I want someone stronger than that. He didn't come after me, not because he fears me, but because he's not ready for me. He's not ready for anyone.' She shook her head, 'You can tell him, thank you. Having you here has been amazing, but I won't go back, there's no point. I'll try to find Jay, maybe travel for a bit afterwards, then head back to England? I don't know, but I can't stay here for a man I hardly know. There can't be a future for us for many reasons. I'd rather leave it.' She pulled away to look at Ben. 'When will you go home Ben?' What was in store for him next.

'Back to Koh Tao?' he shrugged, 'I don't know. My life has not been what I've wanted it to be in a long time, it's time for a change.'

She thought of Rosa's letter and shook her head. 'Go back to England Ben, tell your ex that you're sorry. Trust me, no matter who she's with or what she's doing she deserves to hear it, she may even be waiting to hear it. Don't hide in Thailand, you'll always feel your past stalking if you don't face it. Your parents deserve to have you back in their lives. You're a great guy, the people who love you don't see the person you think they do. Thailand will be here waiting for you if you choose to come back. Maybe we could grab a beer in London when you're home?'

Ben pulled her into a hug as if she were keeping him afloat, 'Maybe I'll see you in another life? Now it's time for you to go get your Swami.' He kissed her on the forehead and walked inside.

Willow stood to go after him, as Bic emerged from his hut. 'Bic!' she screamed unable to contain it. A beat followed, she had no idea what would come next, then he beamed with recognition, beckoning her to join him. She turned back to say goodbye to Ben, but he was gone.

The bridge shook with her strides. Bic's arms were outstretched enveloping her in a hug, the type reserved for the greatest of friends. Her breath escaped her as he leant back, examining her face.

'It is you!' he exclaimed, 'She said that you would come. She promised. I prayed and here you are.' His eyes filled with tears, 'She said a woman the image of her would come. You got her letter?' he stepped back, throwing his hands in the air with glee. His voice was a tapestry of Thai, Indian and English, rich rises and poignant pauses.

The man who had been a stoic, stone figure on the periphery of her life for the past six days was an animated entity. '

It is so good to see that young face again!' He shook his head with blissful disbelief.

Willow grinned, the whole situation was so strange, there seemed little else to do, 'Thank you Bic, it is wonderful to see you too, but I'm afraid that Rosa meant that letter for my mother, her twin sister, not for me.' Tears brimmed, a mix of relief and anxious happiness.

Bic searched her face, 'She intended it for your mother, but it found its way to you, as the universe intended. This is a blessed day.' He shook his head, 'Seeing your face was like seeing her walk into my life so many years ago.' Bic's green eyes, held hers, sparkling like the emerald waxen leaves of the forest.

Willow jumped as something nudged her thigh. She looked down to see Poi Tierake, rubbing against her affectionately. She had forgotten the large cat was even there.

'Hello beautiful,' she murmured, stroking the cat's incredibly soft head, losing herself in the black liquid pools of her opal eyes. She felt oddly calm, despite the strength of the beast nuzzling her with a mouth full of sharp teeth.

'Poi loves Rosa too. She has been watching you every day. She was cross with me for keeping her from you.' Bic explained, leading Willow to join him at the bench on his balcony, Poi Tierake lying at their feet. 'You must be very alike, you and Rosa. I have seen you. When I met her she was plagued by her past too. Do not worry, a plagued spirit can lead a person to do much good in this world.'

Willow nodded, amused, he could read her without them exchanging more than a handful of words. Being next to Bic reassured her, 'I am beginning to see the need for pain, I'm hoping that mine will lead me to where happiness lies. Rosa hurt a lot and went on to do many wonderful things.' Willow smiled, wishing again that she had known her.

Bic raised his palms to the heavens. 'Oh yes she is a wonderful woman. Without her demons she would not have brought happiness to so many. She is very close to God.'

Why did he keep referring to Rosa in the present tense? Surely he meant that she was close to God because she was dead? Her pulse quickened, her hands shook, maybe it wasn't miscommunication? She hardly dared to hope.

'Bic is Rosa alive?'

'Yes, I pray she is well. I saw her a month ago and hope to see her again once the rains have come in strength. Have you had news that she is unwell?' his eyes widened with worry.

The world span, she closed her eyes.

Bic moved closer, resting his hand on hers, 'Please tell me, is she well? Do you have news?'

Willow shook her head, hastening words to reassure, 'If she was well I am sure she is still. I would be the last person to know. I believed she had died in the Tsunami.' She was crying as she spoke.

Bic gripped her hands, 'The water could never kill such a lady. They are special friends.'

It was too much to take in. She had to think logically.

'I saw her death certificate, there was a letter from the government. It said that she and Wan had drowned.' She protested.

Bic shook his head, 'The whole world wanted the loose ends tied up. Bodies were lost in the sea, those that were left were identified in haste, disease was rife, burials and cremations were rushed through. Who gave you this paper?'

Her thoughts were moving in slow-motion, Bic's voice a distant murmur, she tried to focus on his words. Rosa was alive. Bic, content that Rosa was safe, relaxed into his seat and let the silence fall, patiently waiting. Finally Willow pulled sense into a sentence, 'I found it in my mother's belongings.'

'Rosa will have sent it. She always thought that Caroline's life would be better if she didn't have to live in fear of her returning to the farm. The letter I left for you; she wrote that many years before the Tsunami. Perhaps when the wave came she'd grown tired of waiting for Caroline? She set them both free from their bond. She never told me about this. I have been waiting all these years for Caroline to come.'

Bic stopped. 'If you didn't come here for Rosa, what bought you to my home?'

Her mind was reeling. She could only mutter the truth, as if she were reading the words from a paper, robotic, 'I came for Jay. I have a gift for him. That's why I stayed here waiting for you to finish your mediation. I need to find him very quickly. You can help me find him can't you?' A begging tone creeping into her voice.

Bic was still in touch with Rosa, although she was struggling to accept that fact. Perhaps he could lead her straight to them both?

Bic stood and shuffled to the railings. 'Yes I can; but can you stay for a moment with an old man?'

Willow nodded, 'Of course.' She had waited that long.

'When will Caroline join you?'

Willow was caught off guard. He had no reason to know of her mother's death. She swallowed, 'Bic I'm sorry to say that my mother passed last year, at the same time as my father.'

His face dropped, 'I am so sorry for your loss. Rosa will be heart broken.' He nodded, understanding, 'Now I see why you came. Let me tell you about the family you have left.'

He sat down, his aging body struggling to keep up with his wandering.

After a week of silent meditation he was keen to talk, regaling her with stories. He detailed his many adventures with Wan and Rosa and painted a picture of Jay's early life, scrimping on the details of their recent lives; that was for Willow to discover herself.

Willow filled Bic in on the details of the Will. The more she learnt about Jay and Rosa's work the more she knew that she had to get the money to them. It could make such a difference to their lives.

Once the afternoon was upon them, with a heavy heart, it was time for her to leave for the afternoon ferry.

Bic disappeared to his hut, returning with a crumpled piece of paper. 'I cannot give you an address for Jay or the address for *Khrabkhraw*. I will lead you to the school where Rosa once worked instead. This is a better place for you to go. From there you will find your way to Khrabkhraw if it is meant to be.'

During their conversations had she failed some type of test? Why wouldn't he help her properly? Willow realised that she had to be direct with her questions if she wanted a direct answer. 'You must have an email address for one of them? Don't you know the way to *Khrabkhraw?*'

'Yes, of course I know how to reach both, there are many ways, phones, email. I am merely telling you the best way and that is to go to the school first.'

Willow caught his eye, hopeful. They were just an email away. With a few clicks on a smart phone her search could be over. 'Can't you just tell me how to reach them now, or how to get there? I'd love to see the school, but time is of the essence. I've come this far, the letter found me, I'm sure it is *meant to be*!'

Bic stood firm, 'Time is a funny thing. Rosa would want you to go to the school, so you go to the school, from there the directions will become clear.'

Willow had been deprived of her family for too long. They were so close, 'Wouldn't it be easier for me just to go to Rosa? We've been apart for my whole life, I don't want to wait another day. Where's Jay? Why is it so important that I go to that school?' she begged.

Bic took a slow breath, 'You are too quick to fear. The easy path is rarely the right one. The school is on the right path and in the right direction of *Khrabkhraw*. You will go to the school and there you will find answers.' He took her hands looking into her eyes, 'You will thank me later. The end of a journey is just as important as the beginning, you can't rush these things.'

Willow took five cleansing breaths, urging her irritation not to get the better of her. She could see that Bic thought he was doing the right thing. 'I only have six days left. I will not be able to give the money to them if I mess this up.'

Bic didn't falter, 'So you do the right thing, you take your time and maybe arrive with nothing? Who cares?'

The truth spilled from her lips, 'I can't arrive empty handed!'

He nodded as if he already knew her fears, 'You came in to the world empty handed and made your parents very happy indeed I suspect. When you leave you will take nothing. Things are just things. Why not arrive with nothing you will make them very happy?' He shrugged.

Willow began to cry, the truth forming, 'Because I'm scared that I will not be enough.'

Bic gave a knowing look, 'There are only two real emotions in this life: Love and fear. From love comes everything positive. Happiness, contentment, peace and joy all flow from the mouth of this river. From fear flows anger, hate, anxiety and guilt, but like all rivers the tides ebb and flow. It is not possible to feel these two emotions at once. If you are in fear, you are not in a place of love. If you are afraid because of relationships from your past you cannot fall in love again. You should not fear Rosa or Jay. You need to complete this next part of your journey to rid yourself of the fear. Go to them with love not money. It is all you need. If you go to the school you will find more than what you are looking for.'

Willow had to try one more time, 'Bic I am just one woman, even if they are happy to see me, I have £250,000 for them. Think of the things they could do with it.' Surely a holy man would want to help those in need?

'You don't see yet, but you will. There is always money in the world to find if you need it. It won't be gone, if they want it they may have to go on journeys of their own to find it.'

Swami's were tough to crack.

She accepted defeat but had too much to be thankful for to be sad. Her aunt was alive, her cousin would be found one way or another. 'Ok I'll go to the school. I will find them both as soon as I can and one day I will come back here to tell you how I did it.' She pledged confidently.

Bic glowed at her acceptance.

As if psychically summoned Jin crossed the bridge to join them. 'I take you back to the world now.' He instructed.

Once they reached the bottom of the mountain, he took her hand and tied a thin length of thread around her wrist, 'Sai Sin, blessed bracelet for you, keep you safe.'

Willow bowed in response, touched at the thoughtful act. 'Thank you Jin. I hope to see you again soon.'

Jin left her by the same watering hole that Ben had found her. She picked up her bags and her phone, foreign in her palm and called the taxi man.

As she walked away she allowed herself one last glance back to the forest that veiled the sanctuary from the world. Like it or not, she was off on another adventure.

Chapter 25

Willow took a seat on the small decrepit iron school bus, the likes of which she had seen in old American movies. The sun warmed her face through the dirty glass, the open windows serving no purpose as the air failed to circulate.

She fanned herself with a tourist map, shifting over for an elderly lady to sit next to her. The lady wriggled until she was comfortable, no easy task when travelling with a chicken in a coup on your knee. Just another normal day in Thailand.

The journey was long and uncomfortable, but the scenery breath-taking; 164 kilometres of ever-changing worlds. Port-town to grass-land, pineapple fields to inland villages, farm land to coastal oasis and back to port town.

She sat in silence the entire journey, lost in her dreams of family, of Aaron, of Yinga, of everything that had been and what was still to come.

Stepping onto the pavement in Krabi Town, her senses were overloaded again by the sounds, smells and the streets packed with tourists. Spotting an advert for Cornetto's, she found direction. As much as she had loved Yinga's offerings of fruit for breakfast, dinner and tea they could never replace chocolate in her affections!

She bounded into the shop, claimed the ice cream prize and sat by the roadside, devouring the sticky treat.

As she licked the melted liquid from her fingers she opened Bic's note.

Tomorrow interpret directions. Not far to go!

What did it mean?

Beneath was Thai writing, the address for the school?

She had not even begun to tackle understanding the forty-four consonant symbols and fifteen vowel symbols that combined with the twenty-eight vowel symbols and four tone diacritics to create characters that made up the *Abugida*, the Thai alphabet.

Willow glanced around, there was no shortage of Thai people to interpret the text, but Bic had been clear: *Tomorrow interpret the words.*

She stood up, and approached a Thai lady, he would never know if she got a head start. Then she stopped, it just didn't feel right, she would have to wait.

She sat back down with a humph, then smiled, Che was due to be in the Phuket area, not too far away and he had said that he would help her. Maybe he could interpret the address and drive her the next day? She called him, no answer. She texted him a photo of the address and outlined her situation then sat back, Che was never quick to respond.

She consulted her guide book. There were a few hotels Aaron would approve of, away from the main roads, small and hidden. Sod him. She craved normality, a sprung mattress, flushing toilet, a large slice of pizza and a cold glass of wine!

She hailed a cab, told the driver what she was looking for and relaxed as he took her the short journey to Au Nang, a bustling tourist hot spot. Most of the life appeared to be around a beachfront road. They drove around slowly, Willow taking in the souvenir shops, art galleries, spas and tour agents.

Intermingled with the stores were numerous westernised hotels boasting modest swimming pools, restaurants and wide screen TVs with signs promising numerous sports screenings. One caught her eye: *Browns* the sign read; her mother's maiden name. She halted the cab and five minutes later was in her room, spacious, clean and comfortable, equipped with a kettle and *PG Tips*. Heaven.

On the balcony in a bikini, a comforting mug of tea in her hands, despite the heat of the day she watched her fellow guests lounge and swim in the pool. A couple, younger than herself, tossed a giggling toddler between them in the water.

Was it too late for her to hope for that life for herself? She could see more clearly than ever why Rosa had been pained to watch her sister's life and family grow in ways that hers never could.

Her phone sounded, pleased for the excuse get away from the unfolding family tableau, she headed inside, relieved to see that Che responded. He would be with her by lunchtime, whatever that meant in Thai time? She rushed a thankful reply, gathered her things and left, the ocean was beckoning, no sense in waiting inside for the hours to tick by.

The pavements were bustling with pedestrians, vendors and their wares. She walked until she lost the hoards and the beach to her left grew quiet.

The sand lay flat and white, slipping under the lip of the ocean, breath-taking cliffs stood like curtains to the awe-inspiring view. The ocean shimmered opalescent, the surface shifting and glinting in the sun, as the shoals of fish darted about their lives beneath the surface

On the horizon she could make out an island. Her guide book told her it was Aaron's home, Railay. Thankfully he was a safe distance away in Koh Tao.

She unrolled her towel, stripped to her bikini and lay down.

The sun revived her tired spirit as the sound of the sea lapping softly upon the sand cleansed her busy mind. For a moment she was just another carefree tourist catching a tan, but she couldn't lie still for long, the water was too much of a distraction.

She dove in, exhilarated, staying beneath the cerulean surface for as long as her breath would allow. Her day in the sea with Aaron crept into her thoughts but she pushed it away. The ocean on her own was every bit as wonderful. Nobody could ruin it or take it from her. She turned away from Railay, floating on her back, shifting on the waves beneath the sun.

So this is how it felt. Freedom.

That night she sat in the hotel bar, ordered a large Hawaiian pizza with skinny fries and a bottle of white wine, origin undisclosed and enjoyed every bite and gulp.

When she'd had her fill of food, cheap booze and dated electronic keyboard entertainment, she went to bed.

Sleeping between crisp white sheets, unperturbed by mosquitos or calling monkeys was blissful, but she missed having a companion. She texted Ben a lengthily message, goading him with the story of her indulgent dinner and insisting that he call her as soon as he left Yinga.

She was unable to eat breakfast with her excitement and counted down the minutes until she could set-off. It could be *the* day!

She waited outside the hotel from 1pm, eager to go. At 14:15 am Che careered around the corner, leaning out of the window, as he approached.

'Willow! You save me from days running fat camera snappers round temple. They no respect!' he announced at a volume that unapologetically announced his feelings to the busy street.

Willow laughed as he pulled up, people turning. 'Anyone would think you don't like working for the hotels?'

Che continued to yell, 'Hotels pay good. Aaron need time alone anyway. I go to Railay with him in a few day. Horrible time.' His face clouded over.

235

She looked at him and realised that behind the smile his eyes were tired. *What horrible time?* She didn't have time to ask.

The van was blocking the road, disgruntled road users were beginning to make their feelings known. 'Jump in, I tell you where we going.' Che yelled.

Willow climbed in, 'So where are we headed?' she asked, unable to wait another moment.

Che turned on his phone, looking up the photo that she had sent him while pulling out into the stalled traffic.

'This no address. It treasure map. Like seeds on a trail.' Che pretended to be a chicken pecking at corn. 'It says: *find eye that looks over the gold.*'

It was not going to be straight forward. Why did that not surprise her?

She had no idea where they were going, but they were on their way. She had faith in Bic and Che. 'Let's get started!' she yelled.

'You got trainers, food, water? Long walk, maybe some climbing to do.' Che said with a grin. 'I got equipment in case.'

She nodded, alarmed; climbing? 'Where are we going exactly?'

Che shrugged, 'I don't know exactly, but I got good idea.'

If she had been wary Che's driving in the city she had not been prepared for his *skills* on the treacherous mountain paths. They sashayed around winding corners, scurried up impossibly narrow trails and scooted along serpentine expressways.

Willow giggled as often as she screamed, never letting her grip on the seatbelt soften, while filling Che in on her time at Yinga.

He dismissed her concerns over the *horrible time* he had alluded to. Whatever it was could wait. One challenge at a time.

When the tarmac pitted out they stepped out into the pluming dust, amid a rainforest. The canopy was so thick it snuffed out the sun. There were no signs, but the road had come to a definite end.

'Where are we?' Willow asked, hoping that Che had better bearings than she did.

He came to stand by her side.

'We are here,' he whispered.

Willow narrowed her eyes and sized him up. Something about his cheeky face always made her laugh no matter how desperate the situation. 'Where is here precisely?'

'Start of map,' Che pointed into the distance, where a small circle of light was just visible;

'That, *the eye that looks over the gold*?' he laughed at Willow's confused expression. 'Wait!' he ran to the back of the van, pulled out her bag and another overflowing with ominously long ropes and a two large bottles of water. He passed one to her, still laughing, 'Now come, walk, I show you.'

He skipped down the dirt track, leaving nothing for Willow to do but follow.

Her senses told her not to set foot into the tangled mess of a forest, it was sure to be packed full of spiders and snakes, but after a brisk ten-minute walk, mercifully, it thinned and grew brighter. Then things got far worse.

Within twenty strides they were nearing the edge of a cliff. Willow stopped, there was nothing but air as far as she could see.

Che sat on the verge, his legs dangling into the abyss as if he were sat on an arm chair in the safety of a living-room. Her stomach flipped. She shuffled toward him, desperate to pull him away to a safe distance, but not daring to venture that close.

In the far distance was the sea, beneath them a level part of the mountain, an enormous ledge. They were at least forty feet up from more forest and a succession of unexpected huge gilt golden roof tops.

It was the temple that Aaron had recognised, Wat Bang Riang. It stretched out in every direction, more like a village than one house of worship.

Willow stared, astounded, she could breathe in Rosa's photos, they were so close.

Che bowed his head respectfully, spellbound. 'I never think I see.'

'It's incredible,' Willow had no other words for it.

She could make out people moving like ants between the noble structures. Monks?

Che grabbed her hand, a glint in his eye, 'I see next clue!' he pointed to a huge statue, a dragon and pulled Bic's note from his pocket, 'It say here that *dragon looks down upon the chosen children*. He indicated in the direction that the dragon was smiling. 'The school over there.'

Willow squinted into the lower rainforest. There were no signs of more buildings and no evidence of a path or steps anywhere, but if that was where Bic wanted her to go she would.

'How are we supposed to get down there?' she knew before she had finished that she would not like the answer.

Che was already on the floor pulling ropes and harnesses, spiked climbing shoes and a series of locking devices which Willow had never seen before, out of their bags.

'You abseil?' he stated, more than asked, disentangling the equipment. 'You lucky. I have my things. Tourists love to climb, I rent to them and Aaron climbs a lot.'

'Of course he does,' Willow muttered. Aside from relationships was there nothing that Aaron didn't do well? aware that she ought to confess yet another of her own inabilities, but longing to get to the school, she lied. 'Not for a while. Maybe you should just give me a little refresher or we could look for another way? Walk down perhaps?'

Che had managed to lay out both climbing kits neatly, he huffed and stood up, 'We go and pack this up, drive back down. Maybe we find temple again, maybe another road coming from other side of Provence. I no sure. No one know way, not on map. We maybe lose a day and must come back here. What you want to do?' he waited.

Willow bit her lip, thinking of the man she had met in the Bangkok weekend market. If he could climb with one arm; it couldn't be that hard could it? 'I bet you do this all the time right?' she asked, optimistically.

Che was in his harness fixing all kinds of safety ropes and levers to himself, 'Sometime,' he shrugged, peering over the cliff edge. Standing unbearably close, 'I give you pointers and we go.'

Willow was astounded by the woman who was stepping into a harness, she hardly recognised herself and was secretly thrilled to be about to throw herself off a cliff.

Che's pointers were rudimental, at best, but he went ahead, lowering their bags first then making the descent look easy, securing the ropes and expertly navigating the ridges, placing hexes, cams and nuts as he went; all things that Willow had only just learnt the names of.

She lay down at the top of the cliff, crawled to the edge and peeked down, immediately wishing she hadn't.

Che was a small figure, waving up from the ground. Her head swam. Her heart, for once, hammered with the excitement of being alive and for what was to come, not for the fear of it.

'Come down, not too far, it ok.' Che yelled, holding his thumbs up happily.

'Just a minute!' She faltered, looking at her hands.

239

People do this with one arm.

She stood and gipped the rope around her waist with all her strength. She edged closer to the lip of the limestone cliff. Here goes nothing.

She turned around and leant back into the air, using one hand to hold onto the rope over her head and slowing herself with the one around her waist, she took her first few steps.

Quivering like a leaf, she stopped and tried to catch her breath.

Che called up to her, 'Willow you ok?'

She was unable to speak, frozen with uncertainty, she had to trust herself to get down safely.

'I come get you, hold on!' he sounded panicked.

She focused her energy on her arm and forced it out into the air, putting her thumb up and shouting, 'I'm Ok!'

She moved gingerly, gradually descending, the friction device at her waist keeping her in control. Her knees wobbled with each scuffling step but a grin held on her face, she wanted to scream, *look at me world, just look at me!*

She wriggled her toes, feeling the limestone, hard and reassuring beneath them. She paused for another moment, absorbing the warmth of the sun on her face and the breeze in her hair, closed her eyes and exhaled.

'Not far,' Che reassured her, his voice not far away.

'This is amazing!' Willow yelled, continuing her descent, faster than before.

When she reached the bottom Che was there to stop her from toppling on to the ground.

'You did it!' he cheered, collecting their ropes together.

She pulled herself to her feet and shook free from her harness, 'Yes I bloody well did!' she celebrated.

Their voices were loud in the quiet of the basin. The monks were a safe distance away. What would they think to her gate-crashing?

She didn't want to encounter any of them, but the silence made her feel on edge. 'Che are we trespassing?' she could not climb back up so even if they were, they were stuck there.

He shrugged, uncertain, 'Hope not.'

'Excellent.' She laughed. 'At least you're honest.'

They packed away their equipment, picked up their bags and quickly took the path which would lead them in the direction of the dragon's view.

To start with there was nothing more than a silhouette against the horizon. Che called out in greeting as a man stepped from the shadows.

As he came close Willow could see he had a large walking crook in his hand; he wore billowing trousers, a smock top and a broad smile.

Certainly not a monk.

If not a monk; what was he doing there? He walked closer and she saw he was Thai, no older than her and his hair was long, pulled back in ponytail which hung down his back.

When he spoke his English was perfect.

'Hi there. Are you Willow by any chance?'

Was this another of Bic's unexpected tricks?

'Hello,' was all she could think to say.

Che stepped in front of her, protectively.

The man stopped still; his smile so radiant it thawed Willow's reservations.

'It's Ok Che.' She reassured, stepping out from behind him.

The man moved closer, his hand outstretched and spoke again, 'Bic sent me a message to expect you. I've been keeping a lookout since last night in case you turned up early.'

Of course Bic had messaged without bothering to tell her that he was going to. She was hit by a mix of nervous exasperation and relief. 'Yes, I am Willow. This is my friend Che.'

The man shook his head, 'You really look just like her! Bic said you did, but I didn't know what to expect.' His eyebrows raised as he stepped closer.

Che didn't move a muscle, 'Who you?' he asked suspiciously.

The man smiled, 'I am Jay. I think that you've been looking for me?'

Chapter 26

Willow stood and stared, unable to move or speak. Only then did she realise, she hadn't truly expected to succeed. She hadn't planned what she would do or say if she ever found Jay.

Here he was. What to do?

He spoke first to Che, 'Thank you for bringing her safely home.'

The two men shook hands enthusiastically, like it was a normal meeting between friends in a bar.

'You must both come to my home at the school and see the place that brought us to be family.' Jay smiled, stepping forward and wrapping Willow in an embrace that took her breath away.

There was nothing for her to do but cry with relief.

They stayed in the forest crying, hugging, laughing with happiness until Che stood on a twig and the *snap* brought them back to reality. They couldn't stand there all day and poor Che was beginning to look a bit lost.

With Che to her side, Willow walked on, her arm linked though Jays, not daring to let him go for fear he would evaporate into nothing more than the fantasy he had always been.

He led them down a succession of twisting paths to a glade, where, in the distance was the most magnificent building she had ever seen. A huge white, four story, colonial house. It's weathered opulent façade and baroque relief mouldings bestowing European grandeur.

'I was not expecting this,' she gasped, 'Where did this come from? Why is it here?' It was so out of place in the jungle, she could not fathom how the labour would have got there let alone the building materials.

Jay lit up with pride, 'It is something very special. The children who come to live here have no mothers. This school is beautiful, strong and protective. Like a mother should be.'

Willow had tears in her eyes, 'What's it doing in the middle of the jungle?' It felt inexplicably normal to be talking to Jay, like they were old friends reunited after a prolonged absence, not that he was a stranger.

He regarded his beloved school, 'Portuguese settlers came here for tin mining in the around 1511. They bought their style and the Chinese built the houses all over Krabi province. Fantastic buildings sprung up like strange dreams realised from two clashing cultures. It was abandoned, like us all, when Dad and the first teachers arrived. I feel very privileged to live here.'

Willow knew she could trust Bic to get her back to her family. Then a thought occurred to her, 'I assume there is an easier path connecting you to the town?'

Jay nodded, 'Yes we are well connected, but it is well concealed, we don't want just anyone turning up. Our children need to feel safe and the monks in the temple crave solitude. We do not live a secret life, just a quiet one.'

'I assume Bic knows about this easier road?' Willow didn't need to ask.

Jay scoffed, amused, 'Of course he uses it every few months, but if he sent you the other way he did it for a reason.'

She shuffled along under the weight of her bag and climbing equipment, rubbing the sore patch on her leg where her abseiling harness had dug in, but she couldn't begrudge Bic. The journey had been what she didn't realise that she needed.

'Is Rosa here?' she almost yelled, eager. Perhaps Bic had been holding that back too?

'No, I'm sorry, she doesn't live here anymore. She lives just over the water on her island? Bic told you about the island?' Jay asked, leading them closer to the school.

Willow thought of the island which Rosa had mentioned in her last letter, Khrabkhraw. 'Rosa did in a way. Can we go there? Can we go now? You know I thought that she was dead my whole life. I would have come to find you years ago if only I had known the truth.' She was rambling, unable to control herself, her words bubbling over.

Jay put his hand on her arm, 'This is a lot for me to take in. We have plenty of time to talk, the rest of our lives if you like, but I cannot take you to Khrabkhraw today. It would be dark by the time we arrived and it is best not to take the boat out at night. I will explain everything in due time. First you must see the school and eat; you must be hungry? The boys will be having dinner shortly!'

'Yes I like food please.' Che called, happily.

Willow gave him an apologetic look, 'Sorry Che, the least you deserve is your dinner today.'

They'd skipped lunch and had to make do with crisps in the car.

As they approached the large playground and cultivated crop garden Willow saw a few cows wandering in the shady field that ran along-side. Chicken houses stood proud further on. Huge solar panels lay across the roof, such modern technology looking out of place so close to the ancient temple grounds. She was taking it all in when a bell rang, making her jump.

Moments later a swarm of boys of all ages, wearing crisp white shirts and smart shorts, came laughing and shouting from the building.

'Recess,' Jay explained before addressing the mass of children in English, 'Calm down. Come and meet my cousin from England.'

The children ran at them whooping joyfully, trying out their English greetings. Willow was touched by the pleasure she

245

seemed to have brought them, bemused by the way that they pawed at her backpack.

'They think you may have candy for them.' Jay laughed.

Willow rummaged in her bag delighted, 'I do!' she pulled out two packets of biscuits, three large melted Dairy Milk bars and a huge bag of Jelly babies.

Jay smiled, surprised at her stash.

'I learnt to always carry snacks for currency from my friend Lucia.' She explained. As quickly as she had pulled the treats out they were gone, along with the boys, who retreated to huddles to share out the bounty.

She inhaled deeply treasuring the details. The scent of the warm ground, the forest behind them, the gleaming white walls which glowed under the suns watchful eye.

She observed the children, amazed that there was no squabbling. 'They are so well behaved,' she marvelled, as they counted out the sweets and crisps one at time between themselves. 'They share so nicely.'

Che slid past, picked up a football and embarked on a long succession of keep ups, to the joy of the children, busying himself for their amusement.

Jay nodded, 'Most of them have come from nothing, they have had no one in their lives to care for them or to care for. To each other they are the only family they have ever known. They would share their last morsel. Sadly there are always children who will need a safe place to live and learn, but this is a place of happiness and hope. The children need to reflect and deal with the darker issues from their past, they can't forget, but they can heal and prosper. Many of them have gone on to great things. Politician's, teachers, doctors, they have achieved far more than what was ever expected or hoped for them. They are each a credit to my mother. I was just like them once.'

'Oh I know.' Willow said, realising with a start that she had intruded in to his life by reading the letters. She had taken secrets from him that he not offered to share. 'I'm so sorry. I found these letters and…'

Jay raised his hand, 'Don't worry, Bic told me, I know how you came to find us here. I'm glad you know about us, it gives us more time to learn about you.'

Willow's tension floated away, 'This must all be a bit weird for you, me coming to be here out of the blue?'

Jay didn't seem surprised, 'My life has been a series of weird events. It has been all the much richer for it. Now let's enjoy our food with these wonderful boys. Would you like me to introduce you as Sarah or Willow? Bic mentioned that your name was Willow now, but sometimes he speaks in riddles.'

'No one calls me Sarah anymore.' Willow assured him.

Jay kept walking toward the front door, 'Ok. I don't even know what name I was given by my birth parents. I can't remember. I like Willow.' He said waving to another teacher across the yard. 'Chi could you please get take my cousin's and friend's bags inside? Thanks'

'Mimi payha.' Chi, a middle-aged Thai man, called back, *no problem*. He rounded up two of the larger boys to collect up their things, leaving Willow unburdened.

The food hall was a jubilant flurry of chatter and richly-scented cuisine. The long tables and small chairs gave away the school for what it was, but it was like no teaching establishment she had been in, the ceilings elegant and high, the windows huge, looking out over sweeping views of the forest.

A plate was deposited in front of her by a young boy who stopped and surreptitiously stroked her hair. She turned, surprised by his fingers intertwined with her locks and jumped as he pulled a small clump out. His face was full of delight as he skipped away to get another plate for the table.

'Ouch' Willow smarted.

Jay looked up from his food, 'I don't think that Ace has seen fair hair outside of a movie before. He is from a remote hill tribe in northern Thailand, they don't encounter foreigners and he is not ready to go into town. Many of them believe that to touch fair hair is lucky, that your halo has dropped to your hair when you were touched by God.'

Willow nearly spat out her drink. *Touched by God*?

She contemplated Ace, who was grinning at her from across the hall, happy with his plunder.

'Why is he here?' she was unable to believe that no one from his family would want to care for him. He was too young, too small, too vulnerable to have no one on his side.

Jay sighed, 'He turned up one night, about two years ago, left in the playground, filthy and skinny. When I saw him, covered in sores, kicking a ball with bare feet, I wept inside. He was frightened and at deaths door, but all he wanted to do was play football! When all is done he is just a regular kid. Look at him now, with love and food, clothes and education he has thrived. He is very bright, loves gadgets and mending things, when he leaves this place I think he will have a good life. I look forward to seeing what he will become.'

Willow could hear the crack in his voice, see the pain in his eyes when recounting Ace's background. He must have heard hundreds of equally heart-breaking stories but hadn't hardened to the children's torment. She had barely managed to cope with her own.

She looked at Jay, he must have the weight of the world on his shoulders yet he seemed so at peace. She rubbed the sore patch on her head, happy to bring some hope to Ace despite her own discomfort, 'I hope he doesn't become a hairdresser!'

Jay toasted with his glass of water, 'May your locks bring him luck.'

A loud bang sounded from the kitchen.

Jay shot to his feet 'Excuse me, sounds like something I should check on.'

Che finished his food with a satisfied sigh, 'I think I can go now.' He stated happily.

Willow grimaced, 'Sorry Che after everything you've done for me, I've been rude, I didn't mean to ignore you. It's just that this is overwhelming. Please stay.'

He allayed her concern, 'I came for you. You safe. I need get back before it get dark.'

'Of course, you were working. Let me pay you for your time.' She reached in her bag.

Che quickly shook his head and hands, 'My pleasure today. I go Railay tomorrow. No problem. Aaron he needs me.'

Willow paused, 'You can't leave without telling me what is going on. I've been so tied up with myself I forgot to ask you properly.' Had something happened to Aaron? She hated that she cared.

Che considered his next words, 'Aaron say, not to tell you. You happy. I think you not need to know until later. Nothing you can do anyway. I tell you when we next meet. Will you be ok?'

Willow's head span with possible scenarios, each more awful than the last. 'I'll be fine.' she nodded, without a care for where she would sleep or how she would return to civilisation. 'It feels like I've come home.' It wasn't her that she was worried about.

Jay returned, having dealt with what he assured them was a regular drama in the kitchen and read Willow's worried expression. 'Is everything ok here?'

Che stood, satisfied that Willow was safe and keen to avoid her questions, 'All good. I need to go now. Thank you for dinner. We will meet again one day I hope.'

Jay walked Willow and Che out to the playground. 'You take the path to your right, keep walking until you pass the large wooden carved Buddha on the outskirts of the forest, then turn left and walk on for about another quarter of a mile. You will see an ancient stone tablet, about the size of a car door, push through the bush behind it and you will find a staircase to lead you to the top of the cliff. From there you can only turn right. If you keep walking you will find your way back to the only road that can take you down. I assume your car is parked at the opening to the forest?'

Che nodded as a child appeared in the school doorway behind them.

'Mr Jay,' he called.

Jay waved to him and turned back to Che. 'Thank you for bringing her safely to me.' He shook his hand warmly then rushed to tend to the child.

Willow turned back to Che not willing to be brushed off. 'Che what was has happened? I am happy and you don't want to ruin that, I understand, but I'm a grown woman and if something has happened to one of my friends I deserve to know. Maybe I can help? Please tell me the truth'

'There is nothing that any of us can do. There will be funeral there in three day on Railay.' His face was twisted, his light smile, vanished.

Her immediate fears were for Eric. He was well into his sixties, but he had seemed in great health. Lucia would have called if she was in trouble and Che was meeting up with Aaron. Perhaps there had been a diving accident. It must have been someone she had met briefly.

Che took her hand, 'Willow. Ben dead. Jin find him in pool at base of mountain, that lead to Yinga. He take a lot of drug and swim.'

Every. Single. Thing. Stopped.

Willow's legs grew weak, she squeezed Che's hand, needing to feel that he was real, she wasn't in a dream. His lips were moving, but she was deft. He led her to a bench.

'Was it....' She had to know, 'An accident?' Was this the *plan* that he had been hatching all along?

Che spoke gently, 'I think no. He try before, last year. He have diary in bag, he depressed for long time. I'm sorry. I think you make close friends at Yinga, you talk nice about him. He mentioned you a lot, in writing, you bring him some happiness in the end. '

'Yes, I thought we were close.' she whispered, picturing Ben smiling to her from his hammock, writing away. It was incomprehensible that he was gone. She wanted to say more but couldn't think of anything that made sense.

Che squeezed her arm, 'Then you can come to Railay Beach, he want his ashes to go there, he say so many times. *The Lost Sole's Club*, was his most happy place.'

Willow couldn't fully comprehend what he was saying, *his ashes*. 'Do you mean Aaron's place?' she felt she had to ask something.

'His resort, our bar. Long time ago he stop accepting guests, not leave his house when boy and wife die. I go to him and build bar next door. Build bar and friends come. That what happen.' Che explained as if he had thrown a small gesture of goodwill in his friend's direction, not built him a business.

Willow stared at him; she had always liked Che but she had assumed that his life was largely governed by Aaron's generosity, in employing him as a driver and a work colleague. Finally she saw that he was the strength that held Aaron together. She had underestimated him.

'Che you're a good friend to him and to me. What would we all do without you?' she sniffed, surging with affection through the darkness.

Che modest as ever, acknowledged her compliment with a smile and said no more.

'Aaron never spoke about his place much, just that it over-looks the sea. Why is it called *The Lost Sole's Club*? Something about shoes he said?'

She needed the normalcy of conversation to keep her going. How could Ben be dead? She had been with him two days ago, talking about her problems and his plans.

Che didn't appear to know how to guide the conversation either, so he allowed himself to be swept along on her tangent, 'Aaron put Phoenix shoes behind bar on shelf, so we all remember that he walk there one time. His life short, but he had a journey, like us all. One day we see too many shoes have been put on shelf. I hang them up, make curtains for Bar. Aaron say there are a lot of souls and soles in that place. He come up with name and I like it. It stuck.'

'Where did the other shoes come from?' Willow asked, thinking it all sounded a bit macabre.

'Before long many people come to bar. Many lose someone they love. They bring shoes to leave part of friend or family in beautiful place to walk there forever. Some people lose shoes in parties or leave on purpose, those stay too. Everyone go back to real life in office or building families. Nobody go home without leaving part of themselves in Thailand. Their sole's stay up on the hill.

Willow smiled as she remembered returning to her family farm after her parents had died, her mother's wellies were by the door, her father's smart shoes on the rack, still waiting for their owners to slip them on. Willow had worn the wellies, despite them being two sizes too big, and walked the farm for the entire day.

She liked to imagine her parents still there at the farm, walking the land, in the same way she could imagine Ben and Phoenix at peace by the beautiful ocean.

'It sounds special. A good place for Ben. When is the memorial?' she couldn't believe that she was saying the words.

'Four day.' Che sighed. 'But you miss Ben any place, pray, say goodbye anywhere. You stay with family if you not want to leave.'

Willow let the bulbous tears drop from her cheeks to her lap, 'He was part of my family too, you all are.' She whispered, 'I stopped making friends and shut myself away to avoid feeling this way again. It hurts too much to lose people.'

Che grinned beneath his own tears, making her feel as if everything was going to be ok, drawing her in for a hug, 'The price we pay for love is pain. Love worth pain I think.'

He turned his attention to the pathway that would take him back to his van. 'Aaron, he be very distressed, I must get back to him now. You be ok, you be very happy I think. You will see. We lose but we love, this is life.'

Willow nodded, numb. Then realised with a wave of guilt that Che had spent time with her when he was grieving himself. 'Why did you come on this trip? I thought that you had come to escape working with tourists at hotels. Why did you lie? Why didn't you tell me you had all of this going on?'

Che squeezed her hand, 'I feel very bad for Ben, I can cry all day, but I feel better help others, see happiness happening. You and Jay together, I helped to make happen. Aaron want me to help you, it make him smile for a few moments when I say I would be assisting you. Bring others joy, this is better than crying.'

She stared at him, grateful for his kindness, before Jays voice roused her. She dried her eyes quickly and turned to him.

He was standing in the doorway to the school, Ace at his heel, 'Willow would you like to come to my after-hours class? I don't like to think of you alone, but I cannot let the boys down, they love their extra English sessions and you being there would make it special for them.'

'Please come Ms pleassssssse.' Ace pleaded with a grin.

Jay smiled, unaware of her burning grief, 'He won't go to class unless you come.' He explained apologetically

Willow wanted to cry and scream at the world for being a dark and unfair place, as she had many times over the past year but she could hear Che's words repeating in her head, *bring others joy, this is better than crying.* She looked at Jay and to Ace who garnered such obvious pleasure from being around her. She halted her tears and gingerly got to her feet.

Che stood behind her, 'It is my time to leave. You mourn Ben where you feel best. Maybe I see you in Railay, if no, I see you soon.'

Willow turned to him, forcing a smile, 'Thank you Che, you have no idea how much you have helped me. I will think about Railay, it's too much for me to take in now.'

He shrugged as if it was nothing and waved to her then Jay, 'See you again Jay, take good care of my friend.'

Jay waved back 'No worries, we will.' He assured him, his arm around Ace's shoulders.

Che was disappearing in to the jungle before she could change her mind and beg him to stay.

Jay and Ace were waiting, there was no time for tears. She took a deep breath and walked towards them, with each step fighting the urge to crumble.

'Ace can you show me the way to your class room?' she asked, taking his hand and stepping though the school doors, leaving her pain in the courtyard.

Chapter 27

Forty young boys were squashed into neat rows of seats, behind old wooden desks, alert and poised. The room fell silent as Willow snuck in behind Jay, all faces turning then erupting with giggles and chatter.

Jay held up his hand, 'Hush now. You know the rules, only English in this class,' he coaxed.

The boys settled respectfully.

'Ter bing fen cong cun mai?' one of the boys yelled, to the delight of his class mates.

Jay was about to address him when Willow rested her hand on his arm, 'No I am not his girlfriend, I am his cousin.' Her voice was shaky with emotion, but she pushed on determined not to break. 'Do any of you know where London is?' She needed to talk, to distract herself from her aching heart.

A sea of hands shot up.

Jay pointed, 'Yes Rik.'

Rik grinned proudly, 'It's the Capital of England, a long way away in Europe Mr Jay.'

Jay pulled Willow a chair at the front of the class and made his way behind his desk. 'I warned you, these are bright boys! Now we are going to play a game today.' He clapped his hands and rallied them in a game of *I spy*.

Willow was surprised when watching the eager pleasure on the children's faces, a wave of amusement replaced her pain. She even found cause to laugh as the game gravitated toward her as the theme, G – Girl, F – Foreigner and the one she liked the most B – Beautiful.

The children were reviving a latent desire. She had always loved being a teacher, watching her pupils grow and succeed, but teaching adults had been different, if they didn't want to learn there was little she could do. There in Jay's school the children were hungry for knowledge, she could feel it in the air and see it in the complex work that hung on the walls. The difference a good teacher could make was immeasurable. The difference she could make?

As the lesson continued she was drawn to help with structured conversations, phraseology and pronunciation. They conversed about animals and favoured colours, counting and enjoyed sports. From time to time Willow would catch Jay's eye, to make sure she wasn't taking over, he would smile encouragingly and go back to focusing on the other students.

The time flew, until the sound of the bell signalled the end of the school day. The boys sprang from their seats and ran out to play.

Jay nudged her as they collected the text books, 'You are great with them, a natural.'

Willow swelled with pride, but had to put him right, 'I'm not a natural, I was actually a trained teacher.'

Jay wasn't having it, 'That's like saying you *were* a girl. You still are! Once a teacher always a teacher.

Willow had to agree.

What did you teach?' he asked.

She may have turned her back on her job, but the calling was as much a part of her as her hair colour, 'OK I am a teacher. I taught languages, but only ever to adults. It's different teaching children. I never thought that I particularly liked them before, but they are amazing! They absorb everything so quickly. It must be a very rewarding career for you?'

Jay packed away his things, laughing 'You don't like children? I think you might be in the wrong place.'

Willow laughed, realising how ridiculous she must sound. 'I think I was a bit scared of them. I wasn't sure how to talk to them about anything aside from cartoons and games, neither of which I know much about, but these kids are different.'

'Not as scary as English kids?' Jay teased.

Willow smiled but decided not to take the bait, she knew when she was being ribbed. She could see the child within Jay had never fully left him despite his position of responsibility in the school.

'There's more to what I do here, but the best part of my day is being in the classroom.' He said opening the door and leading them down the cool narrow corridor. 'We are looking for a teacher. The pay is small but fair, the accommodation and food are free and as you can see for yourself, the rewards are amazing!'

Willow had been worried that she wouldn't be accepted and there he was asking her to stay, even before she had told him about the money. It had been the best and worst day.

She considered the whitewashed, weathered walls, crammed with drawings, paintings and scripts. She ran her hand across the etched surface, feeling the pulse of the place beneath the surface. The school was a home, a cocoon of safety, full with makeshift family and love. It was everything that she had been looking for, but it would mean turning her back on everything she had known in England.

'I think we need to talk about the past before we can consider the future don't you?'

Jay nodded in agreement, 'Bare it in mind, a qualified language teacher is a rare jewel here, many of the boys will go on to work in the tourist industry, so your knowledge of all European languages would be a real asset. Come and see where I live. See if the accommodation can convince you to stay.' He Smiled, his cards on the table.

Her pace slowed, his comment catching her off-guard. When was the last time she had felt she brought value to anyone? An *asset*. The word sunk in and she realised it was true, there was a lot she could offer.

'Do you live far from here?' she asked, unable to think about her future clearly, she had to change the subject.

Jay was leading her up a series of staircases.

'Up here. There are no other properties fit for habitation for miles, the other teachers have their own flats. I can oversea the boy's wellbeing properly and I'm yet to have a wife. I haven't been too successful with women, I have a lot on my plate, but the boys, they are my family. It all makes sense, but more than that. This is the first place I ever felt safe. I love staying here.' He grinned, happy with his lot in life.

Willow laughed, 'This is all so crazy. Of course I knew that we were around the same age but it hadn't occurred to me that you could easily be married and have a whole separate family. Part of me had been expecting to find the boy from the photos.'

In front of her was a man. She felt foolish, sweeping in to his life, presenting herself as some kind of saviour with fists full of cash. He was clearly content with his life and career. He had a damn sight more than she had.

At the top of the stairs he put his key in the lock and turned to her, 'What photos?'

Willow shook her head, 'We have a lot of ground to cover.'

His spacious loft conversion sat above the school, an unexpectedly modern bachelor pad. She had expected a spiritual hut, like Bic's home. Instead she found a fully equipped kitchen, capacious lounge with a widescreen TV and two bedrooms.

'It's all been redone but this is where I lived with Mum and Dad, when I was little.' Jay explained making his way in to the kitchen, 'Please make yourself at home, I will fix us some drinks.'

Willow slumped onto the large soft sofa imagining what it had been like as a family home. 'Jay I'm sorry about your father.'

She heard a piece of cutlery being dropped in the kitchen followed by a long silence.

'Thank you. I try to remember that I was very blessed to have him for as long as I did, but I still miss him.'

He reappeared with two delicate cups of green tea and settled himself beside her. 'Bic told me about your parents. I am sorry for your loss also. It is very new for you. It really will get better.'

She thought of Ben, how short their time had been, of her parents and all the life they would miss out on. She wanted to cry, but there was so much to say and she sensed that if she gave into tears she wouldn't be able to stop and they'd get nowhere.

She pulled herself together and retrieved Rosa's box of letters and photos from her bag, which was waiting for her in the corner. She handed them to him. It was easier to let the past do the talking.

To begin with he appeared perplexed, then as he dove deeper into the treasures his face lit up, he took his time over each image, particularly the ones of his father, as Willow outlined how she had come to find them.

He was quiet as she filled him in on the lies she had been told about Rosa's death and her confusion over the family rift Rosa had so often alluded to in the letters. They spoke for over an hour.

She was in two minds if she should tell him about the final letter she had received at Yinga, but he was so enthralled in the photos she decided to let him discover the answers in the words if he wanted them.

Then the moment came, 'Did Bic tell you that I have something I need to tell you; well give you, actually.'

Jay shook his head, 'Something else?'

Willow went to the bottom of the box and pulled her mother's will from it. She passed it to him, her hands trembling with excitement. It was not her gift to give, it was better to let her mother explain.

She sat quietly while he read, impatient to see his thrilled expression when he realised that he was a wealthy man.

When he finished his eyes were moist, 'I see.'

His reaction was not exactly what she had expected. Where was the excitement, the gratitude, the thrill? He must be in shock.

Willow patted his arm, 'You must go to the bank in the next two days to cash this cheque. If you don't the money will be lost. You understood that bit right?'

She could not read his thoughts; his expression was blank. 'I can't believe I found you in time, I was so worried that I would be too late and you would lose what is rightfully yours.'

'It will not be lost, it will go elsewhere,' he reminded her, folding the papers. 'It will go to you and Claire. It says so right here.' He was quiet for a long time. 'I didn't know I had another cousin. My mother always suspected, but she never knew for sure. How does Claire feel about your parent's money being shared with me?'

Willow had almost forgotten about Claire, or she had been trying to. How was she supposed to explain that Claire didn't want to know him, that she was selfish and greedy? A selfless man like Jay would find it hard to accept. He had been rejected by his parents as a child, yet he had grown into such a giving and loving man. She couldn't tell him he wasn't wanted again.

'Claire will come around. I have come a long way to give you this money. It was always meant for you. It was what my mother wanted. It is what I want. That's all that matters.' She held up a cheque and thrust it toward him. 'You could buy yourself a house, or hire more staff for the boys, sponsor their further education even. It would make you a wealthy man.'

Jay pushed the cheque away, 'I don't want a house.'

Willow could see that the flat had great sentimental value, but she doubted he could afford to build a house even if he wanted too. He deserved to have the option, 'What if you do have a wife and family one day, this money would help with that, you might want a house then?' She was confused by the amused look on his face.

'This place was good enough for my family.' He reminded her, not unkindly.

Willow was confused 'I'm sorry, have I offended you?'

He smiled, 'certainly not. I'm just surprised and trying to think this through. Your mother would have wanted this money to bring us together and it has. She wanted to heal our family. If I take this money, I will push Claire away and I don't want that. We have found each other and that is all that matters.'

Willow pushed harder, her eyes pleading, 'Jay this is not something that can wait. Claire does not need it. I do not need it. We were left plenty.' She held the cheque, toward him, once again. 'Please take it for the school if nothing else?' She begged.

'I will think about it.' He promised without conviction, leaving the cheque in her hands.

Willow took a deep breath, searching for the words that could reach him. Why was he being so difficult about accepting it; pride?

Jay stood, 'You've told me so much, but I have so much left to explain. I think it's easier for me to show you, then you will understand. We need to make a very early start tomorrow, I've had a bed made up for you in the spare room. I was up most of last night waiting in the forest in case you arrived. Do you mind if I get an early night? I'll be just across the hall if you need me. Feel free to look around the grounds or help yourself to food from the kitchen. The boys and the staff will be up for hours yet and the lights never go out.'

He stood up. 'Willow please do not worry. You don't fully understand what we do here but you will tomorrow and things will become clear. May I take these with me?' He held the box of his mother's correspondence.

Willow nodded, 'They're as much yours as they are mine.' Despite her confusion it felt good to be sharing her family's past with someone, she had hoped for the chance of future but she was beginning to see that where they had come from was as important as where they would end up and both wanted the answers.

When Jay shut the door, her heart seized, she was alone.

Teaching the class had diverted her thoughts of Ben, talking with Jay had kept her from acknowledging the pain that was aching to her core.

With nothing left to occupy her mind she was afraid.

She unpacked and repacked her things. She learnt some more Thai phrases. She toyed with the idea of going for a walk, but grief was stalking her, moving closer. What if she ran in to one of the children? They did not deserve to witness her grief. She considered waking Jay, but for what? She didn't want to talk.

She watched some Thai TV and finally wrestled with sleep, the air was stifling, the ceiling fan doing little to dent its intensity or dissuade the mosquitos.

She gave in, got up and went back to the lounge where she gazed out the window at the darkened rainforest. She sunk to her knees, not praying to God as she had thought that she might, instead she spoke to Ben. She told him she was sorry for not being capable of helping him, she told him about the events of her day and how he had helped her to get there, she sent him love and peace and finally she said goodbye.

In the air she could smell the scent of his ubiquitous spliffs. She could feel his presence as if he were swaying in his hammock behind her, listening as she spoke.

Che was right, she didn't need to be at a memorial to remember, he would always be with her.

'Willow are you awake?' Jay whispered. 'What are you doing on the floor?'

She struggled to sit, her fingers still clasped together and stretched, 'I'm sorry I must have dropped off. I was…'

'You were praying.' Jay smiled, approving, 'You picked a good spot for it. That's where I like to sit to remember Dad.'

'Do you think he's still here?' She didn't want to burden him with her truth, she had arrived with enough emotional baggage.

Jay nodded straight away, 'Part of him. I don't mean like a ghost or anything like that, but he's in the choices I make and the man I am. I try to make him proud so his influence will be here forever.'

'From what I've seen I think he'd be very proud.' She told him, 'Have I got time for a shower?' she blustered, feeling her emotions rising. She needed to clear her thoughts of Ben before she could focus on what lay ahead.

'Sure, I'll fix us some coffee and then I will take you to Mumma.' Jay beamed.

Willow could hardly believe it was happening.

'Ahhhhh,' she squealed as she stepped under the shower, she had not got used to the icy hit of a Thai shower which awakened her senses in a rather aggressive fashion.

She towelled herself dry in seconds, pulled on fresh clothes and joined Jay in the lounge, drinking her coffee in a hurry and forcing herself to eat some of the mango which Jay had laid out for her. Her appetite was meagre with the twisted anticipation and grief, but she had no idea what kind of food would be available on the remote island or how long the trip would be. The idea of eating on a long tail made her stomach flip, she was uncertain if it was the idea of the swaying oversized canoe or that the last time she had been on one she had been wrapped in Aaron's arms?

She was sad to find that the boys were still asleep when they left so she bid farewell to the school in silence, vowing to return soon.

As they walked away the sun was beginning to rise and the forest smelt sweet with the promise of a new day.

In due course they found Jays minivan and with relief Willow found his driving was far more cautious than Che's; tamed by years of ferrying his precious cargo of children to and from town, she assumed.

There seemed to be an unspoken agreement that the conversation would stay light. Willow sensed that Jays emotions were as alert as hers were conflicted. He had read all the letters in the privacy of his own room but said nothing of them. Maybe he was concerned that Rosa would not be as pleased to see her after all?

Whatever the reason she was grateful to be amused with wonderful anecdotes about the boys and what it had been like to grow up at the school among a band of brothers.

Jay gave away precious little about Rosa, but he was fascinated in Willow's early life, something that she had considered to be, comparatively, mundane in the extreme. He enjoyed every detail of her years growing up on the farm and following one story of an Easter egg hunt across the land he erupted with laughter.

'What?' she inquired.

'I too have great memories of such egg hunts at the school, Mumma loved them, she'd travel miles to find a supermarket that sold *Cadbury* eggs. It had to be exactly how her dad did it. I guess no matter how far we travel we take a part of home with us. Our mothers were very different ladies, but both were strong loving and nurturing. It is so sad that they never settled their differences. Don't you think?'

'I've been thinking that since I found the letters. They could have brought something special to each other's lives.' Willow thought he was going to finally talk about the letters but he didn't.

Jay slowed the car, approaching an enormous electric gate, picking his words carefully, 'Willow once all of this is done you must speak to your sister. It's been bothering me all night. Don't let history repeat itself.'

The headmaster in him affected her despite her desire to dismiss his request. She knew that he was right, 'I will,' she promised and meant it.

She wasn't sure if it was Ben's death or their family expanding in such unexpected ways, but she felt like she needed her sister more than she needed to hate her. Thoughts of Claire, as always, led to thoughts of the will.

'Are you sure we can't just go to the bank now before we leave. You will have to race back tomorrow if you don't do it now. What if the rains come again and we are stranded?' she had to give it a last shot.

He shook his head, 'No thank you. I've thought about it and I don't want it, not for me or the boys. It wouldn't be right.'

Before Willow could protest Jay manoeuvred the van carefully up to the gate and swiped an identity card in front of a scanning machine. A voice crackled through the intercom and he issued a series of numbers, before the gates slowly creaked open.

Willow had expected to go to the beach and find a man with a boat. The sea was visible in the distance, but she couldn't make out any signposts or tourists. She hadn't for miles.

She stiffened as a man in a formal blue uniform holding a large gun waved them into the compound. CCTV cameras oscillated this way and that as they parked in a small garage. It reminded her of a military base where extra-terrestrials may be harboured, rather than boats.

She stepped out warily. The man with the gun came to them immediately, a scowl on his serious face, morphing into a welcoming smile when he saw Jay. She could understand fragments of their conversation, which centred around a good weather forecast and something about other people joining them. What other people? Jay hadn't mentioned anyone.

He beckoned for Willow to join their conversation, 'Willow this is Win. He looks after the boats here and most importantly our boat.'

'Hello,' Willow said politely to the soft and happy looking man with his enormous gun. Her mind raced; what kind of boat could Jay have that needed such protection? She had heard stories of islands in Thailand that were used for growing drug crops. She felt a growing urge to run. 'I thought that we would be leaving from a beach or the main pier?'

Jay shook his head, appearing alert. 'We can't travel that way. It would bring too much attention to the island; this bay is closer to where we are heading and some of the patrons need this degree of privacy. We don't want tourists getting wind of it. Be patient. I told you that it will all become clear.' He kept looking to the gate.

Was he checking that they hadn't been followed?

'Why do you need such secrecy? How much privacy can a group of street children and damaged young adults need?'

Willow muttered not wanting to sound rude but feeling deeply concerned.

Jay took her hand, 'There's nothing to worry about, the journey will be a long one. I will explain all I can on the way and the rest, you'll understand, when we reach Khrabkhaw.'

What else could she do? She cautiously followed the men to a short pier which stretched out into the bay where five grandiose yachts were moored. Some small ribs and one enormous boat completed the collection of stunning vessels. Willow was as equally captivated as confused.

The largest of the boats was like something from a rapper's music video, glistening in the tropical sun, bobbing gently on the mornings swell. She scoured the dock wondering which of the small speed boats would be theirs.

'Jay how long will this crossing take? I might just nip to the toilet before we set off?' Should she put in an emergency call to Che; run away to the main road perhaps? Get away while she could?

'Don't worry there are two on board.' He gestured towards the rapper's super yacht that lay in front of them.

Willow rolled her eyes. Why did men have to joke about everything, even at inappropriate times? 'Where's our boat really?

Jay jumped aboard looking out of place with his long hair and billowing linin clothes. Turning back, 'Come aboard,' he requested.

She was hesitant; were they going to get into trouble for trespassing? To her astonishment Win smiled, reassuringly waved to her, turned and left them to it.

Disbelieving she stepped aboard the 120ft brilliant white and chrome boat, speechless, thoughts of drug fields whirling. She waited for an explanation; none came, Jay was too busy enjoying her confusion.

'Let me show you around while we wait for the crew to turn up.' Jay led her towards some steps that lead to the lower floor, before she could say or ask anything more.

Surely it wouldn't hurt to have a look around before they went on their way.

'Oh my god' she gasped as she took in the upper level. There were four upholstered sun beds poised, awaiting their loungers and a hot tub behind a fully stocked bar. 'Jay I don't understand; is this the boat that will take us to the island?'

'Yep. Follow me and we can put your things away.'

He was already walking away with their bags.

She could see that he knew his way around. Perhaps they were traveling as part of the crew?

Willow stepped downstairs marvelling at the interior, the ceilings were tiled with glittering silver surfaces and inlaid lights, the walls clad with mirrors and chrome inlays. There was a huge TV with four cream leather sofas in the lounge area and leading off there were three luxurious double bedroom suites.

As she stood, aghast, Jay disappeared with her things into a room. Willow followed laughing at the surreal site, inside there was a double bed with satin sheets and a fur throw. 'This is just...' She didn't know what to say.

Jay jumped in, looking undeniably smug, 'Not what you expected?'

'No it certainly is not!' she conceded. 'Just what kind of people go to Khrabkhaw? I thought that it was a retreat for the boys from the school, ex pupils, people who had suffered terrible troubles in their lives? This is built for rock stars and actors isn't it?'

She didn't want to admit it, but she was disappointed. She had been under the impression that Rosa was a humanitarian not a hotelier for the rich and famous.

Jay nodded, 'And politicians, but you won't find any there at this time of year. They stick to high season exclusively.

Too much chance of rain for them now. It is a bit excessive I'll admit, but just imagine how even seeing a boat like this can inspire the children and they are far worthier of spoiling than self-important rock stars! Trust me the kids step foot on here, forget where they have come from and focus on where they want to be. Suddenly I'm surrounded by wannabe millionaires all eager to study and get well-paid jobs. It shows them that even wild dreams can be a reality. I was like them once and now I own all of this.'

Willow was struck dumb for a moment, '*You* own this?'

Jay poured two iced waters chuckling, 'Why not?'

To Willow's relief he looked amused rather than annoyed at her surprise.

'Just because a person is born *disposable* doesn't mean they have to stay that way. We are all capable of owning all of this.' He turned in circles, his arms in the air at the centre of the opulent surroundings.

'Some incredible boys have passed through the doors of that school and those children have gone on to become wonderful men. One, Jack, even made it to the top of government - Head of the Environmental Preservation committee. It had always been Mum's dream to have a place like Bic's sanctuary, but somehow along the way, the more that she spoke of it the bigger it became. One of the wonders of being a teacher is that you always have a captive audience. She told us so often that we could have whatever we wanted as long as we put in the hard work, that we believed her.'

He threw himself down onto the sofa.

Willow wanted to slap herself. She shook her head in disbelief 'I've been such an idiot, I imagined every stereotype. I thought you might be desperate for my money and lonely for my company.'

Jay was having fun at her expense, laughing as he drank, his good humour saving her blushes. 'I can't remember the last time I was desperate for anything, but I was keen to surprise you.'

Willow laughed, 'Consider me surprised. Was it Jack who bought the boat?' she had so many questions. Money like that didn't come easily.

'A dream like mums takes a team effort to make it a reality. Jack was like a brother to me and he is responsible for getting us the retreat, the whole island. It was a nature reserve, but like everything in Thailand, it had a price. A hotel had been built on it illegally years ago, bribery would have taken place to get it there in the first place, but that was not uncommon. It had been frequented and exploited by the elite. When the Tsunami hit the Land Rights and Planning Commission was thrown up in the air. When the government finally switched, Jack heard about it. He knew it could be used to inspire boys like him, that Mumma needed a project to keep her going after we lost my father. The island and hotel had fallen to ruin. The jungle and sea had taken over. No one had been permitted to go there, no one seemed to know what to do with it. Jack and Mumma came up with a proposal together, one which would benefit everyone, the government included.' He smiled, 'I bought the boat. I am running the school, but that doesn't really pay. I also do the marketing, the bookings, handle the VIP's special requests, report to the government and environmental lobbies from the retreat. So you see I have no need for your money, but I have need for family, you and Claire are worth far more to me.' He explained sincerely.

Willow was impressed, the island set up was far more than anything that she had imagined. Her preconceived ideas of what was awaiting her were shattered and, yet again, she found herself clueless as to what she was heading into. She knew better than to waste her time asking for details. She'd have to wait.

Jay drained his drink, 'Do you want to have a nap or a bite to eat? You are welcome to use the hot tub on deck if you like? I'm going to set myself up on a sun bed. I've got some work to do, but I can't sit inside on such a glorious day.'

Willow had been washing in cold rain water that morning, the lavishness of the boat was like a dream. She could hardly believe it was true. 'A dip in the hot tub would be incredible.'

The boat hummed to life.

Jay left to check in with the captain and her to change into her bikini. When she went to the deck they were already out in the ocean, the mainland slipping from view; just where was she heading?

Jay was sitting on a sunbed in his shorts, working on his laptop, the successful business man he was and not the poor teacher she had assumed. They bounced along for nearly six hours, in which time Willow indulged in the hot tub three times and slept on a sun-lounger, unable to peel herself away from the view to her cabin.

They shared a fabulous continental breakfast, a fresh sea food lunch and talked endlessly.

When the time came for Jay to return to his computer, she sat back content and thought of how he was filling a hole in her life that had been waiting for him.

When they talked there was an inherent familiarity and comfort born from the fact that he was family. She knew immediately that they would always have each other no matter what. Why didn't she feel like that about Claire? Had she ever tried? She couldn't remember ever sitting down with her for hours and really getting to know her or what made her tick. She didn't know how Claire felt about being a mother or what her hopes for the future were. The truth was that she didn't really know her at all.

When an island came into view, Willow shot to her feet 'Is that?'

Jay looked up, smiling when he laid eyes on Khrabkhaw, 'That's it.'

It was the type of Asian fantasy dreamt up on the covers of travel journals. Palm trees, white powder sands, transpicuous waters of such clarity to show off the other world beneath.

As they grew close she could make out a large hotel-like building of at least four floors with an enormous swimming pool. A few longtails and a large speedboat were anchored, formal pathways twisted from the hotel to a few other buildings, a restaurant and meeting room perhaps? It was a sprawling set up, a resort far away from all the other resorts.

The engine cut and they floated closer. Then there was a woman on the shore. Willow's heart was in her throat, she had been utterly unprepared to look into her mother's face, it was as if she had risen from the grave.

Rosa was the image of Caroline, save for a large scar which fell across her eyebrow. She smiled to her from beneath the swathes of long silver streaked blond hair, waving happily as they moored the boat against the small pier. Jay quickly set off running towards his mother.

'Come on Willow.' He yelled as he went.

She followed suit, speeding down the walkway.

Rosa walked toward them with a limp, her vivid skirt billowing, her face a luminous wash of delight. Willow wondered if she recognised her or perhaps had been tipped off that she was coming?

Then she shouted. *'My boy my beautiful boy!'* and ran toward Jay who picked her up in a hug.

'I didn't think that you were coming back for two weeks. I heard the boat coming in and I just knew. This is a wonderful surprise!' Rosa squealed, peaking around him to look at Willow. She stopped smiling and stepped away from Jay, her hands shaking as they flew to her mouth.

She gasped, 'Is it?'

Rosa staggered toward Willow and embraced her so tightly that Willow thought she would never be able to disentangle herself.

'Sarah!' Rosa exclaimed, pulling back, starring into Willows teared eyes, sobbing with delight, not letting her go as she turned to Jay, 'I told you she would come!'

Chapter 28

Rosa's house was not far from the pier, set back from the sea and away from the main hotel grounds. It was a two-storey wooden structure, nestled into the forest upon a cliff ledge, safe from the tides.

A hammock big enough for two and a selection of beanbags littered the veranda. Playing cards and empty glasses lay, discarded on a low table.

Rosa moved up the front steps with a lopsided walk and started collecting the debris, 'Please excuse the mess, I was not expecting company today. Some of the staff came over last night.' She apologised, disappearing inside, arms full.

Willow loved the house immediately, the views, the ambiance, the way the hammock looked as if it were waiting for Ben.

She had worried that Rosa, as a widower, may have shied away from people and life, but Rosa had gone on with happiness still in her life and it warmed her to see it.

'Never play cards with Mumma, she's a shark. Just ask the secretary of state!' Jay said, raising a bemused eyebrow.

Willow was eager to hear all her Aunts tales.

'You should have seen my mother play Bridge. The neighbours were actually scared to play against her!'

They exchanged a look, each knowing.

'The hearts of the women who raised us had been the same. Their spirits not so different.' Jay summarised.

Rosa returned from the house and threw a wash cloth at him, 'Stop with your gossip, you're still in the doghouse. How could you not tell me you were bringing her? Did Bic know about this? Don't answer that, I already know the answer. Anyway don't scare her away.' She rushed through her thoughts vocally as she collected glasses and hurried Willow to sit on a pair of floor cushions.

Willow didn't know what to think or say, instead she rested her eyes on Rosa. Her eyes were the eyes of her mother, the rest of her face a painting which caught a likeness, but not the soul. Rosa was a different type of lady in every way. Willow tried to imagine her on the farm in Surrey wearing a pinny or her mother living in Rosa's house on the beach. It was incomprehensible.

Rosa took a deep breath and held up a clinking jumble of empty bottles, 'Let me get rid of these and fix us some refreshments. I think we will be talking for a long time! Sarah is coconut juice ok for you?' she said, rushing back toward the door.

Jay yelled, 'Mumma, she prefers to be called Willow.'

Rosa stopped and turned slowly, smiling, 'Of course she does, that's perfect.' She wandered inside muttering to herself happily, 'Well well well.'

Willow was delighted, Rosa understood.

'Have I missed something?' Jay asked.

'There is a huge Willow tree on our family farm. Where our mothers grew up. Our grandmother died sitting under that tree. She had been reading a book in the Sun, her favourite pastime and she drifted away. Grandad always took the girls there to read to them and to remember. My mother would do the same with us.' She explained to Jay. It was a small word, but one that made Willow pause, *us,* Claire was part of her no matter how far she ran. She could see it clearly in Rosa, Caroline was still a part of her all these years later.

'Our family willow tree is strong, it's seen and been through so much, yet it keeps growing. When I boarded the plane to come here, someone asked me my name. I thought, *I don't like who I am or what I have become.* I wanted to be strong, to go on.' She thought of Aaron and the moment that they met. He had bought out the best in her from the start.

'I worry that one day I will wake up and remember my birth name was Barry.' Jay joked.

Rosa returned, her eyes intently on Willow as she lowered herself onto a bean bag with a soft moan. 'How long has it been since Caroline passed away?' Her chestnut skin grew ashen.

Willow was caught off guard. How could Rosa have heard the news of her mother's passing?

Rosa focused on the sea, 'I saw Caroline about a year ago,' she explained, reading Willow's mind, 'She was as the day I left her, so young. I was meditating in the hills and, just like that,' she clicked her fingers, 'Caroline was there, as clear as you are to me now. I thought she was about to say something, then she disappeared on the breeze.'

Rosa sighed, 'I must sound like a crazy woman, but I knew that she was saying goodbye.' She wiped a tear from her cheek. 'Tell me what happened; was it cancer like mother?'

Willow shook her head, 'My Dad was driving to visit my sister Claire, mum was in the passenger seat. A tire blew and my father lost control, the car skidded across the road and they were hit by a truck coming in the other direction. I was told that they were killed instantly.'

It never failed to amaze her how her entire world changed in that moment.

'Peter is gone too?' Rosa's voice came out in a quiver, her hand protectively laid on top of her heart.

Willow cursed herself. Her father had played a huge roll in Rosa's life and she had delivered her the news as if she had been a stranger. 'I'm sorry, I know he meant a lot to you.'

Rosa didn't seem to hear her. 'My lucky sister.'

Willow didn't understand and couldn't help but feel defensive, 'If they had survived I would have been inclined to agree.'

Rosa's eyes were firmly on the sea.

'My sister lived for many years with the love of her life and never had to live a moment without him. She got to see her babies grow to be women. She lived on the farm her whole life, it was her sanctuary, her paradise. She was born into the life she always wanted. Caroline had more than anyone could wish for. Love. Family. Contentment. Lucky Caroline.' Rosa nodded, her face lighting up despite her tears. 'I am pleased to think of my sister's life spent so well.'

Willow reached out and held Rosa's soft hand, thinking of when Aaron had told her that she was *lucky* to be travelling alone, she had seen it as the worse thing imaginable, as was her parents passing. Everything had two sides. 'I'm sorry you never came back to each other.'

Rosa nodded, 'Thank you, but I made my peace with it a long time ago. We were like two pieces of the same cloth, sewn into different tapestries, we never matched up. I doubt either of us would have changed our fate.'

Willow had to agree, her mother was never unhappy, she had truly taken pleasure from every day, but that wasn't to mean that she was unaffected by the rift with Rosa, 'She never forgot you. She kept all of your letters.'

Willow ran to her bag and pulled out the box of letters and photographs, which Jay had returned to her. 'I shouldn't have these anymore, they belong to you.'

Rosa gasped taking the box, lifting the lid and reaching for the photographs. 'Oh Jay look at you!'

She handed over photo after photo of him as an infant.

Jay laughed, 'I've seen these already. I was happy that you didn't have any pictures of that haircut to embarrass me with when I do finally bring a girl to meet you. Put those back in the box.' He instructed as he examined one image of himself, Rosa and Wan. 'That was the day we got my papers to say I was legally yours. Dad was so young. Can I keep this?' he asked Rosa.

A child seeking mother's approval regardless of his position within the rest of society.

Willow glowed, it felt right to reunite the photos with their true owner, 'I would never have found you without those photos and letters, they lead me on quite an adventure.'

Rosa was smiling as she leafed through, absorbing the memories, 'It was quite an adventure creating them. It seems fitting that they have given you memories of your own.'

Willow had lost herself in Rosa's stories and images so many times, she had believed that she knew her life as well as her own.

'I thought that you were dead, otherwise I would not have read them. At first, I was looking for an address, but as you know you didn't leave one for years. Mum left a large amount for money for Jay. I only had a month to find him, by the time I found out.' She cursed Claire again, she could have found them months ago, perhaps her life would not have faltered as it had? 'When I did find him he turned the money down. Now it will be split between my sister and I.'

'Quite right.' Rosa dabbed her eyes, not needing more details, 'I can't believe that Caroline cared about my Jay. I never heard a word for so many years that I cancelled my PO box, checking and finding it empty every month was too much for me. I knew that she could find me if she wanted, the clues were there. Part of me wanted her to work for it, to prove she wanted me back. She didn't.'

Rosa absentmindedly turned the wedding ring that she still wore. 'A well-meaning friend reported me missing after the Tsunami and it spiralled out of control. It's very strange to find out that you are legally dead! It was difficult to convince the authorities that I was alive, I had none of my paper work and my bank accounts were all frozen. Then they told me that my relatives had been informed of my *death* and I was relieved. It was a fresh start, but I never forgot her, or you Willow. Now it seems she had us in her thoughts too Jay.' She reached for his hand, her eyes full with emotion.

'Mumma I am so pleased for you,' Jay stood and brushed himself off. 'I am going to check the monthly reports and take your classes today. You two should have your time together. Were you leading the lunch time mediation on Si Ton beach?'

Rosa nodded, 'Thank you darling.'

She turned to Willow 'He's so kind. Do you know any nice single girls? One day I won't be here and I want him to have a life full with family of his own.' She stopped and dried her eyes, 'But now he has you, a cousin, amazing!' Her relief was audible.

Jay started down the stairs, laughing, 'Mumma don't you ever stop? I will see you both for dinner.'

Rosa's eyes were twinkling, 'We can talk here but come for a walk with me and you'll see what it is we really do here.'

The complex comprised of one main hotel building, twelve luxury town house-style apartments, and twenty separate deluxe beach chalets lining a stretch of the beach. To the West of the island was an impressive farm, where chickens, ducks, cows and pigs supplied the milk, eggs and meat for the guests. A rice paddy and vegetable garden stretched out as far as Willow could see. The workers quarters lay to the east, more modest, but remarkably well furnished. Views of the mountains dominated the shape of Khrabkhaw, the island itself a long dormant volcano, its slopes a blanket of luscious emerald and jade foliage.

As they walked through the plush forest Rosa examined the leaves, checked the fruit trees over and stopped to check on a crop of mangos.

'I never thought I'd run so far from home and still end up a farmer. We can't outrun our pasts' and neither should we want to.' Rosa pointed to the tree tops, where a monkey was swinging from a branch, 'We have our own troop of monkeys, a huge variety of birds and insects, snakes and lizards too. We interfere with the animals as little as possible, although the monkeys have grown fairly tame over the years.'

Willow was captivated. She couldn't find words to explain its unique wonder, but she knew a man who could and she longed to hear his voice. 'I wish my friend Aaron could see this place, he would love it!' she thought aloud.

'Then you must bring him for a visit.' Rosa said, leading the way to a frothing brook. 'This is your home from home now, we might not be too accessible but you must promise me that you will come to see me as often as you can. I rarely leave these days and I can't stand the thought of being separated from you for too long.'

She squeezed Willows fingers gently before dropping her hand and sitting down on the river bank. 'I need to rest my leg a while. It's never been the same since the Tsunami.' Rosa removed her moccasins and dipped her feet into the water with a relieved simper.

Willow followed, the cool brook soothed her aching toes as she stared upstream to where a large pool was being fuelled by a magnificent thirty-foot waterfall. She lay back and watched the natural wonder.

'The pool is really deep. The braver kids like to jump from up there.' Rosa told her with a shudder. 'I think they like to prove to themselves and each other that they are fearless.'

Willow gasped, scared for their safety, 'Wow. The young are either brave or stupid.' She couldn't imagine anything worse than plummeting through the air toward the rocks and dark waters but part of her admired their valour.

Rosa broke the hush, 'If you thought that I had passed, what really bought you here? I don't mean the money, which gave you a cause. What was the reason for a beautiful young woman to leave her life behind?'

Willow recalled the last time that had full control of her life. 'After Mum and Dad died I retreated with my grief. I was home all the time. I lost the energy or desire to go out or look after myself properly. James, my ex-fiancé, was out of work again. He's an actor, but not a very good one.' Willow filled Rosa in.

Rosa lay back next to her, 'They rarely are,' she exhaled.

Willow sniggered despite the bite of the topic, 'He wasn't good for much actually, apart from taking money from me. I should have left him, but I couldn't stand to lose anybody else. I was so desperately sad that I clung to him with a fever. The more he pulled away, the more I grew clingy, needy, fraught, paranoid. I would lay awake while he was out, a sea of images of him with other women tormenting my imagination and clogging up my timeline on social media. I thought that he was so much better than me, that he would realise and leave me. I was terrified to be alone, sick with the stress.'

Willow was embarrassed by her behaviour, ashamed of the woman that she had been.

Rosa looked at her questioningly but, just as her mother used to do, remained quiet.

'I was sending myself crazy with my suspicions, so I opened his computer. The truth was easy to find, reams of emails, all the beautiful things he had ever said to me, his promises and declarations were all laid out for someone else. I tortured myself, I read every email, saw photos of them in bed together, ones of her naked. I was destroyed, my heart broken.

281

Every minute that I was awake and that was nearly every single one in the day, I had to endure the feeling of my heart shattering in my chest. When it got really bad I started sleepwalking. One day I woke up to find I was stood at a drawer in the kitchen taking the knives out and lining them up on the side. Another time I was perched on my windowsill, three floors up. Even in my sleep I wanted to be dead. I finally wound up in a psychiatric ward.' She said quietly, remembering the days that she had woken up in hospital, a prisoner, being forced to go on when she wanted it all to end.

Rosa spoke softly, 'Nobody *winds up* in these places. Who got you there? Someone must have been caring for you?'

With sinking realisation Willow whispered. 'It was Claire. I thought she must have hated me to have me committed to a place like that. Who sections someone they love?' Willow was speaking slowly, thinking for the first time about how hard it must have been for Claire. 'I went to live with her once I was discharged. It was a horrendous year but with medication and counselling I didn't get any worse. I didn't get any better either, but there we go. When I found my Mothers Will and your letters. I thought, *what the hell*, I had nothing to lose and everything to gain.'

Rosa patted her hand, 'It takes a lot of love to do something for someone that you know may make them hate you. I'm sure Claire acted with your best interests at heart. She had just lost her parents to; imagine how she must have felt at the prospect of you doing something terrible to yourself?'

Willow thought of Ben, she had only known him a couple of weeks and the pain of losing him would leave a scar, Claire had been a part of Willow all her life. Willow recalled the phone calls and messages, all the nights that Claire had sat on the sofa watching nothing-in-particular on the TV until the early hours so that she had not had to be alone.

Claire had never left her, despite having three young children, a husband and a job to contend with. Without warning Willow burst into tears, 'I think you are right.' How could she not have seen it before? 'I love her too.' Willow acknowledged, yearning to tell her.

Rosa sought the truth without judgement. 'How are you feeling now?'

Willow shrugged, 'As if I am telling a story about someone else, I am so far removed from the woman that I was, she's a stranger. I'm stronger and happier than I have been in years. Only something so life-altering could bring me to this point, drive me to step on the plane in the first place. I used to blame James for how my life had turned out, now I'd have to thank him. Does that make sense?'

Rosa nodded knowingly as she took Willows hand gently. 'Yes darling it does, but maybe it's Claire you should be thanking? She must be terribly worried about you.'

Willow nodded, overwhelmed by desire to see Claire. 'I will as soon as I get the chance.' She promised not only Rosa, but herself. 'Can I ask you something?' Willow ventured, wanting to move the conversation away from Claire and the guilt it was raising; something had been bothering her since they had met.

Rosa nodded easily, 'Anything. Ask away.'

Willow needed guidance and who better to ask then Rosa? 'How did you turn your life around so beautifully? I mean you had…'

'Nothing. No money, no family, no love.' Rosa finished her sentence.

'When I became a teacher I made a small wage, but I had a roof over my head and I had my boys. I was happy for the first time in such a long time, it was only then that I could fully let Wan in. That's when my life really changed. It wasn't that I needed a man to save me, I needed to love and be loved in return and boy did I love that man! As soon as I let him in others followed, Jay came to be part of our family. Everyone I have in my life are the family I chose and now I have you. If you want to turn your life around you are already on your way, look at how far you've come.'

Willow thought again of the day that she had met Aaron. She had been scared to even get on the plane, to talk to strangers and then to set foot outside of her hotel, to dress up, to have sex, to offer advice, to be alone with her thoughts, to teach. She thought of all the things she had done over the past few weeks. She had come a long way and had a sudden strong feeling of gratitude for it all.

Rosa took her hand. 'Let's go and swim in the sea. Today you are living your memories of tomorrow. Let's make them good ones!'

Rosa led her to a stretch of beach near the workers dwellings, pulling off her clothes, beneath she was already dressed for swimming in her bikini. Her body was a story book, peppered with Tattooed symbols, the Sak Yant, marks and scars. She stroked along one of the larger ones, on her thigh then down to her ankle, mottled with pink and blue tinged skin. 'I survived but I nearly did die in the wave that took Wan.'

Willow smarted, the marks looked painful, 'Do they hurt?'

Rosa waved her fingers over the scars on her legs, 'Not really, only if I'm cold and that doesn't happen much. I like them now. They're part of me. They remind me of what I've been through, how strong I can be. I'm a warrior returned from battle not lost in the fight!'

Rosa ran into the sea laughing. 'I always have to be ready for the ocean, when it calls I must go to it!'

Willow stripped down to her pants and t-shirt and ran after her, thinking of her mother who would throw herself into the lake on the farm, even in winter.

They cooled off in the water, quietly enjoying each other's company and that of the island. Willow cleansed by her earlier admissions, floating on her back, soaking up the sun, so comfortable she nearly forgot that Rosa was there until she spoke:

'Is there a man in your life now?'

Willow thought of Aaron. 'There was someone, Aaron. Things didn't work out. He messed up, but he wants to make things up I think.' Her stomach twisted as she pictured Marcella. Even if she wanted to could she ever forgive him? Should she? 'He wasn't ready. Maybe it was bad timing for both of us?' She conceded, remembering her run in with James the day before she and Aaron had kissed.

'If I know one thing about this life it's that we never have enough time, bad or good!' Rosa stated, with authority. 'Timing can be bad, but it's still time, it will slip through your fingers while you're thinking what to do with it.'

Willow thought of her parents, they could have been richer, they could have seen more of the world, they could have let what they didn't have make them unhappy to live with what they did. She wanted to let them live on within her in the way that Jay carried his father. She wanted to be happy.

She started to remember the things Aaron had done that had bought her warmth, 'He was pretty amazing from the moment I met him actually. He helped me relax on the plane when I was so stressed I was considering hoaxing a bomb threat just to get thrown off. He saved me from a horrible Taxi queue when I was feeling overwhelmed and alone, found me a hotel in Bangkok and introduced me to some amazing friends. He helped me when I was robbed, showed me the beauty of the ocean when I had been afraid.' She thought of Ben, 'He even sent me a protector when I really needed one despite never knowing if he would see me again.'

Rosa's eyebrows rose, 'Sounds like prince charming to me. Marry him immediately!'

Willow dismissed Rosa's eager romantic inclinations, 'He definitely wasn't that. He lost his wife a few years ago and he's complicated when it comes to commitment. There was another woman, kind of, she's gone now, I think. He wants a second chance, but it's complicated.' Even as she spoke she could feel her anger ebbing away. He didn't want Marcella, he wanted her. She allowed herself to feel it in her heart.

'It's not easy to love someone when they're being selfish or stupid, but maybe what they're trying to mask is that they are vulnerable and broken. It seems to me that Aaron was there when you needed him and now you've seen the worst of each other. I wouldn't write him off just yet. Maybe he needs you to be his *knight* and not the other way around? Stay the week and see how you feel at the end of it. This island has a way of showing you what you really want.' Rosa assured her.

Willow wanted her answer to be different, but her mind was made up. She wasn't leaving for Aaron she was leaving for her, for Ben, for what was right in her life. 'I have to leave in two days. There's a memorial service on Railay for my friend Ben. I've only just arrived but…' She fought against the lump in her throat when she said his name. 'I need to be there for Aaron if possible.' Willow sighed loudly, 'I'm so sorry, I know I've only just arrived, but I could stay here and be too happy to go after what I really need. Does that make sense?'

Rosa stood up, her eyes creased, concerned, 'Of course you have to go. I'm so sorry for your loss but let me come with you?'

Willow felt warm, the memories of being nurtured returning to her present, but she couldn't be selfish. 'Don't you have classes to teach, people to look after?'

She chastised herself for hoping that Rosa was not needed as much as it appeared.

Rosa thought for a moment, 'I like to think that I'm indispensable, but Jay can cover, he'll be ok for a couple of days. Besides you've been through a lot and Railay holds special memories for me. Wan and I used to go there on holiday. It seems fitting that you and I go together, to remember the people we've lost.'

Willow saw how Rosa's face clouded when she spoke of Wan, her loss still an evident pain.

'Has there been anyone since Wan?' She asked gently. Rosa was in her fifties, full of fun, love and energy, Willow couldn't imagine her going through life alone.

Rosa submerged herself in the sea, as if hiding from the question, resurfacing her features were rearranged with a light smile. 'I have never met anybody who has come close to him, I doubt I ever will, but that's ok. You are a different matter, you are young and beautiful, you have a lot of life left, there is no reason to do that without a partner by your side. Give someone a chance, give yourself a chance.'

Willow took a deep breath, letting herself believe that she could be enough, 'I might just do that.'

Chapter 29

It was evening by the time they left the forest and still blisteringly hot, but there were rumbles of thunder over the sea and the air was growing damp.

They took a softly trodden coastal path back towards the restaurant, where they sat amongst the staff and guests. Willow could not have hoped for a more welcoming, varied and interesting group of people.

The complex was so grandiose it felt as if she were part of a pack of lost boys who had taken over from the real grown-ups. There were teenagers with pink and blue striped hair sitting upon designer linen-lined seats, impish groups of children drinking from crystal cut glass as the state-of-the-art sound system kept them entertained with music from around the world. Some of the staff were playing musical statues with them.

The playground for the rich and famous was a playground in the true meaning of the word and Willow loved it.

Jay joined them with stories from the day's classes, keen to hear Willow's impressions of the place, checking that Rosa had shown her all his own favourite spots.

Everyone mingled socially with bowls of scrumptious fluffy jasmine rice and an array of colourful zinging curries well into the late hours, with no evidence of a curfew or set bed time. Willow felt as if she were part of a giant sleepover she never wanted to end; but once the last of the children had given in to sleep it was time.

She yawned and rubbed her tired eyes, hardly able to hold them open as she carried some glasses to the kitchen

Rosa caught site of her, clearing a table of her own and rushed over, 'My poor girl let's get you straight to bed,' she wrapped her arm around her shoulders. 'Jay are you coming back with us?' she called to him as he stacked the chairs.

Everyone was at work regardless of status.

'No thanks Mum. I'm going back with Chai to have a beer and game of darts.' He said walking to her and kissing her lightly on each cheek.

Willow wanted to do her fair share of the tidying, 'Let me just finish the glasses.' She yawned.

Rosa scolded, 'Don't be ridiculous, you are my guest. See you tomorrow my love,' She sang to Jay as she led Willow away down the beach.

Too exhausted to argue, Willow rested her head against Rosa's shoulder and enjoyed each step back to the house.

She woke to the rhythmic drumming of rain upon the window. She listened for a while, not wanting to break the spell and stretched. She stepped out of her room into the house, which lay still.

'Rosa,' she called. No answer.

On the table lay a note.

Willow,

I have gone to help the team set up for breakfast. Join us whenever you are ready, no rush. I am looking forward to another day with you.

Rosa
xxx

It was strange to have a new note from Rosa, proof of life going on, the future yet unwritten.

Willow sat on the veranda watching the rain on the sand and the growing storm out at sea. It would be impossible to leave the island if the rains continued, she wouldn't make it to Railay.

Her heart ached for Ben and for her friends, but it was Aaron she longed for. She had been imprisoned by the beautiful island. She stomped up and down on the wooden floor boards, wringing her hands. She tried to meditate, closing her eyes, urging the zephyr to wash through her. It didn't work.

She needed her own form of meditation. She yanked on her running trainers.

Monkeys bounded through the treetops, skittering up and down the trunks between the torrent of droplets. Usually she would enjoy their company, but their chatter and laughter seemed mocking. She kept to a path which led up the volcano.

After some time she stumbled into the path of a young Thai man, she recognised as one of the island rangers. He was carrying climbing equipment, heading downward. He seemed as surprised as she was but edged aside.

'Bai Nai?' He yelled when she did not slow her pace.

His question, *where are you going?* sat with her for a moment before she replied, 'Chan Miru,' *I don't know,* and she really didn't.

'Kuntoe,' he shouted, 'Xantarai!'

Willow ignored his pleas; she knew that it was *raining* and *dangerous.* She would be careful.

There was a growing strength in her legs, where before there had been only weakness and it reassured her. Her legs could take her anywhere, her strength could keep her going, no matter what.

The clouds were black and the birds agitated, but she did not head back. The rain came down harder and harder, pushing through the leaves of the forest which had been shielding her. They drooped under the fall and her clothes grew sodden. She inhaled the damp air, her lungs aching for rest, her legs yearning for flight.

She ran to get away from everyone she was powerless to help until she found herself nearing the top.

She heard it before she saw it, a whooshing bubbling, as she came out from the trees. Before her was a flowing river, the source that fed the brook she and Rosa had dipped their toes in the day before. The same water that had bought her such clarity carved a deep crevice through the hill top, something so angry fuelling something calm.

Without knowing what she was doing she had stepped off the bank into the waters warm tide, moving to the centre of the river, remembering Ben as he swam in the watering hole at the sanctuary, laughing and ducking beneath the surface. Happy.

Looking out to the horizon she could make out where the water flowed to the waterfall. She closed her eyes and thought indifferently of James, safely removed from her life, Claire surrounded by her children and husband, the farm and fields in which she had scattered her parent's ashes under their favourite willow tree and then there was Aaron.

In her memories Aaron was in the caves of Koh Tao where they had shared their kiss, but he was alone in the darkness.

The monsoon rains hammered into her back, insistent and driving. The river flowed about her ankles, the swirl pulling toward the cliff edge. She held her breath, swallowed the pain, and forgot her loss. Then she ran.

The looming jungle palms flew past, panic rising as the edge drew closer, the heavens hung grey and furious above. She jumped, leaving everything behind on the cliff. For a heartbeat she was free, floating on the breeze before she hit the blackened waters and the world stopped.

She sank deeper into the murky water. Rain pelted through the surface, darting past her head like bullets. The water was warm and encompassing. Alone in the depths she felt safe. Her breath began to burn in her lungs, she let it out in one long expulsion, sinking further. She had been in a place like this before, but she had been given a second chance and come further than she had thought possible, filling her life with friends, family, joy and love.

Her feet came to rest on the bottom, she bent her knees and pushed hard, shooting up to the surface. She emerged, rasping, swam to the edge and pulled herself out. The rain was beginning to ease, replaced by the glowing sun.

She made her way to the breakfast hall, her trainers squelching as she went.

Jay spotted her first and walked to greet her with a hug. 'Good morning! I see you got caught in the rain?' he laughed.

Willow smiled, she felt fearless, 'Not to worry, it's sunny now.'

Chapter 30

Willow woke early to meditate in the morning sun. The sound of the gentle waves purring upon the sand stilled her mind and lulled her heart.

Rosa came to join her on the veranda, announcing her arrival with a loud yawn. 'Are you ready for the boat? We have a long way to travel if we are going to make the service at noon.'

Willow opened her eyes and sat for a few more moments, 'Nearly,' She couldn't miss a moment of the sunrise.

Rosa put her hands-on Willow's shoulders, her palms warm and strong, a comforting anchor, 'My home has worked its magic on you.'

Her delight was audible.

Willow let out her breath, 'Yes it has. It has shown me not to be afraid.'

'It seems to me that you have faced some of the worst things in life already; what was left to be afraid of?'

Rosa stood unafraid to ask the questions Willow hadn't dared to ask herself.

Willow placed her hand over Rosa's. 'Living.'

It was noon before they moored the boat. Willow and Rosa hurried into the dingy and raced around the peninsular to Railay beach.

A handful of tourists chatted and lounged on the alabaster sands, acoustic guitars already out in force. Willow hopped from the dingy into the sandy shallows, helping Rosa behind her.

Rosa stood still, inhaling deeply 'It's good to be back.' She gazed upon the land in front of them. 'Wan loved the climbing here and of course the weed.' She chuckled at Willows expression. 'Oh come on; you can't be that surprised? Parents were once children.'

Their skipper had been able to tell them the way to *The Lost Sole's* and Willow was grateful not to have to waste another minute asking for directions. She had text Lucia and Che to say that she was on her way but had not heard back. Neither were good with checking their phones and they were likely to be distracted more than ever.

Did anyone even know that she was coming? The way that she had fled Koh Tao seemed overly-dramatic in-light-of recent events.

Rosa took Willow's hand as they walked away from the beach. 'Are you ok?' she peered at her with the eyes of her mother.

'I was thinking about Claire.' Willow admitted, 'I would do anything to go back, to stop Ben, I would have dragged him to a hospital for help. I would have acted as Claire did. Only now can I see how much she must have loved me. I don't know why I let the rift between us go this far?'

'I will tell you what I tell all my children: It's only when you have recovered that you can see clearly.' Rosa tugged her hand gently, 'Come on, we can still make it if we are quick!'

They raced toward the narrow path that would take them away from the beach. It was a steep incline, cut out of the cliff. Rainforest cloaked the rocky terrain as they climbed higher. Rosa leading the way with a dexterity that surprised Willow, who scrambled along behind, checking her watch again. Ten minutes past and still no sign of accommodation.

The path was dusty, the bushes scratchy against her legs, the heat stifling. Willow was growing flustered, 'Are we going the wrong way?'

Rosa tutted, 'Don't be so quick to give up, look over there,' she pointed to a spot a few hundred yards away.

Roof tops speckled the ridge, the sun gleaming off a swimming pool. Gentle, guitar music reached them, carried on the breeze. Willow followed the melody, in pursuit of the piper.

As soon as she set eyes on the bar she knew it was perfect, a fitting place for Ben to rest.

It was surrounded by curtains made from battered, flip flops and sandals hanging from ropes, each a life, a story to be told. They rose and fell with the zephyr, clattering together in gentle applause as the music ceased. Willow turned to Rosa, not sure what to do next.

Rosa gently pushed her forward, encouraging, 'You need to do this bit on your own.'

Willow had thought her journey would end when she found Rosa but stood in front of her was proof that life goes on, another adventure waiting after the last.

She stepped forward.

Aaron's voice was barely audible from behind the curtain of soles.

'Thank you very much for being here.' He paused and coughed, a tremor faltering his usual confident tone. 'Ben's passing has been hard for all of us to accept, but today we must honour him and celebrate our own lives with a vigour and pleasure that he was unable to garner from his own. Despite all our efforts in his darkest times none of us could reach him or have helped more than we did, I know this because he said so himself.'

Aaron pulled Ben's green leather diary from his pocket. 'Ben wrote in here every day, in the end, I know he was grateful for all of us. The last thing he wrote was...' He opened the diary, '*Today was a good day.*' He read aloud, 'I hope that brings you all some comfort. His last hours were not all pain.'

Willow thought of Ben on that last day. He really had seemed content. She was blessed to have been part of an experience that brought him a respite from his demons even if it failed to alleviate them. She stepped, quietly, from behind the curtain, unnoticed.

Aaron wiped his eyes with the back of his hand, 'I'm sorry, I have never been good with expressing my emotions. I have written a short poem.' He pulled a crumpled piece of paper from his pocket and took his time to straighten it.

Willow looked and then looked again, there on his wrist was a fresh tattoo, an unmistakable small willow tree. Tears gathered in her eyes.

When he spoke his voice was little more than whisper.

'I didn't know your pain or what you were going through.
I saw only happiness in your eyes, because it's what I wanted to.
I take time to remember; The good times, not the bad.
I recall the days you smiled and not the ones I found you sad.
Your torment and your anguish can now be free to cease
and that which caused you suffering I pray has been released.
You made my life far richer, I knew not what for you betide;
Now all I have are memories, and God walks by your side.'

A voice lifted above the crowd, 'Here, Here' shouted Eric.

A ripple of applause followed as the words swamped Willow with emotion, she knew Aaron's words spoke for himself as well as for Ben. She watched him survey the medley of faces before his eyes came to rest on her.

His look so intense she was pinned to the spot as he walked to her. He reached out and pulled her close to him.

She could feel his hands were shaking.

'I can't believe you came.' He whispered.

'Ben wanted me to see you again, I thought that this was a good time to honour his last wish. He thought you deserved a second chance.' She said softly.

Aaron pulled back, his face serious. 'And what do you think?'

'I think that he was better at giving advice than taking it.' It wasn't the time or place to talk about *them*, yet she was unable to do anything else.

He shook his head, disbelieving, 'When I heard that you had found Jay and your aunt, I knew; well I thought I knew, that I would never see you again. You had found what you'd been looking for, you had no reason to stay. I had no idea what Ben had told you. I *really* screwed things up but, if you'll let me, I promise I'll make it up to you'

Willow pulled at his shirt where her hands lay, 'I wanted more than a family, I just didn't see that before.'

A loud clinking tap, cutlery against glass, penetrated the silence, 'Wrap it up, I want to raise this glass.' Shouted Lucia.

Gentle laughter and cheers resonated. Aaron kept his arm firmly around her, looking at their friends. 'Today let's come together and celebrate Ben for all of his wonderful attributes, lets share our fun and sometimes positively unusual anecdotes, as well as a drink or two.'

More soft laughter and murmured agreement fluttered through the familiar, teary faces.

Aaron crouched and picked up a pair of flip flops, which Willow recognised as Bens, then turned to the curtain and tied them to another pair. He closed his eyes in remembrance and raised his bottle of beer, 'Come on, raise those drinks. To Ben.' He shouted

'To Ben!' they chorused.

Lucia ran to her, a whirlwind of pink and orange chiffon. 'I'm so glad you're here. I had no idea that you'd spent the last week with Ben, I didn't know you knew each other well at all. Aaron only told me yesterday. It's so awful.' She dried her eyes and shook herself. 'The last thing he would want is our tears.'

The speakers crackled to life with the commonplace sounds of Bob Marley. 'You must come and dance with me.' Lucia batted her lashes playfully, 'For Ben?'

'Ben was a lousy dancer!' Aaron shouted, as they made their way toward a small group of people swaying to the music.

'Ahh but he liked watching girls dance!' Lucia raised her arms.

'I can't argue with that,' Aaron agreed, before he was pulled into a hearty embrace by Matseuse. He looked back at Willow, his face pressed against his friend's large chest, 'Later,' he mouthed.

The afternoon passed with as much celebration and laughter, as tears and melancholy.

Rosa arrived into the group as if she had been there all along and was not a newcomer. She moved from person to person, learning each one's experiences of Ben and offering condolence where appropriate. Willow watched her offering a motherly hug to Mary, a surge of pride in her chest.

Eric put his arm around her. 'How are you doing kid?'

'Not too bad.' She sniffed, leaning against him, her body awash with conflicting emotions. 'Have you met my aunt yet?'

He nodded enthusiastically, 'I've been talking to her about her sanctuary, I think we may work together in the future. She is a magnificent! The things she has accomplished and the people she has helped!' he shook his head in disbelief, 'She is just like her photographs.' He mused.

Willow observed Eric watching Rosa dance, with a more cheerful Mary and her partner. 'I have you to thank for finding her.'

Eric shrugged, 'I think you would have always found each other. Love is like two magnets; you can't keep them apart.'

Rosa waved over to them.

'I think she wants you to go and dance.' Eric said, taking his arm from her shoulder.

'It's not me she's looking at,' she laughed.

Eric patted down his already perfectly ironed shirt and straightened himself up. 'I do not like to let a lady down and I think there's a man over there who craves a moment of your time.' He nodded to Aaron, who was looking away from his island home upon the sea that had claimed his wife and child.

Eric patted her hand and walked away to join Rosa, who had her arms raised to the heavens swaying to the music, her half-smile growing to a grin as Eric approached.

Like two magnets Willow thought, looking on.

Epilogue

The morning Sun was glorious, standing proud in the celebratory sky. The monkeys seemed to be chattering more than usual and the bird song was more joyous. Bic stood ready to officiate beneath the largest palm on Khrabkhaw, the forest behind him and the sea lying still, beyond the sands, in front.

Her wedding gown was a simple ivory silk slip that brushed the sand as she approached her groom. With hair loose, in curls and a radiant smile, she looked around the huge congregation.

There were yogis and gurus, bloggers and DJ's, shopkeepers and dignitaries, politicians and orphans all sat alike, upon the sands. She clung to Jay's arm while the many children giggled and fidgeted with the excitement of an impending party.

Willow watched her nieces and nephew as they jumped up and down, unable to suppress their joy. It still felt strange to see Claire in Thailand, despite her frequent visits for the school holidays over the past year.

Willow loved that Claire still wore smart shirts and Ralph Lauren tailored shorts, travelling everywhere with a bottle of anti-bac and a smart phone. She unapologetically knew who she was; it was not who Willow was, or would want to be, but she admired her strength of spirit.

One of the smaller school boys ran to Willow and pulled on the length of her dress. 'Yes Rak. What can I do for you?' she whispered.

He squirmed about with crossed legs. 'Ms Willow I need a wee!'

She really didn't get any time off from work, but she wouldn't want it any other way. She moved to take him to the bathroom, relieved when Mary stepped in and took his hand.

'Come on Rak I'll take you. Willow you can hardly miss this!'

'Thank you.' Willow mouthed as Mary swooped Rak into her arms, whisking him away.

Aaron squeezed her hand tightly. 'I wish my teachers had looked like you!' he kissed her lightly on her forehead, the same way that he had done a hundred times before.

Despite the months passing she still got lost in his eyes and glowed at his touch.

'I did not see this coming.' He shook his head in disbelief.

Willow grinned up at him and put her finger to her lips, 'Shhh it's beginning.'

Willow was front row, in pride of place, as Rosa, the glowing bride, let go of Jay's arm and took Eric's hand at the altar.

Author Biography

Debbie Rae is from a family of authors and majored in script writing at university in Southampton. She spent four years living in Thailand and travelling extensively through many southeast Asian countries before moving to LA and then back to the UK.

She has survived life-threatening tropical diseases, hospitalisation following a fall from a waterfall, battled depression and spent a month with orphaned children. She and her husband now reside in Surrey with their two children, where they regularly take time to continue their exploration of the world.

This is Debbie's debut novel and the first in a series of woman's travel stories capturing the beauty, intrigue, humour and, sometimes pain of her many curious global adventures. Although fictional, The Lost Sole's Club was inspired by real people and true-life events.

If you enjoyed this book please share your review on Amazon.

Printed in Great Britain
by Amazon